KNIGHT OF DARKNESS

THE KNIGHTS OF THE ANARCHY
(BOOK 1)

SHERRY EWING

© Copyright 2024 by Sherry Ewing
Text by Sherry Ewing
Cover by Kim Killion Designs

Dragonblade Publishing, Inc. is an imprint of Kathryn Le Veque Novels, Inc.
P.O. Box 23
Moreno Valley, CA 92556
ceo@dragonbladepublishing.com

Produced in the United States of America

First Edition February 2024
Print Edition

Reproduction of any kind except where it pertains to short quotes in relation to advertising or promotion is strictly prohibited.

All Rights Reserved.

The characters and events portrayed in this book are fictitious. Any similarity to real persons, living or dead, is purely coincidental and not intended by the author.

ARE YOU SIGNED UP FOR DRAGONBLADE'S BLOG?

You'll get the latest news and information on exclusive giveaways, exclusive excerpts, coming releases, sales, free books, cover reveals and more.

Check out our complete list of authors, too!

No spam, no junk. That's a promise!

Sign Up Here

www.dragonbladepublishing.com

Dearest Reader;

Thank you for your support of a small press. At Dragonblade Publishing, we strive to bring you the highest quality Historical Romance from some of the best authors in the business. Without your support, there is no 'us', so we sincerely hope you adore these stories and find some new favorite authors along the way.

Happy Reading!

CEO, Dragonblade Publishing

Additional Dragonblade books by Author Sherry Ewing

The Knights of the Anarchy Series
Knight of Darkness (Book 1)

The Lyon's Den Series
To Claim a Lyon's Heart

Knight of Darkness:
The Knights of the Anarchy (Book One)
By Sherry Ewing

Sometimes finding love can become our biggest weakness…

Wymar Norwood understands responsibility. His two brothers have been in his care since his father's death. With his title and lands stripped from him by the usurper Stephen, he aligns himself with the Empress Matilda, the rightful Queen of England. If he can win her favor and become her champion knight, he prays all will be returned to him.

Lady Ceridwen Ward of Norwich is out to prove not only to herself but the Empress that she is more than capable of protecting those she loves. She hides herself in the guise of a knight and follows along with her men to Lincoln to raise her sword for the Empress's cause. But life can become complicated, especially after your identity is revealed.

But Wymar and Ceridwen have a common enemy who is bent on revenge. They will need to search their souls and overcome grief in order for their love to survive life's greatest test.

Dedication

For my niece Courtnie...

I am so very proud of the woman you've become and all you've accomplished.

This one is for you with much love!

PROLOGUE

IN A TIME known today as The Anarchy, England was torn between two enemies each claiming a right to the throne. Some of England's nobles pledged their allegiance to Stephen and declared him king whilst others cast their fate with Empress Matilda, the daughter of Henry I. Such unrest placed most of the country into a state of civil war lasting for almost a score of years. Many knights bore the burden of fighting for one side or the other, each determined to win the land for whomever they served.

Amongst such knights were three brothers who had become hired hands in search of fame and fortune. They swore their loyalty to fight for the Empress Matilda and defend her rightful claim to England's crown. The Norwood brothers were close in age. Wymar was the eldest and jumped at the chance to swear his oath of fealty to the Empress, especially after their parents were killed when Stephen laid siege to their home, Brockenhurst Castle. Ousted from the only home they had known six years ago, Wymar plunged his brothers into the middle of war all in the hopes of having the Empress crowned queen. He prayed, in return for his service, she would bestow upon him the return of his lands, his title, and name him her champion knight.

Theobald was next and the peacekeeper amongst them. He was used to following his eldest brother no matter that he would prefer to sit in front of a fire to rest his weary feet with a mug of ale in his hand. Reynard, the youngest, was always attempting to prove his worth even when the odds were stacked against him. He was more like his eldest brother than he would ever admit, even to himself.

All three swore to remain together as a family as they had no one else besides themselves and for now the land beneath their feet was home. Until they could reclaim their birthright and Brockenhurst was again in their control, the brothers had no plans to marry. They had no time to cater to some woman nor was having a wife as a camp follower an ideal situation. They had sworn their allegiance to the Empress Matilda and until she released them, they were committed to her cause to see her placed on the throne.

But sometimes the fate of man is fickle, especially when you only think of the pleasures to be obtained in life or the jingle of coins to line your coffers.

Every tale has a beginning, a middle and an end for the knights of the Anarchy. This is Wymar's story…

CHAPTER ONE

February, Outside of Lincoln, England
The Year of Our Lord's Grace 1141

WYMAR NORWOOD'S WARHORSE trudged through the muck beneath its hooves whilst thunder and lightning slashed across the early evening sky in an eerie display for any hour of the day. 'Twas almost like a premonition of things to come. He would never admit he was tired, especially to his brothers, but he was. Would the torrential downpour that continued to all but drown him never cease? The road, if that is what you would have called it, had become nothing more than a cesspool of... *shite*! How many men had already traveled this way before him he could not say. 'Twas as though God Himself was displeased with his choice to place his oath of fealty to Empress Matilda. Yet he could do no less, for he swore the Empress was the rightful ruler and not the usurper who had been crowned king.

He spat the foul taste from his mouth. 'Twas as though just thinking of Stephen as King of England had been the cause of his current displeasure and misfortune to be traveling amongst such inclement weather. Yet he could not help but ponder if 'twould be worth it. His way of life and those he looked after would change for the better if he were the man to capture Stephen. Wymar could only imagine the satisfaction he might gain from capturing the man who had sent forces to his home—the man who was the reason his parents no longer lived. The siege on Brockenhurst had cost Wymar and his brothers everything and 'twas all because Stephen wanted to claim more land to rule under his false claim to the throne. For Wymar to have his title and lands restored to him was worth any cost he might pay for pledging his allegiance to the Empress. Surely she would reward him handsomely for capturing her enemy.

Another streak of lightning flashed across the darkness of the night. Wymar pulled at the hood of his cloak whilst memories assailed him. When they'd been forced to leave Brockenhurst behind, Wymar and his brothers had taken whatever they could carry of worth: their swords, a bit of food, a satchel filled with clothes, and more importantly their family standard—a black raven in a field of red. They sold their parents' trinkets and other costly gems in order to live until they began hiring out the strength of their swords. Through the next five years, they journeyed from place to place and gained a reputation of being fierce in battle, earning enough monies to see to their needs.

Word had traveled swiftly throughout the countryside that King Stephen was laying siege to Lincoln Castle. Eager to join the fight for his queen, and to make the most of a prime opportunity to capture the usurper, Wymar had all but yanked his brothers from their beds that morn to begin their travels from the inn they had been staying at near London. The storm they had encountered at the beginning of their journey caused their progress to Lincoln to be tediously slow and overcome with one obstacle after another. At least they were almost to their destination. With his two brothers by his side, Wymar had no doubt they would be on the winning side of the battle once they joined the fray.

Finally arriving on the outskirts of Lincoln, the lights of a distant inn flickered in the dusk of night. 'Twas like a beacon calling him to enter its warmth for a mug or two of ale after hours in the saddle. Rain dripped from his hair and clouded his vision leaving him no doubt as to his decision for a brief respite from the weather. But between the rain and those who had arrived before them, they would be hard pressed to find a place to pitch their tents for the upcoming battle.

He pulled on the reins of his horse causing Aries to whinny. "Theobald! Reynard!" he bellowed above the sound of the storm. Wymar pointed to the inn before covering his face when clumps of mud were flung in his direction after his brothers took off in a full gallop. 'Twas as if they were only awaiting word they could seek their comfort for a few hours of the night. And once they received that word, they would apparently not take the chance that Wymar would change his mind.

"I highly doubt the inn will have any available rooms at this hour. Your brothers care only for their immediate desires and think not of what must needs still be accomplished before they rest their weary heads," Richard Grancourt said, coming abreast of Wymar.

"Aye, but can you blame them?" Wymar replied with a toss of his head as rivulets of water streamed down his brown hair. Wiping the water from his eyes, he turned in his saddle to take in the condition of the rest of the half dozen men who followed him.

Wymar had known Richard for most of his life and did not question his loyalty. Wymar also recognized some of the men who continued to follow him after attending one tourney or another together. But he had far less familiarity with the others he had met on the open road. He only was aware that they, too, went to fight for the Empress. Their number continued to grow the closer to the battlefield they went. Wymar often wondered during their travels exactly how loyal, in truth, they were. Most mercenaries of his acquaintance would change sides faster than Theobald could down a mug of mead if this meant more coins for their purse or a bit of land to call home.

Mayhap one day he would learn for himself if they could be trusted. Until then, he would continue to be on his guard. He did not relish the idea of seeing one of them coming at him with blade in hand in an attempt to gain authority of their group... not that Wymar ever claimed to be their leader. The men just assumed he was the one to look to for their orders. After years of battles, along with tournaments to earn more monies, they would not be the first to attempt to kill him. Wymar was certain they would not be the last and only time itself would prove their worth.

Some of the knights who followed him knew the strength of Wymar's sword and had labeled him the Knight of Darkness after witnessing him fight on several occasions. He could not say he was particularly fond of the nickname, yet he would not complain if his reputation became elevated because of it. Mayhap even the Empress would learn that he would fight to the death for her cause.

"I shall see to finding a place to pitch our tents," Richard stated, interrupting Wymar's musings. "I assume you have no further need of me this night and your brothers will be capable of watching your back?"

Wymar nodded. "I shall be grateful, Richard, for your assistance in seeing to the camp. At this stage of the war, let us hope we can find a spot far enough away from the battlefield to ease our comfort when we are able."

Richard adjusted the hood of his cloak. "'Twill be a miracle indeed and yet I am certain I will be able to find us space. I have not failed in finding us suitable ground to rest our head in the past."

"Nay... that you have not," Wymar answered knowing he could count on Richard. "I promise, just one drink and I will ensure we bring you victuals to see to filling the hole in your belly."

Richard laughed. "If you manage to get your brothers out of the inn after only one drink, I shall take on the task of being your squire for as long as we continue our fight for justice."

"I shall take that bet," Wymar replied with a smirk. "Remind me again why I did not hire that lad back at the last village we stopped at?"

"Because I caught the little thief trying to lift my purse whilst I was perusing a lovely pair of breasts that had been exposed for my viewing pleasure! How could you forget?" grumbled Richard.

"Aye... how could I forget indeed? I would not be surprised to learn those two were in cahoots together." Wymar chuckled again before leaning over and slapping Richard on the back. "I will not be long."

With a flick of the leather reins, he set Aries back into motion until he came to the yard of the inn. A lad came to take his horse and Wymar tossed him a coin. "See that he's taken care of. There is another in it for you if you give him some oats and a good rubdown."

"Thank ye, milord," the boy called out before pulling on the reins to take Aries to the nearby stable.

Wymar entered the inn and was not surprised to find the place overflowing with others who also felt the need for a roof over their heads and a hot meal. A quick scan of the room told him there were none within who held an immediate grudge against him and he relaxed. Theobald called to him from across the crowded room and Wymar made his way toward the table his brothers had managed to claim. He flung off his drenched cloak and nudged his youngest brother.

"Move over, Reynard," Wymar order. "You know I will not have my back to the room."

"*God's blood!*" Reynard complained. "Can you not stop telling me what to do for even a moment?"

Wymar gave the younger man a nudge. "Mayhap you will eventually figure out to follow my orders or learn from the mistakes you have made in the past. At a score and three, I should not have to tell you where I sit whilst in a common room."

Reynard reluctantly slid over upon the bench. "You are but five years older than me, Wymar. Why must you always be such a pain in my arse?" he complained bitterly.

Theobald's laughter rumbled in his chest before he propped his muddy boots across the opposite bench to stretch his legs. "You two go ahead and quarrel if you wish. I plan on ignoring you both and eating and drinking my fill whilst I can."

"Did you order food?" Wymar inquired when Reynard slid a mug across the table toward him. He took a long gulp and sighed in pleasure.

"Of course," Theobald answered setting down his cup. "Thought it wise, given the number of men here tonight. Wait too long and they just might run out of sustenance given the crowd."

"How long has it been since we have eaten a hot meal?" Reynard grumbled into his cup. Taking another sip, he turned his head and licked his lips whilst watching a platter of meat pass by to be served at the next table. "I swear my ribs are rubbing together from hunger."

Wymar laughed. "You are hardly starving, Reynard. 'Tis not our fault you slept late at our last stop and only had time for a bit of bread and cheese to break your fast."

"Bah! We could have waited long enough so I could have at least gulped down some porridge," Reynard moaned.

Theobald banged his mug upon the wooden table. "You know Wymar's rule. Up with the sun to make the most of the day. You had no one to blame but your own self for sleeping so late we had to have a lad sent up to wake you."

"I was sure he was occupied with the pretty wench who had her eye upon him that eve. If such had been the case, he would have been left behind. But nay, not our younger brother. He was only nursing his pounding head," Wymar added casting an eye at his mutinous sibling. "Really, Reynard, I think you should just take advantage of one of these willing whores and ease your suffering."

"Who says I am suffering?" Reynard sneered.

Theobald nodded. "Aye! You should not be mourning a woman for so long, and yet you have not been the same since Lady Johanne's passing. 'Twas not your fault the lady took ill. You are lucky you did not catch her ailment as well. Look around you, Reynard, and enjoy life. There are so many women whose favors can be sampled. Some do not so much as even ask for a bit of coin."

Reynard mumbled a curse and took a drink. A pretty young lass came and brought their food. The aroma of warm bread and meat pie filled their noses. She gave Reynard a wink and a smile. He ignored her unspoken offer and began to fill his trencher.

Reaching for another platter, Reynard broke off a piece of the bread and passed the dish to his brothers. Greedily he began to eat. "You know nothing of being in love and I look forward to the day when you are both struck down by women who pierce your hearts. Until then, I will mourn as I see fit and 'tis none of your business for how long I plan to do so."

Wymar laughed. "Brought down low by some meddlesome woman telling me what to do? 'Twill never happen."

Reynard pounded his fist onto the table. "I shall take that bet!"

Theobald chuckled again, raising his tankard in a silent toast. "You two never cease to amuse me. I just might place a wager amongst the men on who shall wed a beautiful lady first."

Wymar laughed so loud it caused those at the next table to stare at them. "Save your monies, Theo!" he answered waving to have his cup refilled. "Until our lands and my title are restored, I have no desire to settle down. And I have no intention of ever seeking love, which is for fools by the way. Mayhap someday a woman will cross my path where I can find a common accord and live out my days at Brockenhurst. But for now, I can have all my needs satisfied easily enough without the commitment of marriage."

Reynard gazed at Wymar with an obnoxious smirk set upon his face as though he knew some inner secret. "Mark my words, brother. Love will find you whether you wish it or not and I for one cannot wait to see you fall!"

Wymar just snorted at the very idea as he began to eat his fill. *Love! Bah! 'Twas for fools*, he thought again and had no doubt in his mind such an emotion would thankfully pass him by.

CHAPTER TWO

Lady Ceridwen Ward took a sip of her wine whilst her eyes kept a constant vigil upon the occupants of the tavern. Concealed in the shadows of a corner table, she took no chance she may be discovered as being anything other than one more knight, albeit a young one, bent on eating and drinking his fill. She was thankful she was at last dry whilst the storm continued to rage outside.

Now that her meal was finished, her men continued to consume the remaining food to satisfy the Empress's entire army. She would not, however, complain on the coin well spent to fill the table. Aye, she would spend all she had and more as long as they remained at her side on the off chance she had need of their aid. True, she was more than capable of personally rousting any ruffian who chose to take advantage of her person, but it was good to have others she could rely on. No one could stay vigilant all the time.

She glanced at the men at her table. All had been loyal to her family for many a year. When she fled Norwich to join the Empress's fight for the throne, many of the garrison knights had joined her. They had not left her ancestorial home defenseless but she was thankful for the number who decided to accompany her. Extra men on her side could only benefit her and she did not question their loyalty. She could not ask more from them.

She took another long sip of her drink whilst pondering her fate. How she had managed to hide her identity as she traveled the countryside must surely be by intervention from God Himself. She would not forget to give her thanks during her morning prayers. The months since she joined the Empress's calvary sometimes worn her thin with the trials she faced, but there had been no serious problems as of yet. She eyed the crowd yet again but still no one took notice of her and for that she was grateful. Everyone seemed to see only what she wanted them to see—just another knight eating their fill.

'Twas a constant worry that she might be recognized as the daughter of the Lord of Norwich or simply as a woman. Her father had protested when she insisted on joining the Empress's ranks, and not simply for the danger she would face on the battlefield. He swore that Norwich would be secure if only she would marry the son of their neighbor. Ceridwen grimaced knowing that such a fate would only see her miserable. Nay, she could not marry the choice her father offered. Instead, she sought to earn enough monies by her sword, in service to the Empress, to ensure the security of their lands. She seized the opportunity to change her fate and had reached out to her captain of the guard. With his help, she had enough men to comfortably ensure her safety whilst she traveled. And her efforts thus far had been fruitful.

She checked her attire for what must have seemed like the hundredth time but all was in order. Her chainmail helm hid her length of long blonde hair whilst her tabard concealed any hint of her bosom, not that she had much to boast of. The hood of her cloak was pulled down low masking the majority of her face. Her one feature she could not hide were the color of her eyes, for they were a vivid shade of aquamarine that many a suitor had remarked upon in her past. If she were to encounter any of those men, there was a very real risk that they would recognize her. Luckily, the hood of her cloak, or the helm she wore upon the battlefield, concealed her face and gender.

Her thoughts wandered to home. Inwardly she sighed wondering upon the fate of her father and their estate whilst she had been gone. Mentally she counted the months she had hidden within the Empress's army of men and came to the realization she had been gone far longer than intended. Had it really been half a year since she last crossed the gates of Norwich? Even now, was her father so worried that he sent out scouts to find her and bring her home?

His insistence that she continue her duties at Norwich was proof he had come to rely on her much as if she had been the son he never had. As an only child, her father kept her close despite the obvious fact she should have wed long ago. Most men would not care to take a wife who was aged a score and three, but her father had constantly put off finding a husband for her, saying there was more she needed to learn first.

He had taught her the inner workings of the estate, ensured she understood the importance of keeping accurate accounts of the monies spent or coming in to support their home. They often rode the land to oversee the serfs or inspect the fields so she learned what to look for in the fields for when crops should be rotated if the land needed to rest. Over time, he had passed many of his duties over to her, trusting to see them well handled. But when it came to making choices for herself about what her future should hold…that was where his trust ended.

She inwardly sighed remembering her last night at Norwich. His arguments had continued into the late evening hours, mainly due to the fact she was indeed a woman who had no place fighting amongst seasoned warriors.

But Ceridwen had fought back stating he had been the one to first thrust a sword into her hands at the tender age of ten summers. At the time, such a deed had but amused him until he had seen for himself she was skilled with the blade. Since that day, Ceridwen had never been far from the lists and her sire should not have been surprised when she had thrown caution to the wind and joined in the fight to help Empress Matilda ascend to the throne.

A bolt of lightning slashing across the evening sky lit the common room with a burst of brightness as though 'twas daytime and brought her out of her musings. Yet the brilliance causing her to shield her eyes lasted but an instant before the inn was again plunged into dark gloom. She quickly glanced around, wondering if someone had mayhap seen what she had been hiding—that she was a woman in a man's world. But no one came to her to call her out once she was again hidden in the darkness of the booth. The shadows of those within the tavern were again cast upon the walls from the candles and fire within the hearth causing Ceridwen to breathe another sigh of relief. She was still safe, for now.

With the next burst of lightning, the door was thrust open and a knight filled the space giving evidence to the man's height. He held her attention as he shook off the rain that continued to plummet downwards from the sky.

Ceridwen watched his progress whilst he all but swaggered across the room. 'Twas not often a man gained… nay, *earned* her appreciation, but this warrior seemed to have a commanding presence about him that few of her acquaintance possessed. He threw off his cloak, reminding her of a wet dog as he shook the rain from his shorter than average brown hair. She had the impression such a color was subject to the sun and once dry 'twould become lighter. Where such an assessment came from, she knew not, but this warrior continued to hold her interest when he began striding toward a table near her own where two men had just recently taken a seat. Since they had not given her a second glance, Ceridwen did not think she had to worry about them. They seemed more interested in food, drink, and the chance to get dry than anything else.

Murmurs as this stranger made his way through the room began to grow louder. Word that the Knight of Darkness was in their midst began to circulate amongst those in the tavern. *A man with a reputation it seems*, thought Ceridwen, though she was unsure how impressed she should be. Still, she continued to watch him as he stopped at the table to briefly converse with the two men seated there. Was he evil? Was that why the word *Darkness* had become associated with him? Or mayhap he was called this for another reason? Curiosity began to gnaw at her insides. She had lived a fairly sheltered life at Norwich and had not had a chance to learn very much about the notable knights who were fighting for the Empress's cause. Clearly the men here knew of this man but 'twas obvious she would receive no answers as to why he was called such a name.

Although she could not hear the conversation going on at their table due to the noise in the tavern, 'twas clear he was heckling the other occupants already seated. He was a cocky one, for certain, and she stifled a laugh as she took another sip of her wine whilst she continued to watch his antics in amusement. He at last folded himself onto the bench with his back to the wall, much like Ceridwen herself was sitting. The man was wise for she also would never sit with her back to the room.

"My lord…"

His laughter rang out and she watched the pleasure that lit his striking face once he took a long hard pull of the drink filling his cup. Once he set his tankard down, his eyes scanned the room and Ceridwen held her breath when his gaze momentarily flitted in her direction. She could not be certain the true color of his eyes from this distance, but they must be some shade of blue. She stifled the sudden urge to get up and cross the room just so she could end the mystery. She chuckled to herself knowing she would appear the fool if she actually braved such an act. Still…

"My lord…"

… he was handsome in a rugged sort of way, she would give him that much, but he nevertheless presented a puzzle to her. Why did she feel this sudden interest in this total stranger? Tilting her head gained her no further answers and yet the black raven in a field of red on his tabard looked oddly out of place. She did not recognize the crest and she pondered if he mayhap pilfered the emblem and garment. He reminded her more of a wild lion than a simple bird of prey.

He smiled at the pretty maid who came to place their food upon the table and her stomach churned that she was not the one who had earned such a reward. *God's Bones, where had that thought come from? Was she going soft? What was the...*

"Lady Ceridwen," a voice hissed drawing her out of her musings and her attraction to a total stranger.

"Quiet, you fool," Ceridwen warned, "else our relaxing evening will turn into a full brawl given the limited amount of female company that can be found here."

Arthur Chamberlayn, the captain of her guardsmen, watched her carefully before his eyes followed hers across the room. "I tried to address you as *my lord* more than once, but you appear distracted, my lady," he said with a furrowed brow.

"If I do not respond at first, you must simply try harder. There is no excuse for behaving so recklessly. Must I needs again remind you I am as any other ordinary knight here this eve?"

Arthur choked on his ale whilst he burst out into laughter. "I would hardly consider you ordinary, Ceridwen."

Her brow rose, along with her anger. "Are you trying to start a fight? Cease addressing me by my given name or as *my lady*! Will not the morn be soon enough to test your prowess with a blade with the next phase of the battle? I am to be addressed as Lord Elric and nothing else."

Symond Godwin, another one of her guards, thumped his mug upon the table and called out for more ale. He waved a young woman forward, her hips swaying as she made her way across the room. "Let us be merry and forget for one eve what awaits us in the morn."

Thomas Montecute, another of her guards, nodded in agreement. "Aye! Surely there are more pleasant ways to spend a night than worrying over what the morrow will bring." He pulled the woman forward into his lap and a squeal of delight passed her lips when he nuzzled her neck.

"Hey, now Thomas, I saw her first," Symond complained attempting to pull the woman from Thomas's grip.

"Sod off," Thomas returned with a smirk before giving the woman a quick kiss. "She liked me better the moment we walked in the door, you fool."

Ceridwen rolled her eyes and saw how the attention of the room was beginning to focus upon them. "Enough," she fumed, tossing them a glare in the hopes they would behave.

"'Tis just a bit of fun, my lord," Symond replied.

Ceridwen wagged her finger at both men. "Neither of you will be sampling the fares of anything more than the ale in your cup and the meat on these platters. Best leave the maid to finish her duties, Thomas. You must needs seek your comfort another night. We must all get a good night's rest so we will be ready for the battle on the morrow."

As he let the woman go, she bent to whisper in his ear and Thomas let out another burst of laughter. He gave the woman a swat upon her bottom and she left with a smile of promise on her face. Symond grumbled into his cup apparently knowing a lost opportunity when he saw one.

Ceridwen shook her head as the men returned to their meal. Her captain, however, continued to wear a fierce frown of displeasure upon his visage. "What?" she murmured even whilst her gaze continued to once more rest upon the stranger.

Arthur placed his cup upon the table after taking another long pull. "What is he to you?" he asked, leaning forward so their discussion would not be overhead. "Do you know him?"

"Nay, our paths have never crossed before now."

"Then why is it you continue to gaze upon him as though you wish to remedy such a situation?"

"There is just something about him that I find intriguing…" Her words trailed away into the nothingness of the night and she clamped her lips tight when she heard a low growl from her captain.

"You have no more time for a dalliance than the men do, *Lord Elric*, not that I would allow such an occurrence," Arthur warned in a low forceful tone. "I have guarded you from unsavory advances for years and have not once faltered in my duty to protect you. Your father would see my head upon a pike outside his gates and the rest of my body scattered across all of England if you are not returned in the same condition in which you left."

'Twas Ceridwen's turn to frown as Arthur talked as though he was in charge of her and the choices she made in *her* life. "You know damned well my virtue is still intact, Arthur. And I shouldn't need to remind you that you have no say in how I spend my days or nights," she murmured in annoyance. She reluctantly took her eyes from the warrior across the room. She would not admit it, but for one brief instant she felt a sense of freedom from duty. Her father expected her to marry someday to bring further wealth to the estate. A brief liaison with some lowly mercenary was out of the question.

"We should not even be having such a conversation," Arthur grumbled into his cup.

"Then why bring up such a subject? You know I would never—"

Arthur held up his hand to halt her words. "Aye, I know. Let us change the focus of our talk."

Her brow rose in amusement seeing her captain uncomfortable for 'twas a rare occurrence. "Would you care to have speech about the weather?" she laughed.

"You are being cheeky. Nay! I do not wish to have speech about the damn weather but a bit of sun on the morrow would be most welcome."

"Then what is on your mind?"

Arthur scratched at his chin. "What is taking Ratcliff so long, do you suppose? I would have thought he would be here long before now."

Ceridwen leaned back against the wall before reaching for her cup and bringing it to her lips. "Why are you wasting a perfectly fine eve by bringing him up in conversation?"

"Keep your enemies close… well… you know the rest," he said.

She leaned forward to rest her forearms upon the table. "I sent him on an errand to see to the camp," she murmured attempting to hide a smirk of satisfaction.

"That could not have gone over well," Arthur declared with a laugh.

"I am sure I shall pay for it upon his return. His disposition is ornery on most occasions. Being sent about like a squire will certainly not improve his mood but I could not resist the temptation. He vexes me."

Arthur nodded in agreement. "I still do not know why your father insisted he join us."

Ceridwen sighed and attempted to relax again against the wall. "My sire favors Ratcliff's suit. But do not ask me why, for I care not at all for the man. I would think father would be able to see him for what he is… a man after more money, land, and power who sees a wife as nothing more than another possession to acquire. It is not a marriage where I could ever find contentment."

Before Arthur could form a reply, the door to the tavern burst open again. All eyes turned toward the newcomer before they went back to their food and drinks. Ceridwen tried not to shiver in distaste of who stood before them. 'Twas as though by speaking of him, she had conjured up the man herself.

CHAPTER THREE

Sir Sperling Ratcliff threw open the door to the inn and let his eyes adjust to the dim interior light. He would like nothing more than to demand a room for the night and seek his comfort with a willing woman beneath him instead of a bedroll upon the cold hard ground at the campsite where he had set up his tent. But 'twas not to be, at least not this night. When he had tossed a coin to the lad who came to take his horse, he had been told the inn had no rooms to spare. He had lifted his fist to the heavens, feeling as if everything was against him. But while a warm bed was not to be his for the evening, there was still the chance of a hot meal and something to drink. That was enough to reconcile him to heading toward the inn. A good meal was the *least* he deserved after spending hours running about like nothing more than some nameless, worthless knight carrying out errands for his lady. For Ceridwen *was* his lady, no matter the woman continued her sham of cloaking her identity. He looked forward to the day when he would take her to wife and he could at last keep her under his complete control.

Slamming the door, he scanned the room before he espied the lady of his current irritation. She was a feisty one. He was tired of taking orders from her when the situation should be reversed. If only he had been able to convince her sire for them to wed before she decided to go in search of fame and the favor of her Empress. His only choice had been to follow along in her entourage. At the very least, if he was there with her then he could keep an eye upon her. Ensure she did not fall in battle before he could make use of her. A life such as hers should not be snuffed out in service of the useless woman they called Empress.

Bah! Empress. Anyone with any sense knew that King Stephen was the true ruler of England. Sperling had long since chosen his allegiance, certain that it was the winning side. And yet he would play this game of pretending to serve the Empress to its fullest potential if through it he could win Ceridwen's hand in marriage. Her estate was adjacent to his own and would double his wealth if they were to marry. Their marriage was a logical choice and would benefit both families. 'Twas but one more stepping-stone in his plans to amass the power he craved—along with his king's favor.

Pretending to favor the Empress was but a ploy. Sperling planned to trade the information he learned whilst in Matilda's camp to Stephen. He could only hope that the information he shared would hasten the end of the war—at which point they could all return home, where he would marry Ceridwen, expand his holdings, and earn true respect from the king. Surely, with the information he could impart to the king and the land he would own in Stephen's name, Sperling would be rewarded handsomely and would be able to show his monarch how valuable he was to have on his side. He silently vowed he would be victorious in gaining all he deserved. Wealth and power were undoubtedly what the Lord intended for him. Of *this* he had no doubt!

Taking off his drenched cloak, he draped the garment over his arm and strode toward Ceridwen's table. The men seated with her were never far from her side and he swore they sniggered into their cups as he drew near, the bastards! None of them treated him with the respect he was due—but that would change when *he* was their lord and master. He could bide his time until then.

Knowing what was expected of him, he swept down into a low bow that would have mimicked someone at court paying homage to his or her king... or empress depending on whose side you were on. "My lord," he said loud enough for the entire room to hear his words. This situation continued to irk him that he must appear to be in service to some young lord out to seek his own glory. By rights, he should have a score of knights dancing attendance on *him*.

Ceridwen nodded toward him in acknowledgment. "Ratcliff," she said his name with a low tone giving those within hearing evidence to this *lad's* youth. "All is in order with the camp and men?"

Sperling bit back a sharp retort. The woman had had him running errands like some squire doing the most menial of tasks. Meanwhile, she was inside drinking and eating her fill, not to mention being dry for the first time in days. He should have been here, too, enjoying a hot meal and a cold brew to quench his thirst. "Aye, Lord Elric," he replied briskly using the name she went by publicly. "Everything you have asked for has been accomplished."

"Good! Symond, move over and give Ratcliff room to sup with us. He has earned the privilege," she proclaimed raising her chalice of wine in a silent salute.

Privilege? Damn the woman. Her blue-green eyes sparkled like jewels in her amusement and he knew full well she had been pleased to send him running about and debasing himself by fulfilling her commands. He reached for his dirk strapped to his side and stabbed at a piece of meat, thankful there was still something left for him to break his fast.

"Best be quick about satisfying your hunger, Ratcliff," Arthur commented pointing to the remaining victuals. "We had just about given up you would join us and were getting ready to leave."

"Have you any notion how fierce the storm is outside?" he grumbled tossing those before him a frown.

"Lucky for you there is still meat upon the table, Sperling," Thomas mocked.

"Best eat up and enjoy the view of the serving wenches here whilst you can before Lord Elric sends you on another errand," Symond chuckled.

"Cease your jesting with me," he warned. "I have little patience for you or anyone else since I was the one running from one end of camp to the other seeking a place to pitch our tents. At least let me enjoy a few moments to eat in silence. I do not relish being the subject of your *witty* conversation."

Ceridwen leaned forward with a smirk. "I am certain you found us adequate space else you would still be out in the night searching for one. Will I be pleased?"

Sperling swallowed hard, the meat sticking in his throat. *God's Blood* this woman was beyond annoying. "Aye, I would not be here otherwise," he answered with clenched teeth. He would not tell her they were as far away from the battlefield as he could put them. The morn was soon enough for her to learn the truth when the dawn appeared on the distant horizon. Their location would hopefully ensure that she would not be able to reach the front lines where the fighting would be fiercest. He knew she was eager to show off her devotion to the Empress, but he had no interest in allowing her the opportunity to fight at all if he could help it. His intention was to keep her far from the action so that she would survive uninjured. It wouldn't do to lose his bride to some hulking brute's blade on the battlefield before he had the chance to wed her. It was an added incentive that keeping her a distance from the fighting would stifle any possibility of her getting recognized for her swordsmanship. He wanted that glory as his own.

Not that she seemed to care one jot for his glory or for what he was owed. She spoke to him as if he was no more than a common knave. He would not stand for such a thing. Aye! He would have much to say to her once he got her alone but until then he would cease further speech with her. He would not allow any woman to humiliate him, especially one who would one day be his wife. She was clearly enjoying their banter all too much for his liking.

Sperling continued to gulp down his meal and barely had time to finish his ale before Thomas rose from the bench. "Let us away whilst we can make a quiet exit," he said scanning the room for threats as the crowd became more rambunctious the more they drank.

Arthur stood as well. "It appears Ratcliff has had his fill. The dawn will greet us soon enough. Best get some sleep whilst we may. My lord…" he waved his arm in the direction of the door.

Ceridwen swung her leg over the bench. "Lead the way, Sir Arthur. Ratcliff can watch my back."

Sperling hid a smirk as Arthur, Thomas, and Symond left the table and made their way out the door. Before Ceridwen followed them through the portal, he grabbed hold of her arm and gave it a mighty yank. A squeak escaped her that was far from *manly*.

"A word, Ceridwen," he hissed in her ear.

"Let go of my arm, Ratcliff, lest you are left with a nub," she warned.

"You would not dare, my lady." His words were meant to threaten her but she smiled as though they held no weight.

"Surely you do not wish to test me, sir." Her free arm went to the sword swinging from her side.

Before she could pull the blade, he captured her other arm and gave her a shake. "Defy me all you want now but, once we are wed, you shall no longer be so free as to treat me like your lackey." He gave her a shove and she bounced off the frame of the open portal. Her feet slipped out from under her from a pool of water the rain left in the entryway. Amusement filled the common room when she landed in an undignified heap at his feet. Even Sperling was surprised—and amused. She must have been caught off guard for she would normally hold her own against him. She raised her head to stare upon him with angry blue-green eyes.

Sperling smiled in satisfaction when she managed to kneel upon the floor. Ceridwen belonged beneath him, in more ways than one. One day soon she would be groveling for his affection and approval as she waited for him in his bed. She certainly had no place on the battlefield.

Arthur returned to the door. "Lord Elric," he began.

"I am fine, Sir Arthur," Ceridwen declared through clenched teeth.

Her chin rose definitely as she stared up from her position on the floor as though daring Ratcliff to have the audacity to touch her once more. The thought of being inferior to a mere woman infuriated him. He nudged her shoulder with his boot, just for the sake of putting her in her place. Her glare told him much when she reached for a knife she had hidden in her boot. She held the weapon before her.

"Here now! Leave the young lord alone," a voice yelled out.

Sperling spun around to see who dared to interrupt his pleasure. A man strode rapidly across the floor with a determined stride. Two others followed close behind and, from their appearance, Sperling guessed them to be related. "What business is it of yours? Go back to your drink," he ordered, not giving the men another thought. But 'twas a mistake to think they had enough sense to go back to their table.

'Twas clear this knight had no thoughts of heeding Sperling's warning. He gave Sperling a shove as he passed by and offered his hand to help Ceridwen from the floor. She declined his help and stood on her own accord quickly adjusting her hood to cover her face. The man was a fool if he could not see for himself a woman stood before him instead of a young lord.

"Are you all right, sir?" the stranger asked casting a glance between the two of them.

"Aye, my thanks," Ceridwen ground out before fleeing through the door.

The knight once more turned to face him. "You should not have pushed the young lord. Once was bad enough. The second was uncalled for. Do you serve him?"

"'Tis none of your concern what is transpiring here this eve."

"I despise those who bully others. Is this not right, Reynard?" the man asked not taking his eyes from Sperling.

"Right enough, brother," the man called Reynard smirked. "The last one you fought with ended up with a busted nose and then face down in a pile of cow dung if I remember correctly."

The tavern erupted in laughter as wagers began to be made on who would win a fist fight. Many began siding with the other man, who was apparently called the Knight of Darkness. Ratcliff's eyes narrowed at the man before him. He was unfamiliar with anyone going by such a moniker, but then again, he had never been to Lincoln prior to now.

Sperling crossed his arms over his chest. "Who are you?" he said briskly wondering about the man behind his reputation.

"No one of import. My name has no bearing on the fact you should not pick on people either under your care or smaller than you."

Sperling's hand lowered to the hilt of his sword. "I should like to know your name before I kill you for your interference."

The other man next to Reynard came forward and began laughing. "Why is it we can never have a quiet evening without someone threatening you, Wymar? If you are going to brawl with this cur, take him outside and be done with it quickly, if you please, so we can go back to more pleasant entertainment."

"Wymar…?" Sperling frowned trying to place the name. He didn't believe he had heard it before.

"Aye, Wymar Norwood, and I shall be more than happy to oblige you by showing you a lesson or two in manners. Since we are exchanging pleasantries, mayhap you shall also tell me your name?" he asked with a smirk whilst looking him up and down as though he was assessing his worth and finding it lacking.

"Lord Sperling Ratcliff," he said scowling. How dare this man look upon him in such a manner? Clearly this warrior was nothing more than a mercenary for hire. And were that to be the case, that meant he was far beneath him.

"And the young lord who just left?"

"Not that it is any of your business, but he is Lord Elric Bartone. He is the brother of my intended," he stated, to make it clear that this was a family matter and was thus none of Norwood's business.

Norwood walked around him before facing him once again. "Brother? If I were you, and thankfully I am not, I would take more care with the young man who will one day be a relation."

"You know nothing of the situation so enough of your pestering me, lest you wish to test my blade!" he roared.

Norwood had the nerve to laugh. "Mayhap I am making it my business. Never did like to see someone taken advantage of. And if you're so eager to have your blade tested, then I'd be happy to oblige you. Let us take this outside and settle this among us, since you seem so very anxious for a fight. It is odd, though, for I somehow thought we would be fighting on the same side. Mayhap I was mistaken thinking those who dined here were faithful to Empress Matilda, considering her army is camped close by."

Sperling glanced around the room as all eyes became focused upon him as if awaiting him to declare himself a traitor to the woman they saw as their queen. Seeing no one else present who would come to his defense, he knew he had no choice but to concede. "My Empress knows I am loyal to her cause."

"Good!" Norwood declared crossing his arms. "'Tis gratifying to know we are on the same side and all seek to do whatever is within our power to restore our Empress to her rightful place upon England's throne!"

A loud cheer went up as those present raised their drinks in a salute to their queen. Sperling held onto his temper knowing now was not the place for a confrontation with the man before him. Not when the odds were stacked so heavily against him. He was not opposed to an unfair fight—but he preferred to hold the advantage on his side. "You and I can then settle this between us at another time, unless you remember to stay out of my affairs by then," Sperling stated.

"'Tis unlikely, so I will be at your service whenever you are ready to take me on," Norwood mocked with a jaunty salute.

Sperling gave a short nod and fled the inn. He knew when he was outnumbered. The morrow would be soon enough when the battle began anew, if by some slim chance he came across Norwood.

Drawing his cape around him, he made a vow Norwood would pay for interfering just when he had Ceridwen where he wanted her. If luck was on his side, the bugger would already be dead by someone else's hand. If not, it would give him the greatest pleasure to perform the deed himself!

CHAPTER FOUR

Wymar perused the tavern door with a scowl as it slammed shut. Something about the man who just left perplexed and unsettled him.

Reynard began chuckling. "Ratcliff... he certainly is living up to his name."

"How so?" Wymar asked, still curious why this man in particular irritated him.

"Did you not see him? He looks like a drowned rat with those beady brown eyes and his black hair plastered to his head," Reynard answered with another amused laugh.

"We most likely do not appear in much better condition, brother."

"Nay, none with our grand titles could ever be as ridiculous as that man!" Reynard protested.

"Knights of Darkness... Chaos... Havoc. We are not immune to what those in the heat of battle have come up with to call us," Theobald chimed in. "But those names do not provide us with any protection—or absolution. Our past misfortunes continue to follow us to this day."

Reynard's bellow of amusement left his lips. "I do not mind a misfortune or two in the service of building our fame. And I quite like those names. Makes us sound fierce for others to leave us in peace. But do not leave out Richard's name. Who could ever forget the Knight of Mayhem?"

The three brothers looked to one another before another burst of laughter between them rang out in the inn. Wymar cracked his knuckles before pulling his leather gloves from his belt and donning them. "Theobald, pay our bill," he ordered, after tossing a glance to his brother. "I wish to make certain the young lord will find his tent without being further accosted."

"Come now, Wymar," Reynard protested whilst eyeing the warmth of the fire inside the tavern's hearth. "Must we really rush away, back out into the rain? The night is still young and surely the knight will be just fine."

Wymar's gazed turned to his younger brother. "We are done here. Gather up what remains of the meal for Richard and let us go. 'Tis not subject to an open discussion."

"Best listen to him, Reynard," Theobald stated whilst he fished out the proper coinage to pay for their meal. "You know he will not change his mind. We were lucky enough to have sat here for as long as we did. We could have been eating whatever meager offerings we had left in our saddlebags instead."

With their bill paid, the three brothers pulled up the hood of their cloaks to give themselves whatever small protection from the elements they could find. The wind was fierce and Wymar held on to the neck of the garment to keep the hood from blowing back whilst his eyes adjusted to the dim of the night. 'Twas folly to attempt to even find the young man in weather this foul, especially when he had no way of knowing where the lad had made his camp, but he just could not shake the feeling he had in his head that this Lord Elric may have need of his help. 'Twas certainly none of his business as Ratcliff had said but still…

Paying the stableboy another coin for the extra care of Aries, Wymar mounted his horse and the brothers began trudging their way once more through the muck in the road. With the next bolt of lightning, he caught a quick glimpse up ahead of the young lord of his musing who was making his way upon a striking white steed. He was not alone with Ratcliff but was surrounded by a number of men. Seeing he was accompanied by others set most of Wymar's fears to rest.

They began winding their way through camp. When Wymar spotted his standard, he halted beside his tent and jumped off from his steed. "Do me a favor, Theobald, and see to Aries."

His brother took the extra set of reins. "You go alone and on foot? You should know better. Who will watch your back? You are not so foolish as to think there is no danger that could find you here, even though we are in a camp of allies."

"I will be fine and will not be long. If any try to accost me, I can see to myself—though I doubt any will. As you said, we are among allies for our Empress," Wymar declared. "The walk will do me good after all the riding we have done these many days."

"I do not like it. Take Reynard, at the very least. He may be young, but he is still good with a blade. You saw to his training yourself, after all."

Reynard slapped his thigh as he, too, jumped from the back of his horse. "I cannot believe I heard you give me a compliment about my competence with my sword arm. But you are right, of course. 'Tis impressive."

Wymar attempted to hide his smirk but 'twas hard to remain indifferent to his younger brother. He was only hard on him so Reynard would learn from Wymar's own mistakes in his youth and not repeat them. "Impressive? What was impressive? The compliment or your strength and skill with a blade?"

Reynard's hand went to the hilt of his sword and pulled it from the scabbard to swing the blade in front of him. He sliced at the air with an amused smile. "Ha! Both, of course," he boasted.

Wymar gave the younger man a playful shove. "Go and rest your head, you insolent pup," he taunted, "lest you be too weary come the morn to even lift such a heavy weapon of war."

His brothers led their horses away to seek a place hopefully out of the majority of the storm whilst Wymar continued following the young lord's group. He frowned as they moved throughout many of the campsites for their Empress's army. Aye, something was strange, indeed, and Wymar cared not that their group still pressed forward.

Their group at last stopped and Wymar saw for himself they had indeed pitched their tents on the very edge of the Empress's defenses, as far as possible from the battlefield. It didn't seem likely that there had been no positions closer that they could have taken—not when the lord and his men had already been at the tavern when Wymar arrived. Nay, their placement here, far from the action, had been chosen deliberately—and not by command of the lord, himself. He continued his observation of the group from a distance and saw that mayhap they, too, had figured out for themselves their situation. A shoving match began between two of the knights before the young lord came between them. He sent one of them on his way and Wymar saw he was Ratcliff. Mayhap the imbecile would be standing watch the whole night long.

The young man at last went into his tent alone and Wymar debated on whether or not to intrude and offer his services if he was needed. He paced back and forth for several minutes in indecision before he made up his mind and trudged forward through the mud.

>>><<<

CERIDWEN SWORE. HOW dare he humiliate her like he did! They had not made an official announcement that they would wed and yet he treated her as though they had already sealed their vows before a holy priest of God, leaving her as his to command. She would have much to tell her father once she returned home about the character of a man he thought should be her husband. The man was a vulgar beast and she would ensure she would not be forever tied to someone of his low character.

Tossing off her cloak, she pulled at a fur pelt and wrapped it around her shivering body. She should have called Arthur to return and help her remove her chainmail but she had wished to be alone with her thoughts, which at the moment were full of nothing but anger and frustration toward Ratcliff. Not just for the way he had treated her at the inn but for his utter failure to adequately perform the task she had given him prior to that. Did he have nothing but air between his ears that he would make camp so far from where the battle would take place on the morrow? How could he have missed something so glaringly obvious no matter how hard the rain pelted the ground, or the wind whipped at the branches of the trees?

There was no doubt in her mind Ratcliff had done it on purpose, but what she couldn't begin to fathom was what his motives could have been for their current location. Was it just to spite her?

There was the sound of raised voices above the riotous storm outside her tent and the noise pushed Ceridwen out of the musings. She had just about reached for the flap when it was flung open by Arthur.

"You have a visitor, my lord," he announced for the benefit of whoever awaited outside. Arthur was clearly upset. Though it was too dark to be able to tell for certain whether he was frowning, she could hear the tension in his voice.

"I have no wish to spare any further energy this night arguing with Sperling. Send him away and I shall deal with him on the morrow if there is time."

"'Tis not Ratcliff but another knight from the inn. He wished to see for himself you suffered no harm and he would not take no for an answer."

Her brow rose. Curiosity got the better of her. "Then send him in," she said waving her hand toward the flap of the tent.

Arthur hesitated. "Are you certain?"

Rolling her eyes, she waved her hand again toward the closed flap. She understood his caution, since she usually avoided letting any but her own men see her up close, but it was mostly dark in the tent. Surely that would be enough to protect her from detection. "If I am to see even a hint of sleep this night, then show the man in so I can be done with this matter. 'Tis late and I wish to seek my slumber," she fumed. She could not imagine who might be wishing to see her unless...

She pulled at the chain helm in order for the metal hood to once more cover her hair. She barely had enough time to ensure she looked the presentable *lord* before *he* filled the tent with his presence. *Damn...* despite the darkness, she could tell that he was even more handsome than when she saw him sitting at his table. If she wasn't disguised as a man she just might have swooned for the first time in her entire existence. He made her want to feel like a woman with his nearness.

He offered her a bow that would have done anyone at court justice. "My lord," he murmured in a deep baritone, "I am Wymar Norwood, most recently from Sheffield."

Ceridwen gave a brief nod. "I am Lord Elric Bartone," she replied, not giving any location from where she hailed. Nor did she trust herself to speak more for fear of giving her true self away. She may be attracted to this man but she knew him not and there was no reason for her to trust him as yet. She folded her arms across her chest and tilted her head to study him further. A convenient bolt of lightning illuminated the tent, and she was able to see the blue-grey of his eyes. She almost smiled seeing the color. Such a shade further complimented the man standing before her as though he in truth commanded the Empress's entire regiment.

Wymar cleared his throat and looked about her tent. She dare not peer behind her on the off chance she left something feminine in sight, not that she carried much with her as a reminder.

"You are well?" he finally inquired.

There was genuine concern in his voice as he observed her and she realized she needed to dismiss him as quickly as possible. She had a feeling in her gut this man was smarter than most. "I am," she answered curtly.

"I thought mayhap you could use further assistance. You seemed distressed."

A snort escaped her. More like irritated than anything else for allowing a puddle of rain to be her embarrassing downfall, along with a shove or two from Sperling. "I can handle Ratcliff."

"If you are certain…" His words lingered in the air whilst he waited for her reply.

"I am," she replied waving to the entry to the tent. 'Twas as though Arthur stood within hearing for the flap opened wide for Norwood to take his leave.

He watched her carefully before giving another nod. "Then as long as you are safe, I bid you good night. I am at your service, if you ever are in need of my assistance. Godspeed and may you remain safe on the battlefield come the morrow."

"And you, Norwood."

The handsome devil took his leave and a rush of air left her lungs in a huge sigh of relief. Arthur continued his vigil at the entryway to her tent for several moments.

"He is gone?" she asked in a breathy whisper.

Arthur let the tent flap fall into place closing off the outside world. "Aye, you are safe for now from any further intrusions for the night."

"Let us hope so." Ceridwen finally pushed the metal helm from her head and pulled out the long braid of blonde hair. "Help me with this chainmail. The gear feels unusually heavy this eve."

He lessened the distance between them. "I can imagine," he grumbled. "Lean forward so I can help you."

Ceridwen did as her captain bid, and relief flooded her to no longer bear the weight of the heavy chainmail that had protected her all day and night. "I suppose I shall be donning it much sooner than I would like. Dawn will be here before we know it."

"We can always go home instead, let others carry the fight," he suggested taking the chain linked armor and placing it over a wooden chest near her pallet.

"You know I cannot just up and leave."

"Why not? 'Tis not as though you are under orders to appear. Indeed, the Empress does not even know you are here amongst all these warriors, and praise God for that. She would not be pleased."

"Aye, I know," she hissed rubbing her eyes. "But I swore a vow pledging my sword arm to do all I was capable of in order to fight for her throne. I cannot in all good conscience forget such a commitment. Besides, if I were to return home, my father would think I was weak. I would rather die upon the battlefield then to allow him to condemn me in such a manner."

Arthur sighed. "You know very well he would not think of you as weak. You are the son he never had."

"He may think of me as such at times but he also has no issue to press the suit of a man not worthy of me. I hope upon my return home that I can convince my father of Ratcliff's true nature. I cannot image being condemned to a life with Ratcliff. Surely my sire will see reason."

"Indeed, he loves you so dearly that I cannot imagine him forcing you to wed against your wishes. All he wants is for you to be settled and happy."

"And so I shall be, with the husband I will find *after* the Empress is crowned queen. Until then, my place is here."

Arthur sighed. "You cannot blame me for trying. I sometimes wonder if 'tis worth the effort. Perhaps we are fighting for the wrong side."

She gasped and her eyes narrowed. "'Tis treasonous to even suggest Stephen should be king. Tell me I have not unjustly placed my trust in you. I thought you believed as I do that Empress Matilda is the rightful queen as the daughter of Henry I!" She gritted her teeth to prevent herself from shouting.

Arthur raked his hair back from his forehead. "You know I am faithful to her cause and to you. Mayhap I am just tired of it all and missing home, along with the comfort of my own bed. Sometimes I feel I am too old for this *shite!*"

"Bah! Old? You? If a score and ten is old then what will you feel like when you are old enough to be a father or grandfather for that matter?" she teased, thankful that her captain had only a momentary lapse of homesickness.

"I have to marry before such a miracle will happen and I am too busy fighting and keeping you safe to wed," he jested in return. His again went to the opening of the tent to peer out into the darkness. Closing it once more, he stood in silence as she went about putting the rest of her gear in place. "He is dangerous."

"Norwood?" she asked continuing what she was doing and not looking at Arthur.

"Who else would I be talking about?"

"Ratcliff." She pulled at a blanket and tossed it to Arthur who always slept at the entrance to her tent to continue his vigilant guard over her.

"We already knew him to be trouble from the moment he joined up with us. Nay, Norwood is far more dangerous, and I have the feeling he will change your life in unfathomable ways."

Ceridwen laughed before lying down upon her pallet. She would not confess that she, too, was tired of sleeping on the ground. "Norwood is as any other man," she answered dismissing any further thought as to the warrior's importance. She pulled the pelt of fur up to her chin and turned on her side. "Sleep well, Arthur."

Arthur blew out the candle and went to his pallet by the door. "Just be careful where he is concerned, my lady, and remember to guard your heart."

'Twas not long before Arthur's gentle snoring filled the tent. But such was not the case for Ceridwen as sleep evaded her. Her thoughts turned again and again to the way that Norwood had come to her aid this night. Even though she was more than capable of taking care of herself, it spoke of his character that he would rise so quickly to another's defense. And furthermore, to come through camp and the rain to check on her... a small smile escaped her thinking the man must have a sense of chivalry engrained in his soul. It mattered not to her that he thought of her as just another man. He had a sense of honor, enough so that he had taken the time to ensure she was safe. A man like that would be hard to forget.

Tossing and turning far into the night, a pair of blue-grey eyes continued to haunt her causing her to fret that perchance it was too late. Mayhap, and God help her if such was the case, she had already lost her heart to a handsome stranger.

CHAPTER FIVE

An eerie fog blanketed the early morning hours that would leave most with a premonition of spine-chilling events to come. Already a se'nnight had passed since his arrival at Lincoln, allowing Sperling to spend his days swinging his sword for the Empress in spite of his best attempts to avoid the battlefield. Yet Sperling had only one purpose in mind this morn and 'twas not to serve the Empress—nor would worry over the ghostlike weather deter him from his task. Nay, he would use the mist to his advantage to move about camp for the most part unseen. There was only one who stopped his progress over the line of defense set up by Stephen's army. But the sentry on duty was aware of Sperling's dealings with the king at such an ungodly hour and let him pass without a word being said once he recognized who approached.

He would be considered a traitor if captured by any of the knights who fought for either side considering the many times he had traipsed across to both camps during the Battle of Lincoln. Those in Matilda's army would slit his throat without a moment's hesitation if they knew he had been passing on information to King Stephen... or that he was, in truth, loyal to his king. And 'twas not as though all of King Stephen's men knew Sperling was on their side. 'Twas a dilemma he prayed would end soon with a victory for his king.

With the sighting of the king's tent, the knight standing guard gave him a leery look before allowing him entrance by holding open the flap. *The insolent cur*, he thought before bowing low upon entering.

"Your most gracious Majesty," he murmured respectfully.

"Rise, Sir Ratcliff," the king bade with a wave of his hand.

"I am your most humble servant. How may I be of service?" he asked rising to watch his king's fingers drumming restlessly upon the arm of his chair.

"You could have this blasted siege be over and done with if you truly wished to please me... but I suppose that is asking much for just one man."

"If 'twas in my power, I would grant you victory of the battle, Your Grace."

"What news do you have of *her* camp?" King Stephen inquired refusing to even say Matilda's name.

"There is not much to report, Your Majesty, since my last visit. Her army is prepared to wage war for the entire year if need be to win their cause."

The king stood and began pacing the confines of his tent. "That damn woman will not win what is rightfully mine," he swore raising his fist.

"Of course not, Your Majesty," Ratcliff bowed, lowering his eyes.

"What news do you have of her half-brother, Robert, first Earl of Gloucester? Has he joined her ranks?" the king questioned.

"Not to my knowledge or that I have been privy to overhear."

The king walked over to a table and motioned for Sperling to join him. He began pointing toward a map. "I have plans for you, Ratcliff. There are several castles between Lincoln and London where it would be beneficial to me to know I have a loyal man who supports my reign, especially with those near the coast. Several are currently in my control and their lords have now pledged their fealty to me. This one here I believe you shall recognize because 'tis adjacent to your own land."

Sperling's eyes traveled across the map to where King Stephen pointed. There was no mistaking the estate. "Aye, of course I know of it since we are neighbors."

"Once the battle is won in our favor, make your way home and pursue a marriage between yourself and the daughter. Kill her father if he will not agree. I hear he is a traitor and favors my cousin so 'twill be of no matter to me if his head sits upon a pike outside his own gate. How you deal with the woman is up to you but wed her and secure the castle in my name."

"'Twill be done, Your Grace," Sperling replied with a smile of satisfaction. He knew that God had blessed his dreams, and this was just further proof, since the commands of his king aligned so perfectly with his own wishes to control Ceridwen by any means possible.

"Then be gone with you before this infernal mist disappears and you are spotted as a spy," his king ordered with another wave of his hand. "You have served me well, Ratcliff. I would hate to lose such a cunning man."

Sperling bowed again and left the tent eager to be amongst the fighting this day. If all went according to plan, he would be wed once this battle was over and at last have Ceridwen right where he wanted her… in his bed.

⇢⇉⇉✕⇇⇇⇠

WYMAR DUCKED, BEFORE dropping to his knees when he narrowly missed the battle-axe aimed at this head. "You bloody whoreson," he shouted when he regained his feet, swinging his sword in a wide arc.

"I will spit on your dead body and claim to be victorious over the Knight of Darkness," the cur retorted, full of arrogance that his poor swordsmanship certainly didn't warrant.

Wymar smirked knowing the knight before him would fail in his boast to kill him. He lifted his sword. A howl of pain erupted from his adversary when the blade came in contact with the man's arm, severing it cleanly at the elbow. The knight fell to the ground, screaming. Taking his life would likely be a mercy at this point, but there was no time to waste on his fallen foe, not when another easily took his place.

'Twas rumored that the Empress's half-brother had joined their forces bringing with him his own army of men. Surely, the battle would tilt in their favor with the additional knights to fight for their empress and ensure Stephen's defeat.

But as far as Wymar was concerned, today's battle was no different than the day before. The enemy continued to press forward in their desire to win the day. Those who fought for the Empress Matilda were just as eager to secure her title and claim the battle as a victory in her name. Yet all Wymar saw before him was blood and death. The stench of it sickened him but still he continued swinging his sword.

A movement caught his eye and his attention was drawn to one of his brothers. Theobald was holding his own for the most part but he was so focused on the man in front of him that he paid no attention to the one coming at him from behind. The fool!

Wymar dodged a blade and shoved his shoulder into the knight who was facing him, catching the man off balance and knocking him to the ground. He jumped over him, running in his attempt to reach his brother before a blade was thrust into his back. The idiot had had no time to put his chainmail on this morn before the call to arms was raised. Theo's leather jerkin would provide little protection against the steel coming closer by the second.

With no further thought, Wymar began running to reach his brother. Reaching behind him, he pulled a dirk from his belt and flung the blade. Wymar watched in satisfaction as the knife hit its mark right between the eyes of the unsuspecting mercenary who fell in a heap to the ground.

Theobald must have heard the man's cry as he was struck, for he appeared stunned as he swerved to miss another blade. He thrust his sword forward. The enemy before him groaned as he fell to the ground and Theo pulled his weapon from the dead man's belly before turning to glimpse the man at his back who had nearly taken his life.

"My thanks," he called out to his brother.

Wymar met him upon the field and then clasped arms. "Be more mindful next time. I may not be there to save your sorry hide."

Theobald grunted, before he elbowed another knight in the gut. He gave the man a swift kick in his arse and watched in satisfaction as he went tumbling forward. "Take care of yourself as well. We might just win this day if we are lucky," he shouted.

"Where's Reynard?" Wymar yelled back, swinging his blade again and again. The sound of swords meeting swords rang out in the air along with the moans of the dying.

He brother raised his shield to deflect another blow. "There!" he bellowed swiftly pointing his sword toward the left before throwing himself back into battle.

Wymar swung around and was satisfied his younger brother appeared to be holding his own. He may be young but he was an exceptional swordsman, even better than Wymar had been at that age… not that he would ever admit such to Reynard.

He had no further time to worry about his brothers, not when the enemy continued to press forward to gain every inch of land. Time and time again, Wymar lifted his shield or swung his blade. For each foe he struck down who attempted to take his life, another took his place. A moment seemed like an hour in the endless sea of knights fighting for whichever side they belonged on.

A sharp, childlike cry rang out. It was an ungodly sound amongst the battle weary. Wymar paused to get his bearings and to search for the source of the cry, for no one of such tender years belonged in the bloodbath before him. He ducked from another sword aimed at his head before he at last espied the person who had drawn his attention.

A young squire, no more than ten and four summers, held a dirk to defend himself whilst he stood guarding another knight lying upon the ground. He watched as the boy was backhanded and 'twas a grim reminder of the incident that happened the night at the inn. With no further thought, he plowed through the men standing in his path of reaching the boy who swayed yet continued to hold his ground. The boy had some fight in him, and was clearly willing to risk his all to give his master a chance to recover. Alas, a glance was enough to tell Wymar that no such recovery was possible. The knight who the boy was so valiantly defending was already dead.

Wymar charged into the mercenary who was about to kill the boy, knocking him to the ground. Mumbled curses came pouring forth as they continued to wrestle in the mud to gain the advantage. But Wymar had had enough of those showing such unfair and excessive aggression toward people who were too young to be well equipped to be upon the battlefield. He found himself thinking of the knight he had met when he first arrived in Lincoln, treated so appallingly by a man in his service. The young lord deserved better—and so did this squire. Fumbling for a knife he saw laying on the ground, his fingers at last grabbed at the hilt and he plunged the blade into the man's leather jerkin, thankful this one was not wearing steel chainmail.

He saw the man's look of surprise before his face went slack with death. Wymar rolled off him and retrieved the knife. Wiping the blade on the dying man's clothing, he gave no further thought to him but turned his attention to the young boy still reeling on the ground.

"Get up," Wymar bellowed, taking the boy's elbow to help him rise. Making a fast assessment of the situation around him, it appeared as though no one was immediately going to make another attempt on his life… at least not as yet.

"But my master…"

"…is clearly dead. Have you no sense, boy, to be here where you do not belong?"

The lad shook his head still dazed. "I was to follow him…"

Wymar sighed and began pulling the boy away from the field.

"And you have done your duty but, unless you wish to join him in the afterlife, you need to get yourself to safety."

"I have nowhere else to go," he cried out and Wymar was reminded of when he and his brothers had been in the same predicament.

Thundering hooves caused Wymar to shove his charge away from the massive war horses that carried their knights away from the battlefield. *The cowards*, Wymar thought whilst he saw what appeared to be Stephen's cavalry deserting him.

"Damn Welsh!" he murmured whilst another all too familiar scene flashed across his mind. How many years had it been since he had lost his home? Only six, in truth—scarcely more than a handful—and yet they felt as if they had been too many to count. At times, it was as though they had been living from place to place longer than they had called Brockenhurst their home. The only remembrance was the family standard he had been able to save, and he continued to have the image of the black raven sewn into his tabard when the opportunity presented itself.

His father had been beheaded for treason when Stephen's men broke down the barbican gate and seized the keep. Wymar had rushed to gather what he could before he quickly ushered his brothers into a hidden passageway only known to the family. There had been no time to gather any of the other household staff to ensure their safety. Though it pained him to his soul to leave the rest behind, protecting his brothers had to come first. The servants' lives might be spared, depending on the mood of their captors. But sons of the keep would be made an example of. With their sire dead, Wymar knew it had been imperative to escape as quickly as possible.

Once they had made their getaway and were far enough away from the madness that had befallen them, Wymar had turned back to look at what was left of their home. Their estate surrounding the keep burned until there was not much left to salvage. And yet his eyes had observed how the keep still stood proudly in the distance even though the outbuildings were no more. Even the title that should have rightfully been his birthright had been stripped from him and he watched angrily when Stephen's banner was raised at the top of one of Brockenhurst's turrets.

From that day forth, Wymar was suddenly a parent to his brothers, wandering the lands and hiring out his sword arm for a bit of coin in order to help them survive. Mayhap 'twas a blessing their mother had died giving birth to Reynard. He would have not wished her to see their fate if she had yet lived that awful day their father's life had been taken.

Another cry from the boy had Wymar coming out of his memories. Whirling around, he finally noticed that another knight was charging in his direction with battle axe raised. With the boy clinging to him in fear, Wymar was unable to lift his sword or shield to protect them. He saw his life passing before his eyes until the warrior suddenly started to drop face down into the ground. Puzzled, understanding at last dawned in Wymar's mind when he saw the reason for the man's demise. He could not miss the sight of a long knife protruding from his adversary's back.

He looked up thinking he would see one of his brothers, only to come eye to eye with the young lord he had been thinking of only moments ago. 'Twas obvious he had just saved Wymar's miserable life. He gave a brief nod, the man acknowledging him before clicking his heels to his horse's flanks. Leaning low in the saddle, he reached forward to pull his weapon from the warrior's back and proceeded to maneuver his white steed back into the fray to chase after the disappearing cavalrymen.

His arm around the squire, he pulled him further away from the battlefield. "Think you can find my standard amongst the camp, boy?" he asked showing him the blood-soaked tabard he still wore.

"Aye, milord," the boy replied.

"Then get yourself to my tent and stay there. We shall talk more once the battle is over."

Wymar watched the boy scamper away. Once satisfied he was done saving children for the time being, he went back into battle. 'Twas not long afterwards that the sound of raised voices began to be heard and men on both sides lowered their weapons of war to figure out what was occurring.

The unmistakable sound of laughter and rejoicing began to fill the air. 'Twas something so out of place yet the sound spread the news as quickly as a brushfire burns out of control. Stephen had been captured by none other than Robert, Earl of Gloucester, the Empress's half-brother. Wymar swore. Kicking the dirt in front of him, he sheathed his sword when he realized he had missed his opportunity to impress his Empress by capturing the man himself.

Men from Stephen's army began to scatter in every direction to avoid being captured by Matilda's forces. But Wymar's only concern was to ensure his brothers were safe. Afterwards he would need to once more seek out the young man to whom he owed his life. He could only begin to ponder what Lord Elric would demand as a life debt payment.

CHAPTER SIX

DEFIANCE RACED AFTER the Welsh horsemen as they fled not only the battle but their supposed king. *The traitors*, Ceridwen thought as she flicked at the leather reins in her gloved hands. Her horse knew her well and stretched her neck to run at a full gallop in pursuit.

She was not the only one riding to catch up with the fleeing army. Arthur, Thomas, and Symond also rode with her. Where Ratcliff was hiding no one could be sure, not that she cared where the bastard had gone. She could only pray he was either dead upon the battlefield or scurrying his sorry arse back home. If luck remained with her and with the Empress's victory, Ceridwen would soon be riding to Westminster Abby to see her sovereign crowned as the rightful ruler of England.

Or would she?

She could not hide under this guise forever nor could she put off for long her return home. If the fighting was over and the Empress was crowned queen, then Ceridwen no longer had any excuse to not return to Norwich. She could not avoid her father's dictate that the time had come for her to be married. In truth, it was not so much the idea of marriage that Ceridwen objected to so much as the man her father had chosen. Ceridwen's only wish was to speak to her father and convince him that Sperling Ratcliff would only run Norwich into the ground. Nor did she trust him to treat his wife with kindness or his children with consideration. He was a man who cared only for himself. Surely, she could make him see reason upon her return.

She could only hope that her return would come at her own time and not because her identity had been revealed. She had succeeded in hiding it for all these months, but any day could be the day when her true identity was unmasked. Bad enough if the men in the camp were to learn that there was a woman among them. But it would be far worse if the queen were to discover it. Her Empress would be furious that Ceridwen had come to fight for her. It would not matter that Her Majesty knew how well trained she had become. After all, 'twould not be the first time her queen had learned of Ceridwen's desire to fight alongside the best of her men. Her Majesty had visited Ceridwen's home many times over the years and had watched from the side of the lists whilst she trained.

"Lord Elric…"

But just like her father, Empress Matilda had only approved of her sword work with the understanding that she would use it solely to defend her estate. She had expressed quite clearly that she would never approve of Ceridwen wielding a sword on a distant battlefield. Once she had departed, Ceridwen swore she would fight for her queen and prove her worth so as to demonstrate that she could fight just as well as any man in Her Majesty's forces.

"Lord Elric…"

She was proud of how well she had fought, but she did not know if she had done enough to distinguish herself. There had been many excellent fighters on the battlefield… such as Norwood. She had seen him fighting with ferocity, day after day. And then on that very day, her heart had been in her throat when she witnessed him so preoccupied with a mere boy that he had no clue he was about to be run through with an axe! His nod across the battlefield had a promise that he would seek her out after the battle… or mayhap she should be thinking he would be looking for the lord he owed his life to. A smile lit her face. *God's Blood* she would love to reveal herself to him just to see his reaction to the news that a woman had saved him.

He was even more handsome in the light of day with his blondish brown hair blowing in the breeze after his helm had fallen back from his head. She wondered if the neatly trimmed beard would be soft to the touch. Would he mind that her hands were as calloused as his from years of holding a sword? What would it be like to—

"Damnation, Lord Elric, hold up!"

Arthur's shouting quickly brought her out of her musings of the handsome knight and she pulled back on the reins. She watched the fleeing horsemen as they continued onward from the battlefield. They were too far out ahead—there would be no catching them now. Very well, then. Let the cowards go back from whence they came.

"What is it?" she bellowed once Defiance came to a halt and Arthur was abreast of her.

"I could ask you the same thing considering I said your name several times before you heard me. You may be chasing after those traitors but your mind was somewhere else, I think," he replied whilst watching her with a quizzical gaze and furrowed brow.

How easily he reads me, she thought, although why should he not? He had been by her side protecting her for more years than she could remember. They were more like brother and sister than captain and lady. "I do not know what you are talking about," she said irritably before pulling on the reins to turn her steed back toward the battle.

"You cannot fool me, Ceridwen, even if you wish to try to convince yourself that your mind was completely focused on chasing down the Welsh riders," Arthur taunted.

Thomas paused to look at the riders who were disappearing from view. "Perchance this is a good omen that we shall win the battle."

"Aye," Symond joined in. "Mayhap the rest of our enemies will also come to realize they fight for the wrong ruler. If those Welsh are so cowardly to up and leave their *king*, then perchance his soldiers shall do the same!"

Ceridwen chuckled. "Well, let us not waste any more time. Shall we join in the fun to send the rest of them on their way, men?" Flicking the reins, she sent Defiance into another gallop with her men following close behind.

But there was no reason for them to hurry. Nay. By the time they made their way back to the battlefield, the Empress's army was in the process of placing any of Stephen's troops under guard. They slowed their mounts to take in the scene of those who had perished.

"You there!" Ceridwen shouted at one knight checking to ensure those upon the ground were in truth dead. "Have we won?"

The knight looked up after stabbing one of the fallen in front of him. Hearing the man's last breath, he stood. "Where have you been that you have not heard Stephen has been captured? Half the army is already in their cups celebrating our Empress's victory."

Ceridwen dismissed him from her mind. "Praise be! We are victorious," she yelled standing up in her stirrups.

"Does this mean we can now go home?" Symond asked.

Thomas reached over and clasped his arm. "I would not mind heading in that direction myself. Arthur?"

Arthur pulled off his helmet and placed it over the pommel of his saddle. "You know I go where our leader goes. 'Tis up to Lord Elric," he said briskly.

Ceridwen looked between her men. "Can we not just savor this moment for a few minutes before you all start hounding me on when we shall return home? Do you not wish to see our Empress crowned Queen of England?"

Symond pushed off his helm as they continued walking their horses. "Are you sure you wish to continue riding with the Empress's troops, my lord?" he inquired.

"He brings up a valid point. The longer you ride with these men, the easier 'twill be for Empress Matilda to learn you are here," Arthur stated the obvious.

Thomas nodded. "Aye... let us not forget the last time she saw you training when we were home and what happened when you offered her your service to fight on her behalf."

"She will not be pleased to learn you disobeyed her," Symond agreed.

Ceridwen pulled hard on the reins causing Defiance to whinny in protest. "Enough! We can discuss this at length later this eve or the morn for that matter. For tonight, we shall celebrate our victory and let the rest fall into place as it may."

"But Lord Elric—" Arthur began, but clamped his lips shut when she put up her hand to halt his further protest.

"I said *enough*. In either case, the ride to Westminster will take us south which is the direction of home. Let us drink tonight and be merry. We can discuss the matter of our return home whilst we travel."

They had not gone far when they came upon Ratcliff who was traipsing through the blood-drenched field. He looked as though he had been to hell and back given the amount of blood staining his attire. He looked none too pleased as he slapped his leather gloves against his side.

"Get down from your horse," he ordered whilst looking up at Ceridwen and her men from his placement on the ground.

"Excuse me?" she hissed, peering down at him with furrowed brow.

"You heard me," Sperling spat. "You have had your fun playing the loyal soldier, but now that the fighting is over, 'tis time you play the dutiful wife."

"My father never agreed for us to wed and neither did I."

Sperling burst out laughing. "Think you I care one whit whether you agree to our marriage or not? You shall do as you are told."

Arthur inched his steed closer, his hand holding the hilt of his sword. "You forget yourself, Ratcliff."

"And all of you will be the first thing I remove from Norwich once

I am established as lord and master there," Sperling hissed.

"You can try but you will not succeed," Symond said moving his horse next to Arthur's.

"Aye. We know the meaning of the word loyalty," Thomas said as he, too, came to the other men to show a united front.

Ceridwen was glad to see her men coming to her aid. Their loyalty was to be commended. Still, it surely wasn't needed. Sperling was spouting off, but she couldn't believe he would do anything truly rash. "Stand down, men. I am certain I can handle Ratcliff."

"God's Blood, you will not handle anything where I am concerned," Sperling cursed before he continued his rant. He pointed toward Ceridwen. "We shall wed posthaste as soon as I can find a priest to see the deed done. Then we shall make our way home."

"I am certain any good man of the cloth you come across will be too busy giving last rites to have time for a wedding... a wedding I have not agreed to. Nor have I any intention of making such a commitment to you of all people—now or ever."

"You will obey me, Ceridwen, elsewise everyone will know you have disguised yourself as a man these many months. I have no issue exposing your deceit to the Empress and to all who will listen if you do not do as I demand."

"Nay... I think not. You think you may have the upper hand over me but your ploy will be useless if I declare my real self to Empress Matilda," she informed Ratcliff, leaning her arm upon the pommel of her saddle. "I will also ensure my father learns your true character when you are not trying to impress him. Think you that he will welcome your suit when he learns that you tried to blackmail his daughter? Any talk of marriage to you will cease posthaste. I shall even go so far as to assert that he will ensure you never set foot on our land again. Now move aside... I have better things to do than waste my time having speech with someone who cares only for himself."

With their conversation over, she clicked her heals setting Defiance back into motion. As her horse passed Ratcliff, her steed reared up as though she had commanded him to do so causing mud to go flying all around. For good measure, Defiance swished her tail, hitting Ratcliff in the face. He looked furious, but he said nothing as he stormed away. She patted her horse upon her neck causing her to nicker.

"We have not heard the last of him," Thomas declared as they rode.

Arthur nodded. "Aye. He cannot be trusted."

Ceridwen grimaced at their words. If Ratcliff told all in sundry that she was in truth a woman before she could reveal herself first, 'twould not take long for such news to reach the Empress. She could only image the ramifications. The Empress would not be pleased.

"Ratcliff could *never* be trusted. Since he is threatening me, I believe my guise of being Lord Elric Bartone is most likely at an end," Ceridwen finally answered as she came to terms with the idea of revealing her true self. "I will have to pay the consequences when my actions are common knowledge with our Empress but have no fear, men. I will take full responsibilities for having you all take part in my ruse."

They continued riding in silence. She did not look to see where Ratcliff had gone. She had no interest in attempting a reconciliation with him. Instead, she left him and the battlefield behind, and never once looked back.

CHAPTER SEVEN

WYMAR ENTERED HIS tent with Richard and his brothers following close behind. Immediately, the lad he had saved from the battlefield stood. He had to admit, he had almost forgotten about the boy until he saw him standing there, rushing to assist him with his gear.

"What is this?" Richard asked with a chuckle. "You have gained a squire in the course of one day?"

Wymar unfastened the belt holding his sword and handed the weapon over to the boy. He faltered slightly from the weight but still held the gear firmly before setting it down upon a small table. Tall, lanky, and with a crop of curly black hair, the boy looked as though he weighed little more than his sword. "Aye, his master died upon the field. The lad might have met his maker as well seeing how he was risking life and limb, trying to protect the man's remains with nothing but a dirk and stubbornness."

"Will you help me find him, sir? And also, a priest to see to a proper burial," the boy asked.

Wymar gave no hesitation as he nodded. "Of course, but first things first… tell me your name. I cannot call you *boy* for as long as you are in service to me."

"'Tis Turbert, but my friends call me Turb."

Reynard laughed. "They call you Turd?"

"That is unfortunate," Richard replied ruffling the boy's hair.

"Nay, not Turd but Turb for Turbert," the boy's face reddened in embarrassment as the men around him chuckled.

"Then Turb it is," Wymar stated before turning a raised brow to the rest of the men in the tent, "and stop teasing the lad. He has had a rough time today and he is now under my protection."

Theobald stepped forward placing his hand upon Turb's shoulder. "Welcome to our group. I am certain my brother will treat you well. You are well trained in the duties of a squire?"

"Of course, milord," Turb answered, nodding eagerly.

"Call me Theobald. Since my brother Wymar has forgotten his manners, I'll make the introductions myself. This is our younger brother Reynard and our friend, Richard."

Wymar pulled the bloodstained tabard from his body. "You shall forgive my manners or mayhap not. I have other things on my mind."

"Like celebrating our Empress's victory with an ale or two I hope," Theobald replied, clapping his hands together in anticipation.

Wymar waved Turb forward and the lad assisted him with removing the chainmail. Fetching a small basin of water, Wymar washed some of the grime from the battle away. "Nay not necessarily, although a drink may be in order before the night is done."

Richard grabbed a stool and sat. "What could be more important than celebrating our success and victory in battle?"

A goblet of wine was pressed into Wymar's hand and he took a long pull before he motioned for Turb to fetch drinks for the other men. "I owe someone my life. If 'twas not for him, Turb and I might be lying dead upon the field."

Reynard was about to sip his drink but froze at these words and tossed him a startled look. "You owe a life debt?" he whispered as though barely believing that his brother would owe a stranger his life.

"Aye," Wymar replied with a frown.

"To who?" asked Theobald and Reynard at the same time.

Wymar finally sat. "The young lord from the inn. His name is Lord Elric. I must needs seek him out for I know nothing about him or what he may ask of me before he feels the debt is paid."

Richard set his cup down. "His act of saving you was in the heat of battle. Surely he will not ask much of you. You are most likely not alone in helping another when you saw the chance that someone from our side might perish."

"Aye, this is true but you know how I feel about such things. If nothing else, I must needs seek him out and find out for myself what payment he might expect of me." Reynard and Theobald both began drinking and chuckling at the same time. "I do not know what you think is so humorous. We agreed to stay together so wherever I might go to repay this debt, then you both will be traveling there as well," Wymar smirked in satisfaction as he watched the laughter die from his brothers' faces.

Richard rose. "Then we best make ourselves as presentable as possible."

Wymar gulped down the rest of his wine. "Your journey can end here if you wish it, friend. 'Tis not you that owes the debt. You need not come with us."

"You insult me, Wymar," Richard grumbled. "We have watched each other's backs for how many years and obviously I failed you, especially if you claim you owe another your life."

"No insult was intended, Richard," Wymar stated. "I just wanted to give you the option to travel wherever your horse may take you instead of staying with us."

"Stop trying to get rid of me, you dolt," Richard said coming over to Wymar and punching his arm good-naturedly. "Wherever you go, then I shall follow."

"Turb," Theobald called out. "Come see that your new master has fresh clothes to don and let us go meet this knight who saved my worthless brother's life."

With Turbert's help, the men cleaned themselves up, donning fresh garments. Once presentable they began making their way past numerous tents. 'Twas certainly a far different air about camp now that they claimed the victory at Lincoln. Capturing Stephen was more than enough of a reason for everyone to rejoice. Wymar had only wished that he had been the one to turn him over to his Empress. Still, he could still hope that he had fought valiantly enough to merit some share of her attention and praise.

Following the path from the previous night, he was almost to his destination when the one he sought came riding up from the opposite direction. He reined to a stop in front of his tent but remained on horseback. Two of his men dismounted and came to the front as though protecting their master. The other—the same one who had been guarding his master's tent the night that Wymar had visited—continued to keep his seat in his saddle and frowned at Wymar.

Not sure why the guards were on edge, Wymar bowed and cleared his throat until his brothers, Richard, and Turbert did the same. "My lord," he began, "I have come to have speech with you on a small matter."

"You mean the matter of me saving your life. *That* small matter?" Lord Elric sounded amused. Wymar was uncertain whether to take that as a good sign or a very bad one.

"Aye."

"I would not think saving a life is so insignificant, unless you do not value yours as much as I value my own," the young lord murmured low.

God's Blood! Hearing the tone of this fledgling knight, Wymar could only guess as to the age of the person he now owed a debt. Had this man even reached a score of years? Wymar doubted such was the case.

He stood upright, stepping forward even whilst the lord's guards reached for their swords. Wymar held up his hands. "I mean you no harm. Indeed, I wish only to know how I may give service to repay the debt I owe you. Mayhap we could negotiate terms that will be agreeable to us both."

The young knight before him took off his helmet and handed it to one of the men waiting on the ground. "Stand down, men. I do not think Norwood means me any harm. Go tend to your horses. They have served us well this day."

"If you are sure, my lord," one of the warriors said never taking his gaze from Wymar's group.

A bit of bubbly laughter erupted from the lord sitting atop his steed causing Wymar to frown. The light, *feminine* sound was as unexpected as the fact that Wymar owed his life to another. *What the bloody hell?*

"Arthur is here with me, should I need protection. But I believe I have proved my worth this day upon the field. Is this not so, Norwood, or should I call you the Knight of Darkness?" he inquired lifting but one brow. One corner of the knight's mouth quirked up in amusement at his own jest.

"Aye, my lord, you have more than proved your worth, especially in my eyes. No man could ask more from another than to defend one's life. I owe you a debt, sir, and one I shall humbly pay." Wymar fell to one knee paying homage, continuing to wonder what the man would ask of him.

Wymar was not expecting laughter to erupt from the knight, especially as the laughter still did not sound manly at all. He watched as Lord Elric pushed off his chainmail helm and reached behind him to pull a long braid of blonde hair free. A gasp arose from all who were witness to the transformation taking place for everyone to see Wymar's shame.

"I am no man, Norwood!"

The knight slid off the horse and came to stand directly in front of Wymar who did his best to hide his shock of who was standing confidently before him. By *Saint Michael's Wings*... a woman had saved his life!

CHAPTER EIGHT

As she watched the man before her paying his respect for the way she had saved his life, Ceridwen had realized this was the best possible way of letting those around her, and Norwood, learn the truth that she was in truth a woman. His shocked expression was worth the strain of hiding her true self away for so long. And others who had also witnessed her act would spread the news, leaving Ratcliff's threat of exposing her useless.

The rumblings that grew in volume were proof that everyone was, indeed, discussing this surprise—but they were also noisy enough to cause for Ceridwen to wish to continue the conversation with Norwood in private where they could talk without needing to shout. She motioned for Norwood and his group. "Follow me," she ordered and turned her back to proceed to enter her tent.

Arthur was close on her heels. "Are you mad, Ceridwen? What the hell were you thinking?" he hissed before pouring himself a goblet of wine.

"Pour me one," she said whilst starting to unbraid her hair. "I have the feeling I shall need a cup, at the very least. More likely, I shall need two."

"You think?" he all but growled handing her a cup. "'Twas not wise to reveal yourself in front of half the men you have been fighting beside."

"'Twas either reveal myself now, on my own terms, or have the choice taken away from me. Better to be the first to reveal it than let

Ratcliff have the upper hand. The moment felt right to let my ruse be at an end. Besides, did you see Norwood's face?" His reaction had been worth the risk she had taken and she would regret nothing.

"'Twas reckless," Arthur added. "I can see the reasoning behind not leaving the secret as a weapon for Ratcliff to use against you, but you could have revealed yourself directly to the Empress without exposing yourself to the entire camp. Mayhap Empress Matilda would have been gentler in her response if you had gone to her directly. As it stands, 'twill not take long for the Empress to learn what has taken place. She will not be pleased."

"Then I shall pay whatever price I must for my indiscretion. I can only hope she will appreciate the efforts I have gone to in order to fight for her cause." Ceridwen gave a heavy sigh before taking several sips of her wine. Watching the entrance of her tent, she continued waiting to see if Norwood would enter or not. "Do you think he will come?"

"A man like that has chivalry and honor engrained in his soul. He will not shirk what he owes. And yet, if I were him, I would probably be wondering how in the hell I would ever follow a woman, even if only in order to repay my debt."

"You have had no problem doing so," Ceridwen replied as she finished unbraiding her hair. She gave her head a shake, feeling a sense of physical relief after having her tresses tightly bound and hidden for days on end.

"That is because I am in service to your father and your well-being has been entrusted into my care."

"And I appreciate your service to me," she said making her way toward the entryway and opening the flap slightly to peek outside. "Let us see what is taking him so long, shall we?"

"You are playing with fire, Ceridwen."

Ceridwen gave a short laugh. "I have never been one to live a docile life, as you very well know, Arthur. There is nothing wrong with a little excitement to spice up your life."

Arthur shrugged. "You have enough of that by just breathing, Ceridwen. Do not let it be said I have not warned you. You may very well get burned, my lady."

She shivered as she realized her captain's words had more than a hint of truth in them. She flung open the flap and took in the scene. Norwood was arguing with his men, two of whom—his brothers, as she recalled from the inn—were laughing. He was clearly not happy with his situation at all.

"Well?" she called out. "Do you plan to keep me waiting all eve to have speech together, Norwood, or should we dismiss your vow from but a few moments ago?"

Norwood ran his hand along the back of his neck before he began making his way toward her. As his men began to follow, he stopped and turned. "Wait here. No need for you to witness this humiliation."

"You never let us have any fun," one of the younger men called out.

He pointed his finger toward the man. "Go tend camp and our horses, Reynard, and you best do a good job of it. Take Turb with you."

"Still cannot believe it! Saved by a woman," Reynard laughed, taking the boy about the shoulder. "Come along, Turb, elsewise you may lose respect for your new master whilst he grovels at the feet of a lady."

"Reynard!" Norwood bellowed.

"I am going!" he returned as he began to leave. "Have fun, Wymar."

Ceridwen tried not to laugh herself as she returned inside. She leaned up against a table whilst Arthur thrust her goblet of wine back into her hand. She had only taken one gulp before Norwood filled her tent... again.

My word, he is enraged, she thought watching the burning fury in those blue-grey eyes.

"You could have told me," he at last growled out.

"Told you what?" she teased. If his eyes were angry before, they were scorching her right on the spot the more she taunted him as she picked up where his brother had left off.

"That you were a mere woman," he finished.

"A *mere* woman?" She echoed his words before setting down her cup and folding her arms in front of her. Nothing would get under her skin more than some man thinking she was incapable simply because of her sex.

"Aye."

"We should set things aright between us now, Norwood. The first thing you must needs learn about me is that I am no *mere* woman."

"That, I will concede. But you *are* a woman nevertheless," he smirked, as if giving her this half smile would have her falling down at his feet. He may be handsome but he was far too arrogant with it. He seemed like a man who would expect a woman to bend to his will. She would never do such a thing. Ceridwen would have no issue to bring him down a notch or two.

"And the one who saved your sorry arse!" she seethed.

Norwood shrugged. "The situation could have easily been reversed."

"And yet you came to my tent of your own accord to settle your debt to me."

"Aye, I did when I thought you were a man."

Her eyes narrowed. "And now you think that because you have learned I am a woman you have no problem going against your own words that you owe me a life debt?"

Norwood sighed. "I never said that."

"Good!" Ceridwen said taking her goblet and giving him a salute with the cup. "I would hate to have to call you out to test your sword arm against my own."

A half snort, half laugh escaped his lips. "You would lose."

"Do you think so?"

"Aye!"

A corner of her lip turned up. "Well, we may just have to put such an event to a test after tonight's celebration."

"I will not lift my sword against a woman."

"Yet if we had met just this morn, you very well may have been fighting side by side with someone who you, and everyone else for that matter, assumed was a young lord."

"You played the part well."

Ceridwen smiled. "I shall take *that* as a compliment. Do you care to know my name since we shall be spending a considerable amount of time together?"

Norwood shrugged. "If it pleases you, I will not gainsay you."

"Fair enough," she replied. "I am Lady Ceridwen Ward of Norwich."

He watched her for several moments as though her name meant nothing to him. "What do you wish from me?" he said although the narrow glint in his eyes clearly indicated how much he hated being at her mercy.

A small laugh erupted from her lips. "I have no idea. I never thought I would be revealing myself to anyone in the Empress's army let alone having one of her men claiming he all but owed his life to me." There was no cause to share with him that she had been forced into the decision to reveal herself. "'Tis a new challenge for me and I shall need to think on the matter. Until I come to a decision, you must needs remain close by. I will send one of my men for you on the morrow."

"Fine!" he said between clenched teeth and began to take his leave.

"Norwood!" she yelled out.

He spun around to gaze upon her. "What?"

"Did you forget something?" she asked needing to remind him that he owed her respect, if nothing else. She waited whilst attempting to remain indifferent to his charms. Her heart raced within her chest with his nearness and yet she continued to remain calm whilst he came to some inner decision. She had not enjoyed herself this much in a very long time. Goading him was such a pleasure but even more so she wanted him to remain close as she came to grips with her emotions wreaking havoc in her mind.

He cursed beneath his breath but not quite enough that Ceridwen did not hear several foul words pass his lips. "My lady," he said with a short bow, the words issued from between gritted teeth, "I am at your service."

"Enjoy the celebration this eve, Norwood. I shall call for you on the morrow." She waved him off. Once he was gone, she reached for her wine and gave the departed man a silent salute whilst Arthur only shook his head. She swore she continued to hear Norwood grumbling and cursing her name to hell as he walked away from her tent.

CHAPTER NINE

WYMAR KICKED A stone in his path as he trudged through the ranks of his Empress's army. His mind was filled with the woman he had just left, and he was unsure how he would ever face his men again. No doubt, word had already spread of who had saved his life. He could already imagine the sound of their laughter. He could still hear *her* laughter ringing in his ears, high and sweet. Lovely, for all that it had been mocking him.

Once he had entered her tent, he had been momentarily stunned, not that he would show such an emotion to her. She had undone her braid and had stood there with a confidence most women would not show to a stranger. With her blonde hair cascading down to her waist, Wymar would have needed to be blind to not see the beautiful woman hiding beneath the garments of a man. 'Twas not hard for him to imagine what she would look like dressed in a gown and with the grime of battle cleansed from her body. And those eyes… aquamarine and as clear as a tropical sea. Aye… she was a beauty and Wymar would be hard pressed to keep his wits about him when he was once more back in her presence.

Richard fell into step with him. "Dare I ask what she demanded of you?"

Theobald slung his arm over Wymar's shoulder. "Aye, brother! Tell us… did she ask you to grovel at her feet or, even better, to service her?"

Wymar elbowed his brother and chuckled in gratification hearing the air rush from his lungs. "She asked nothing of me as yet, but that does not mean she will let the matter rest. She seemed to take considerable satisfaction from the fact I owe her my life."

Richard gave Wymar a nudge. "Who would have thought the young man we saw at the tavern was in truth a female? She certainly looked the part at the inn."

"Aye, I more or less reminded her of such a fact. She could have easily told me she was a woman when I went to her tent to inquire if she was in need of my aide."

"Ratcliff certainly knew who she was," Theobald added.

Wymar halted in his steps and peered over at the army of men. "Which makes the fact he had no issue pushing her around all the more upsetting. No man of honor would treat a woman that way. I did not notice him lingering near her tent with her other men, or did I miss his presence?"

Richard shook his head. "I did not notice him, but I was not really looking for him either."

"'Tis curious, is it not? One would think Ratcliff would be keeping an eye on a woman who is the sister of his intended. Unless he lied about the connection—perhaps 'tis Ceridwen himself who he means to marry. But that would give him even more reason to stay close to her side." Wymar replied scratching at his beard. "Theo, do me a favor and take a stroll amongst the camp and see if you can find the cur."

Theobald glanced at his brother with a frown. "I would rather be drinking my fill to celebrate our success than searching for a man I would just as soon not come upon. I am telling you, Wymar, there's something I do not like about him."

Wymar patted his brother upon his back. "Aye, I agree, but that is all the more reason to keep an eye on him, if for no other reason than to satisfy myself that he is up to no mischief."

Wymar watched his brother take off knowing he would do a thorough search of the knights who were already in the process of getting drunk. If the Empress was not careful, her entire army would be careless enough to become worthless come the morn with aching heads and roiling stomachs.

"You are upset," Richard said as they continued onward toward their own camp.

"Owing a debt to a woman does not sit well with me."

"I think owing the lady is but one of the reasons you are angry."

Reaching his tent, Wymar motioned Richard to enter. He proceeded to fill two goblets with wine. "I had hoped to capture him myself," Wymar confessed swiping at the back of his neck.

"Stephen?"

"Of course, Stephen! Do you not ken how much of an advantage his capture by my hands would have given to my quest to win Empress Matilda's?" Wymar sat and hung his head in his hands. "I had hope that if I had been the one to have seized him, the Empress would reward me by returning my title and my lands."

"All is not lost, my friend," Richard said pulling up a stool. "You can still plead your case to her."

"Aye… if she will grant me an audience but I have the feeling she will be too busy making her way to London to be crowned and seeing that her prisoner is kept someplace safe. Who am I but a hired sword?"

"'Tis certain she knows of your name. And I am certain she will feel sympathy for her cause. Stephen stripped many a nobleman from their titles and lands and claimed them for his own—singling out in particular those who were most loyal to her."

"Indeed, for such was the cause of my father's death, at the hands of Stephen's men," Wymar growled out.

"You have carried the burden of his death for many a year, Wymar. At some point you have to let the matter rest and live your life."

Wymar stood and began to pace his tent like a caged animal. "How do I let my sire's death rest? 'Tis still as fresh in my mind as though the deed but happened yester morn instead of nigh unto six years ago. My brothers and I were forced to escape our own keep lest the same fate should meet us. We had no chance to collect but a few things. All else, the relics of my family, gathered over the course of generations, were looted or burned."

"You forget I was there with you afterwards," Richard claimed. "I know all too well what you lost. But 'twill not help to continue dwelling on a matter that cannot be changed. Brooding upon how another captured Stephen will not make your father return."

Wymar gave a heavy sigh. "Aye, I know. I had hoped that if I had been the one to imprison Stephen myself, I could return to our homeland and my brothers would no longer have to hire out their swords for a bit of coin.

"And that still may happen. If not today, then someday."

"Let us hope so. Brockenhurst may not have been much, but 'twas our land and must needs be returned to us. In the meantime, I still have Lady Ceridwen to deal with."

Richard chuckled. "She is interesting, to say the least. I wonder what *her* story is?"

"What makes you think she has one?" Wymar asked sitting back down and taking a sip of his drink.

"A woman masquerading as a man, fighting alongside them, and no one the wiser? She has a story of her own, I assure you."

"Mayhap you are right. 'Tis amazing she has gotten away with her charade," Wymar said draining his drink.

"She is beautiful," Richard declared.

"Is she? I hardly noticed." The lie did not sit well with him for the woman was indeed beautiful… but he dare not say it aloud to his friend. He could take no more jesting this day. He stole a quick glance at Richard whose lips twitched in amusement. He knew Wymar all too well.

Richard laughed. "You must be blind then! How could you not notice she is very fetching?"

A bitter sense filled Wymar. "Perchance I was too angry at being duped by a woman to notice."

"Ha! Get over your own worth, Wymar. You may just have found yourself a treasure for the taking if *you* are deemed worthy of *her*," Richard pronounced as he rose and went to the entrance of the tent. Folding back the flap, he looked back toward Wymar. "Let us go and celebrate with the men."

Wymar slapped his thigh and followed him. If anything, he would see for himself how many of his men remained or who left with the traitors who departed the battlefield once their cause was lost. He must needs also find a priest to fulfill his obligation to Turbert so his previous lord could rest in peace.

He supposed taking care of the business of seeing to a burial should take priority over everything else. Afterwards, he would drown himself in drink to stop himself from thinking too long on a fair-haired lady with sparkling aquamarine eyes. Just thinking of the lady caused his heart to lurch in his chest. *God's Bones!* Had she somehow already weaseled her way into his heart? He raised his hand and saw his fingers tremble just from recalling his brief time with the woman. How would it feel to trace that porcelain skin? To wrap his arms around her waist and bring her into his muscled chest? To feel her naked skin up against his own?

Wymar inwardly cursed as his mind wandered from where he should be concentrating. He must find a priest first, and then see to his men. Thoughts of Lady Ceridwen could wait until far into the evening hours, when he would be alone.

<hr />

FAR INTO THE night Sperling traveled, racing his horse as though the devil himself was fast on his heels. He was not certain such was not the case. He was still stunned the battle had not gone in favor of his king.

And for His Majesty to be captured! *God's Blood* who would have thought such a thing was possible.

His thoughts momentarily went to Ceridwen. As soon as the battle had ended, he had attempted to take her in hand. King Stephen had been captured, but surely he wouldn't remain that way for long. In the meantime, Sperling still intended to see his plan through. He had thought by threatening to expose Ceridwen to the men and the Empress that this would have the desired outcome… the lady coming with him willingly. Had she done so, it would have ensured he'd be able to take Norwich easily, with the lord's daughter in tow. Her defiance rattled Sperling causing him to lose his temper. That, he was forced to admit, had been foolish of him. She had a lifetime of being spoiled and indulged. As a result, she would respond with a tantrum whenever anyone attempted to show their rightful authority over her. She was too headstrong for her own good, but he vowed she would come to him even if he must force her hand!

All of this was more difficult than he had anticipated. Instead of Ceridwen by his side as he carried out his king's commands, Sperling would have to use more drastic means to achieve his ends. But he would not falter in his purpose, nor in his commitment. Ceridwen would be his, as would Norwich. The rightful king would end up back on the throne where he belonged, and Sperling would reap the benefits of his loyalty. Such was surely the will of the heavens—and Sperling would see it carried out. With a fair number of the king's men traveling with him, he had no reason to not believe he would soon be lord of the keep. He would then earn his king's favor and have Ceridwen in his bed as his wife, whether she liked it or not.

CHAPTER TEN

CERIDWEN WAS RESTLESS after a nightmare that would not allow her to return to sleep. 'Twas hours ago that camp life had at last settled down from a night of merrymaking. After Norwood had left, she had sent a dispatch out with Thomas to ensure all her men were accounted for. She had learned, unfortunately, that several had lost their lives and only a few remained of those who originally traveled with her.

She had willingly pulled out several coins and tossed them to Thomas, asking him to see to their burial needs and for a priest to bless their graves. They deserved as much in recompense for their years of loyalty to her and her family.

Such loyalty could not be claimed by that worthless cur Sperling who was apparently last seen riding out with any number of men from Stephen's army. Traitors, each and every one of them. Deserters who deserved to be stretched from a rack and their entrails scattered to the four corners of the earth. She shuddered with thoughts that the same could have been declared in her case had the battle gone in the opposite direction. Thankfully, they had claimed victory for the Empress and but awaited word on the direction she wished to travel.

She pulled a feather from her pillow that had been sticking her in the face for at least the past hour. The nightmare she had experienced had rattled her head with worry for her father. She knew she should not pay too much attention to a dream, but the vision had felt so real, so terrifying, that Ceridwen had awoken with a racing heart. How could she not when the dream had shown her standing over her father's grave? The sound of his ghost taunting her that she had failed him echoed in her mind until she let out a low growl of frustration. 'Twas not true! Her father yet lived. She would be reunited with him soon, and all would be well. Yet somehow, she could not seem to convince her speeding heart to calm.

Frustrated that she could not return to sleep, she tossed off the coverlet and began pulling on her boots. She slept in her hose and tunic, which left her covered enough to be seen outside. Perchance a brief walk amongst the stars would settle her soul enough for her to claim a few hours of sleep before the dawn.

Ceridwen grabbed her cape and pulled the garment over her head. On silent feet, she crept toward the entryway of her tent. Carefully, she stepped over Arthur's vigilant guarding. She had just gone to lift her other foot when he made a grab at her ankle, almost causing her to fall atop him. A gasp escaped her when he would not release her foot.

"Where do you go at this hour, my lady?" he said as though he, too, had been fully awake all the time she had attempted to remain quiet.

"I had a bad dream, and I cannot sleep so decided on a brief walk around the camp to clear my head. I shall return shortly."

"'Tis not wise you should do so unguarded, given you decided to show yourself to all the men. They will be watching for you."

Ceridwen let out a frustrated huff. She knew that a walk was not wise… and yet she felt so anxious that she did not think she could settle without some fresh air to brush the remnants of the dream away. "Arthur, do not overreact. The men have all fallen into a stupor and will be nursing a sore head come the morn. No one will notice but one *man* taking a walk to clear his head."

"Do not be so sure your identity is not now the talk of the entire camp. Wait but a moment for me to get my boots on and I shall accompany you. 'Twill put my soul at ease that you are safe."

She bent down and removed his hand from her ankle. If Arthur accompanied her, he would want to know about the dream that had her in such turmoil. The thought of sharing the dreadful words said by the ghost in her nightmare made her stomach wrench. Besides, now that she was awake and moving about, she became aware of a physical situation that needed to be seen to sooner rather than later. "There is no need. I will be gone but a few moments. Rest," she said giving his arm a pat, "I shall not be long."

Not waiting for a reply, she left her tent and began making her way around the outskirts of the tents and toward the trees. A few moments of privacy to take care of her personal business and out of earshot of all the men would be a welcome relief.

She paused but a moment before she plunged herself into the darkness of the forest. Not seeing anyone that may come upon her, she quickly scooted behind a large oak and took care of her needs. Having time to oneself had not been a luxury in so long that Ceridwen began to wonder if she would ever be so carefree again. Images of her dressed in her finest gowns and jewels seemed at the very least two lifetimes ago. If Sperling was not lurking in the shadows of her keep hoping for an alliance between their families, she just might wish to be home instead of traipsing about the countryside dressed as a knight, even if her cause was righteous.

With the sounds of a nearby babbling brook, she adjusted her clothing and thought she could refresh herself further with a few splashes of water to her face. Mayhap that would allow the nightmarish scenes to leave her head. She was so distracted from the ghoulish vision of her dead father that she missed the hole in front of her and her boot became stuck. As she struggled to release her foot, the sound of footsteps came closer. She was such a fool to become so distracted—she had not noticed their approach until they were nearly upon her. Two mercenaries walked out from behind the trees and stood there licking their lips. She reached for her sword only to realize that in her eagerness to leave her tent, she had foolishly left her blade behind. *Imbecile!*

"She does not look very prepared for battle now, does she, Martin?" one said to the other.

"Nay," Martin said with a laugh and rubbing his meaty fists together. "I would say 'tis a vast improvement over what she used to look like. Come here, sweeting, and give us a kiss."

Ceridwen yanked hard on her leg and her boot finally came free. She looked about her for some form of weapon knowing she would quickly be overcome if they decided to come at her together. They began to move as if they had read her thoughts. The closer they came, the further Ceridwen backed away. She would not give them the opportunity to accost her by closing in around her and cutting off her escape.

"My captain will be looking for me. You best leave now whilst you can do so in one piece," she ordered. Reaching for a stick she found upon the ground, she waved the makeshift weapon in front of her only causing the men to laugh at her antics.

"You think a measly piece of wood will stop us from taking you right here?" the one called Martin replied with a jeer upon his lips.

"Go ahead and try it, you miserable whoreson," Ceridwen shouted back.

"We like them feisty, do we not, Martin?"

"Aye, that we do, John. The more they squirm the bet—" His words were cut off when Ceridwen slashed forward with the stick causing a large scratch to run the length of Martin's face. There was just enough blood for him to howl in outrage.

"Take that," she called out with a satisfied grin when she successfully defended herself. Yet such a grin quickly faded as the other mercenary caught her arm and pulled her into his burly arms in a crushing embrace.

"You are going to pay for hurting my friend," John sneered, bringing back his arm.

His palm landed on her cheek in a slap hard enough to cause her skin to feel as though 'twas on fire. A scream erupted from her mouth before his descended upon her own. She gagged as his tongue made every attempt to penetrate past her closed lips. She refused to be taken here in the forest with no one around to hear her call for help. Thinking quickly, she lifted her foot and jabbed the heel of her boot into the knight's leg. 'Twas enough for him to loosen his grip and yet she was far from done with him. Lifting her knee, she jammed it with all her might right into his unprotected manhood.

Howling from pain, he fell to the ground. "You bitch! You shall pay for this," he managed to bellow out before he pulled himself into a fetal position.

Ceridwen would have laughed in triumph but she had no time for Martin quickly took his friend's place. "I shall teach you a lesson on how a proper whore behaves," he sneered before shoving her onto the ground whilst his knife made quick work of her hose. His mouth attacked her neck whilst he fumbled with his own hose.

She pounded on his back for all the good it did her. His strength was no match for her own meager frame. "I am no whore!"

"You will be by the time we get through with you," he laughed pushing her legs apart.

Ceridwen continued to struggle but she was tiring and clearly not about to win this battle. Unable to push this beast of a man from her body, tears ran unbidden down her cheeks with the thoughts of her virginity lost to rape. She clenched her eyes shut waiting for the inevitable… but instead she heard a deep grunt from the man atop her before she felt the full, slack weight of his body upon her. She could not breathe and again she pushed at Martin who barely budged. Of a sudden he rolled off her but 'twas only because of a man towering over her who had used his boot to kick him off.

She expected to see Arthur had come to save her. Instead, Ceridwen viewed Norwood standing in the cool night air shirtless and dripping wet. His arm held his sword toward the other ruffian upon the ground. The one who almost defiled her had a knife sticking out of his back, clearly dead.

He held out his spare hand toward her. "Get up," he ordered pulling her to her feet. She stood there numb, unable to even utter a word. "Are you injured?"

"N-nay. I am w-well." Was that really her voice stammering her answer as though she was some defenseless female?

"You do not appear, nor sound, *well*," Norwood growled out before pulling her into his chest as though to protect and keep her safe. She could hear his heart beating rapidly beneath her ear and yet his outward appearance showed he was nothing but calm.

"Let me go. 'Tis highly inappropriate for you to be holding me thusly," she huffed yet he only tightened his grip upon her.

"Be still and let me dispatch our unwanted company." He pointed his sword at the mercenary attempting to gain his feet. "If you are wise, which I doubt you are, you will leave now unless you wish to join your friend in death. Never bother the lady again or you shall answer to me. She is under my protection."

"I am not," Ceridwen murmured trying to wiggle from his grip but he held her firmly yet gently all the same.

"Be quiet," Norwood stated as they watch the man scamper away. "Where is your sword?"

Ceridwen muttered her answer so low he repeated his question. "I forgot my blade in my tent," she at last said.

He placed his sword within his scabbard then took her by both arms and gave her a shake. "Have you no sense, woman? What made you leave your weapon behind? 'Twas careless and could have cost you your life."

"I was unsettled by a troubling dream and was not thinking clearly. I am truly thankful for your intervention, Norwood, but the scolding is unnecessary. I am well aware of my foolishness. I do not need you to reaffirm how much my negligence may have cost me."

"Dream or not, I would not have thought you capable of making such a costly mistake. Come with me," he said as he began pulling her deeper into the forest.

She was alarmed but only briefly. "Where do you think you are taking me?"

He continued onward in silence until he came to the small stream Ceridwen had heard earlier. His appearance now made sense since he, too, had apparently wished to clean himself in the water. His tunic had been left on the rocky bank and he went to pull the garment over his head. He picked up a drying cloth he had left behind and looked her over. "Do you wish to wash yourself?"

"Will you stand guard?" she asked for she would like nothing more than to wash away the foulness left behind by the two men who had been bent on taking her.

"Aye. Do not be long." He tossed her the cloth and turned his back before taking up his stance to ensure her privacy.

Ceridwen hurried to the stream and began splashing water upon her face and arms all the while thinking Norwood's debt had now been repaid in her eyes.

CHAPTER ELEVEN

WYMAR WAITED SOMEWHAT impatiently as he heard more than saw Ceridwen whilst she cleaned herself in the stream. Earlier, he had barely taken advantage of the water himself before he heard the screams of a woman in danger. Since there were not many women roaming about camp at such an hour, Wymar had had no doubt in his mind just who had been in peril.

Coming upon her when she was about to be taken had caused fury to erupt inside Wymar like he had never known before. Men who took advantage of a woman in such a way had never sat well with him. But to see Ceridwen on the verge of being raped had almost been his undoing.

Tossing his dirk into the back of the unsuspecting man gave Wymar no remorse nor did he feel any sympathy for the dead man when he kicked the cur from the lady's body. He could not miss seeing how her hose had been cut away from her body and hung low upon her legs. She had been shivering, most likely not from the cold but fear.

"Are you almost done, my lady?" he asked.

"One m-more m-moment, please." Her tone was soft and he was unsure if she now stammered because she was in truth cold or from her ordeal.

"Are you decent?"

"Of c-course!" she said a little too loud.

Wymar whirled around and gathered his cloak he had left on a nearby rock. Strolling toward the bank, he saw Ceridwen sitting upon a boulder hugging herself and rocking back and forth. He came before her assessing her situation. Decision made, he took hold of one of her hands and yanked her up. Before she could protest, he placed his cape upon her shoulders, took her place upon the boulder, and then pulled her into his lap. His hands briskly attempted to rub some warmth back into her.

"N-Norwood, t-this is h-highly inappropriate!"

"The way you are shivering I assumed you were cold," he said whilst continuing his administrations. "Stop fussing and let me help warm you."

She stopped squirming upon his lap but he could still feel her quivering after several minutes.

"I cannot seem to stop shaking," she at last admitted.

"With good reason, Ceridwen," Wymar murmured pulling his cloak closer about her. He pushed her head down upon his shoulder expecting her to protest yet she did not do so.

"I have not given you leave to call me by my given name." Her hushed tone pulled at Wymar in a way he never thought possible by a woman he barely knew.

"Given all that we have been through, you and I, you should call me Wymar at least whilst we are alone. I would not think the effort should inconvenience you overly much."

"'Tis not a matter of inconvenience but more of what is proper."

He gave a short laugh that ended with a snort. "Proper? You go to war dressed as a man and you are worried we are not being proper by calling one another by our first names?"

"I see your point," she said raising her head to gaze upon him.

He watched her for several minutes whilst he pondered what she was thinking. "Do you?"

"Aye, I do."

"At least we have something to agree upon."

"My thanks for saving me this eve, Nor... Wymar." She reached up and her fingers brushed along the stubble of his beard before she cupped his cheek.

He shivered at her touch for 'twas most unexpected. He was even more surprised when she leaned toward him. She hesitated but an instant before she placed a chaste kiss upon his lips. She must have realized the inappropriateness of her impulsive gesture for just as suddenly as her kiss had occurred, she jumped from his lap and began to leave the river's side.

"I should not have done that," she tossed over her shoulder as she climbed up the bank.

"Ceridwen," he called to her.

"Here is your mantel," she answered, barely looking at him as she tossed the garment into his face.

He whipped it away and reached for her hand. 'Twas then he saw her tears cascading down her cheeks when she raised her face to meet his. "Tears on so fierce a warrior as you?" he teased her gently as he wiped them away with his thumb. He hoped the words would spark her indignation. Surely that would be enough to distract her from her sadness and fear. But to his dismay, her tears did not abate.

"I am a woman before all else and even I can have a moment of weakness." She turned away from him even though he did not let her go.

"You are hardly weak, Ceridwen. In fact, I have never met another woman with the courage to enter battle as you have done."

"But I was weak back there," she shouted pointing toward the river. "I should never have kissed you, let alone gone into the woods without my guards to protect me."

"Are you truly crying over such a little kiss or are you more upset with yourself for what almost happened to you?" he questioned. He turned her around and saw the anguish upon her visage.

"Perchance all of it! I do not make it a habit of kissing men, I assure you."

He tried to make light of the situation. "I never assumed you did with the meager sampling you gave me. 'Twas not the kiss of an experienced woman."

"'Tis not the first time I have been kissed." She defiantly lifted her chin as though to prove the truth of her words.

"Then 'tis apparent you have only been kissed by a relative or someone who knew not how to pleasure a woman."

"Are you mocking me?"

"Mayhap I am. I have the distinct feeling you should be kissed often and I may be the man to show you how 'tis properly done." He pulled her closer.

"Do you honestly think you are man enough?" She did not seem to object to him pulling her closer into his embrace, although she was not agreeing to anything like him giving her a demonstration either.

"Now 'tis you who are but jesting with me. I can assure you that you will not go wanting whilst in my bed."

"I never said I would bed you. We were talking about a simple kiss, and nothing more," she protested.

"There is nothing simple about a kiss, when it is done properly. Why, I am told if you put in enough effort, the act can be most pleasant." He took a step closer and heat radiated between them like a burst of fire.

"What is it you are doing?"

His arm snaked around her waist and he pulled her completely up against his body. "Testing the theory that I am man enough for the likes of a Viking shield maiden like you."

"I am no Viking shield…"

"…who talks entirely too much."

Wymar lowered his head and he watched whilst her eyes widened in surprise. She may be fierce on the outside but he had the distinct feeling that despite what she had said, she had not much experience with a man. His lips gently brushed against hers. Teasing her to awaken the woman hiding just beneath the surface of the fierce warrior she had chosen to become. His name passing her lips whispered between them on her breath. He almost smiled in satisfaction that he had been right.

'Twas enough for him to continue his exploration of her mouth and from her response as he deepened their kiss, she was more than willing to allow him to instruct her on the art of kissing.

CERIDWEN WAS UNCERTAIN what was happening but she did not wish for it to end. Never had she felt such a rush of emotions as when Wymar began to kiss her. She knew she should be putting a stop to what they were doing but mayhap tasting such sweetness a little longer would not hurt her… or would it?

Her arm made its way up around his neck and her fingers began to play with the hair at the nape of his neck. He tightened his grip upon her even whilst he deepened their kiss. *Merciful heavens, what is he doing to me?* she thought. 'Twas more than exquisite and she was more than happy for him to be her teacher on what he liked—especially since *she* found she liked it exceedingly well.

She began to mimic what Wymar was doing with his tongue and upon hearing his moan of pleasure she was certain she was learning this business of kissing very quickly. Aye, she would have smiled if such a feat were at all possible but such was not the case when her mouth was being all but devoured. He was magnificent and she was more than willing to continue on with this lesson.

He broke their kiss as abruptly as he had started it. 'Twas then she heard their labored breathing. Wymar was just as affected by their play as she had been and such knowledge satisfied her immensely. "Why did you stop?" she asked in disappointment and watched when he took several steps away from her.

"Only someone naive enough or too young and inexperienced would fail to realize that to pursue the course we were on a moment ago would be foolish," he said quietly.

"Are you telling me you regret kissing me?" She took a step backward in disbelief that something that was so earth shatteringly wonderful to her was nothing to him but a mistake.

"I regret nothing but I will not take what you seem to be offering here on the ground like some common harlot."

Her eyes narrowed. "And now you insult me," she fumed.

He winced, looking genuinely regretful. "I did not mean for my words to sound as they did. My only thought was I did not want to be like one of those fools who would have taken you and not given you another thought come the morn."

"'Twas only a kiss, Norwood," she hissed.

"Wymar," he urged. "We agreed to call each other by our given names."

"I am not certain we actually came to such an arrangement."

"Was that not your voice whispering my name but moments before?"

"'Twas a slip that shall not be repeated."

"Aye, it shall when we are alone," he ordered. His tone was firm as though he thought he had won their argument.

"I am not one who takes orders well. Generally, I am the one giving them out."

"That was before tonight. I have now repaid my debt to you."

She distanced herself from him. "Have you?"

"Saving you from rape, or worse, should have more than evened the score."

"Mayhap I shall demand more. I could have taken care of them myself," she huffed with another lift of her chin. True, she had concluded for herself that Wymar had indeed settled his debt by saving her, but she did not feel inclined to say as much now. Not when he was behaving this way. That debt was the one bit of power she had in the situation, and she found herself far from willing to let it go.

"Then it must have been some other damsel in distress I saved because the one whom I rescued was indeed in need of saving." He came to her and placed his cloak once more upon her shoulders. "You might as well take this meager offering. You cannot go through camp only wearing your tunic."

She gathered the edges of the garment to cover herself. Not trusting herself to speak further, she began to walk back toward camp. Wymar followed close behind.

"You need not follow me. I can find my way to my own tent," she stated.

"You do me a disservice if you think I would not accompany you to ensure you return safely."

"There is no need," she insisted.

"There is every need," he declared whilst taking her elbow as though she could not walk on her own.

Wymar continued to escort her through camp and Ceridwen realized that going straight through the middle instead of skirting around the edges meant that it took far less time for her return. She had barely placed her hand upon the opening of her tent, when Arthur flicked the fabric open.

"Lady Ceridwen… Are you unwell?" Arthur asked.

Before she could answer, Wymar stepped forward. "If you are her captain then I suggest you do a better job of seeing to your mistress's safety. I may not be around the next time."

"That is uncalled for, Norwood," she snapped.

Wymar gave a short bow. "We shall settle this between us come the morn, my lady."

"There is nothing to settle."

The bastard actually gave her a wicked grin. "Aye, there is."

He began whistling a merry tune before his shadow disappeared into the night. Ceridwen went into her tent with Arthur taking up his stance once more at the entrance. His eyes widened once she took off Wymar's cloak and tossed it upon her trunk, showing the true state of her clothes.

"I will kill him," he began before she held up her hand to halt any further insults she knew would be pouring forth from his mouth.

"'Twas not him. Thankfully, he came in time to interrupt the others."

"Who are these others?" Arthur asked grimly. "I will see to them."

Ceridwen shook her head. "There is no need. 'Twas but two men—one of them dead by Norwood's knife, the other scared away. From the terror on his face, he has likely run halfway cross the county by now. There will be no finding him, and I see no point in trying. Let us rest whilst we still have a few hours," she murmured. Pulling off her boots, she crawled into her bed.

And when she finally found her slumber, she dreamed of a tawny haired warrior who held her in his arms and kissed away all the worries of her life.

CHAPTER TWELVE

THE EYES OF a hundred men swept over her as though she rode her horse completely naked... or so it seemed to Ceridwen. Her chin defiantly rose. She would not regret her decision to show Wymar and the others that she was in truth a woman. Not when Ratcliff could have done more damage by revealing her identity himself. But there was no mistaking the looks she was receiving, nor could she pretend they did not unsettle her.

Every knight now knew she was a woman amongst them. She and her blade had battled alongside these warriors with no complaint when they had thought her a man but now they did not look upon her the same. Aye, she was attired as she had always been but this made no difference. Her position amongst this army was a dangerous one now that they knew her true nature. Ceridwen might need to rethink her decision to remain with the Empress all the way to London once she joined her troops. Word had traveled swiftly that the Empress was riding from Gloucester. 'Twould only be a matter of time until she caught up with those who supported her.

More news of the battle continued to swarm through the ranks. The Earl of Gloucester was currently on his way to Bristol Castle with a contingent of men to see that Stephen was imprisoned there. Now, nothing stood in the Empress's way to becoming Queen of England.

Ceridwen was thankful to be on the winning side of the battle. They broke camp early in the morn the night after she had experienced her first real kiss and had now been riding for several days.

Arthur, Thomas, and Symond stayed close but at times she felt as though they were highly outnumbered. She may not like to admit the truth of her situation but unfortunately 'twas a fact she was only now beginning to face.

Ratcliff had escaped with those fleeing with Stephen's army who had evaded capture. On one hand, she was happy to no longer have to see him. On the other side of this dilemma, his treasonous desertion worried her of what trouble he was up to once he returned home. Since his land and her father's joined boundaries, she should be making her way home. 'Twould be the smart thing to do, so why was she still traveling with this army?

She knew why and the thought irked her that she wanted to be near *him*. 'Twas no matter that in truth his debt was repaid when he dispatched the mercenary who had attempted to take her against her will. She still wanted more time with him. And only part of it was because she felt safe with him—in contrast to many of the other men present. There were already whisperings running rampant within the army that she was no more than a whore following the camp. How easily some of these men forgot she had spilled the blood of their enemy just as they had done. They only thought of one thing now that they knew she was a woman. Only with Norwood had she felt that desire did not have to be a frightening thing. What the other men wished to take by force, her fevered imaginings could picture giving to him, willingly.

They had had no further opportunity to have speech since the army broke camp. For once Ceridwen was content there had been no occasion to do so. She had to admit, if only to herself, that she had enjoyed sparring with him. Such an endeavor tended to sharpen her wits whenever they were together. And then there was that kiss... she began to wonder if any other man would make her feel as Norwood had done but she doubted such would be the case. She was drawn to him from the first night she had seen him at that tavern in Lincoln.

Her attraction to him had only intensified since then. She had never believed in love at first sight and yet all things were possible where Norwood was concerned.

He came alongside her horse as if he had known her thoughts had fallen upon him. He gave her that cocky grin she was beginning to hate despite how much he continued to intrigue her. She barely acknowledged him.

Wymar chuckled. "You cannot ignore me all the way to London, Ceridwen."

"Aye, I can and we are not alone, Norwood. You best address me differently if you want me to answer you."

"Then be so kind as to tell me how I should address you. Do you prefer my lord or my lady?"

"I believe I would prefer silence instead."

Wymar gave a laugh low in his chest and Ceridwen's heart leapt into her throat. *The damn cur. Does he do this on purpose?* But he at least held his tongue. The silence was indeed preferable to his mocking conversation as though he held some secret only he knew for sure.

"Your horse is beautiful and well trained from what I have seen. Her name?" he asked whilst still keeping his stare upon the road.

"Defiance."

"Ah, I see. Much like the defiant lady she carries. The name suits her."

Ceridwen gave her mare a pat upon her neck. "She has served me well. I have never regretted my decision to bring her, even though I am well aware that most would have chosen a heavier warhorse much like your own. His name?" she inquired for the black steed was indeed as magnificent as the knight who rode him... not that she would confess such to him.

"Aries."

"Like the god?"

"Of course. Is there another who would go by such a name?"

"The name suits him as well. He is a beautiful horse."

Aries bobbed his head as though he were agreeing with her words. "Do not fill his head or he will become most ornery."

She muffled a laugh but the twinkle in his eyes told her he heard her. "You act as though he is a misbehaving dog instead of a horse."

"He does tend to act like one when the mood suits him." The two horses began nickering together as though in conversation. "I believe they like each other. They are like night and day or mayhap white lightning flashing against a midnight sky."

"Do not be ridiculous," Ceridwen replied as she watched her horse interact with Wymar's. She pulled on the reins and moved Defiance over upon the road.

"Do not be so mean-spirited. They were just having fun."

"They do not need to be having *fun*," she fumed, wondering if there was an underlying message to his meaning. They were discussing their horses, were they not?

"Do not be so serious, Lady Ceridwen. Life is to be enjoyed, is it not?" Wymar asked, before turning in the saddle. "Reynard! Theobald!"

Two of the men who had been with Wymar on the day he had vowed his service to her came abreast of them. They were indeed his brothers, and Ceridwen could easily see the resemblance. "There is a tavern ahead," Wymar told the other two. "Go procure a table large enough for us, along with Lady Ceridwen and her men."

"We could have seen to our own table," Ceridwen replied whilst nodding to Thomas who also took off heading in the same direction as the Norwood brothers.

"We may as well share one. Besides, best to get there quickly. With an army this size upon the road, the food will surely run out before everyone is served, and I rather fancy some time to indulge in the fare to be found inside a comfortable inn. We have spent far too much time living off the land of late."

"I can take care of myself and my men. I do not need you to see that I am fed."

"Humor me," Wymar replied before waving his hand again. "Turbert! Care to get off your horse for a while? Richard, shall we?"

Wymar's squire let out a loud yelp and the three men took off at a gallop.

Arthur came abreast of her after Norwood had left. "I am reminding you again, Ceridwen. Be careful with that one," he warned.

"I am being careful," she answered watching the trail of dust disappear off in the distance.

"You best try a little harder, my lady."

She gazed upon her captain. "You are almost as irritating as he is," she tossed her head in the direction ahead of them.

"You have never before objected to me voicing my opinion. I assume nothing has changed on that score just because of Norwood."

Ceridwen sighed. "Nay, I value you speaking frankly with me. Besides, I doubt I could stop you even if I tried."

He laughed. "You have that aright. 'Tis why your father appointed me your captain. He appreciated the fact I could put up with you and not allow myself to be wrapped around your little finger."

"Your candor is appreciated, Arthur, but for once leave me to my inner thoughts."

"As you wish, my lady." Arthur gave a nod of his head, and after that, she was thankful to only hear the sound of an army on the move.

They had not traveled far before the inn came into view. For once, she might indulge herself and spend her hard-earned coins on a room for herself if one could be had.

"Arthur... See if a room is available. If I am to be condemned for being a woman, I might as well take advantage of the situation and feel a bed beneath me for a change."

Arthur went inside the inn whilst Ceridwen saw to the stabling of their horses. She went to one of the packhorses and pulled at a satchel.

Grabbing the leather bag, she slung it over her shoulder whilst she made her way into the inn.

The tavern was crowded and she noticed Thomas and Symond were already sitting with Norwood's men, although Wymar was not amongst them. They raised their cups to her but instead of joining them, she waited by the stairway in the hopes a room was vacant.

Arthur joined her several moments later and took her bag from her. With a nod toward the upper floor, she followed him up the stairs. The passageway was dimly lit as they made their way down the hallway. After passing several doors, he came to what she assumed was her room and shoving open the portal, they entered. 'Twas a small chamber, but in her eyes 'twas a huge luxury for she had not pampered herself in such a way for a very long time. The room would more than suffice for the night.

"I paid for water and a tub to be brought up. I assumed you wished to bathe," Arthur said whilst he placed her satchel upon the bed. "'Tis small but at least 'tis clean."

"My thanks, Arthur," she replied whilst she pulled off her tabard. He came to her and helped her remove the heavy chain mail and she felt as though the padding beneath the links was plastered to her body in sweat.

Before she could answer, a knock echoed in the chamber. Arthur swung open the door to admit several servants who carried in a large wooden tub along with pails of water. One bucket was placed by the fire to keep warm. One young woman stayed to assist Ceridwen.

"Do you have need of anything else?"

"Nay. I will be down shortly to enjoy a hot meal."

"Bolt the door after," he ordered, "to keep out the curs who are currently waiting to pounce upon you. Do not doubt that there are many."

"Of course."

He left and she slid the bolt into place. She gazed upon the metal and frowned as she gave the loose hinge a wiggle. Such a flimsy piece of ironwork would surely not protect her very well. She had best sleep this night with her sword close by her side.

Pulling out a dress from her bag, she gave it a shake. 'Twas the last truly clean garment she owned. Even though 'twas wrinkled, she hardly expected the linen to be perfect packed at the bottom of her bag, beneath all the other clothing she'd been wearing these many months. With the servant's help, she slid out of her remaining clothes and sank into the warm water that sloshed over the edge of the wooden tub. She sighed in pleasure whilst her hair was unbraided.

She began to wash and took delight in feeling completely clean for the first time in many se'nnights. Her only complaint was the tub was not big enough for her to stretch out and just relax. But, so be it. Her bath complete, she seated herself by the fire to attempt to dry her hair as she began to ponder if Wymar would even notice she had taken such an effort to look presentable. There was only one way to find out.

CHAPTER THIRTEEN

WYMAR WAS IMPATIENT. He paced back and forth from the stairs to his table and back again. How long did it take one woman to cleanse herself? He had heard Ceridwen's captain asking for a room for her, and for a bath to be drawn, and Wymar had the sudden urge to see if another room was available for him, as well. Alas, she had taken the last chamber but the thought of leaving her unattended left Wymar with an uneasy feeling in the pit of his belly. She seemed to bring trouble to her side whether she willed it or not.

Her captain continued to watch him warily. Wymar could not truly blame the man since they did not know one another. Small talk seemed beyond him whilst he continued to intently watch the stairway. Wymar had even given up his seat at the table and instead watched for Ceridwen to appear from the upper floor.

After arriving at the inn and hearing there were no other vacancies, he had taken himself out back, plunged his head into the freezing horse trough and cleaned himself up as best as he could. He had donned a dark blue tunic that had been mended several times but still looked presentable despite the fact he had not changed hose. Why was he bothering to tidy himself up he could not say, at least out loud. That woman had stirred something in him that he refused to acknowledge even if only unto himself.

She was a lady… he was without title or land, although that had not always been the case. Where did he actually think their relationship could progress besides the two of them going their separate ways?

'Twas that damn kiss he had given her to teach her a lesson that had started his downfall. But how was he to know he would relive the feel of her lips upon his own for what had remained of the night—and for all the hours of the day?

His patience at an end, he had just put one foot upon the stairs to go and fetch her himself when she appeared upon the landing. *By Saint Michael's Wings!* This woman was going to be his undoing. Her eyes widened when they met his own and she appeared surprised he was waiting for her. He looked her up and down and then noticed her long flowing blonde hair freely cascading down her back. Her dress was the same color as his own tunic as though they had coordinated their attire. A golden chain hung low on her hips and the end swayed whilst she descended the stairs.

He held out his hand for her and she willingly placed her cool fingers within his palm before he tucked her arm in the crook of his elbow once she was level with him. "Beautiful," he whispered wishing they were dining alone instead of with their men.

She blushed from his compliment and he had the distinct notion she was not used to receiving them. "You have changed as well I see," she murmured gazing up at his still wet hair.

Wymar shrugged. "It seemed appropriate," he answered whilst he began escorting her across the room. A room that was eerily silent of a sudden. Some of the men had their mouths gaping open whilst they viewed the vision before them. He could understand why they were as stunned as he was to view Ceridwen attired in a gown instead of being dressed as a man. But while he could understand it, their staring still aggravated him.

"There is nothing to see here, men. Go back to your food and drink," he ordered.

The noise of the room went back to a normal level and Wymar assisted Ceridwen to her seat. Her captain slid over upon the bench when Wymar gave him a silent look that spoke aloud his thoughts. His brothers and Richard sat at the far end of the table and he gave a nod in their direction. Wymar called for food and he filled a trencher for him and the lady to share. When Ceridwen began having speech with those on her other side, he waited for her captain to voice whatever was on his mind. Wymar did not have long to wait.

"I do not trust you," Arthur said low enough for only Wymar to hear.

"You have nothing to fear from me. I vowed my service to her and that includes protecting her to the best of my ability."

A grunt spilled forth from Ceridwen's captain. "She has me for that. I have been watching over her since she was a wee lass. Do not think you can so easily replace me."

"I never said I was replacing you. I am merely fulfilling my vow and therefore 'tis about my honor being at stake if I should fail. Surely you are familiar with such a trait."

"You know damned well you are attempting to fulfill more than just your vow of service. I swear by all I hold dear, if you harm her in any way, you shall answer to me," Arthur replied in a low warning.

"Are you threatening me?" Wymar asked, taking a sip of his wine. He watched the room, not the man grumbling at his side.

"I am cautioning you to stay away from her. Her sire put her in my care and I shall return her in the same condition as when she left her estate."

Wymar set his goblet down and turned on the bench to face him. "'Twill be hard for me to stay away when the lady herself has not released me from my vow to repay the debt I owe. Until she does so, I shall stay near."

"Yet you are hardly pleased about being beholden to a woman for a life debt."

Wymar shrugged. "Aye. I cannot gainsay you on such a fact but that does not mean I will forsake my vow. I may no longer have my title or lands but that does not mean I am not honorable. Besides, I fight for the Empress's cause and she is, as everyone here can attest, a woman."

Arthur held his knife out toward Wymar before he stabbed at a piece of venison upon the platter in front of him. "Just remember my words. I, too, took a vow to her father. If you are so honorable then you ken my meaning and we shall have no need for further speech on the matter of the lady."

Wymar gave a brief nod and conceded. After all… he had no intention of furthering any form of a relationship with the lady other than fulfilling his debt. He pondered how many times he would have to remind himself to leave the lady alone before such an obligation was over. He took another sip of his drink, as if that could quench his thirst for her.

His arm was brushed, and he saw Ceridwen intently watching him. "What were the two of you discussing?" she asked peering at him over the rim of her cup.

His gaze swept across her face. The last thing he wanted to discuss was her captain's complaints against him. "Nothing of note. Surely there are far more important topics that we can mull over?"

"Like what?' she asked. Her sparkling eyes silently voiced her amusement as though testing him to come up with a witty response.

Wymar chuckled. "Mayhap the weather?"

Her laughter rang out like the sweetest song. "Surely you can do better than that, kind sir?" she teased before pointing to their food. "You should at least eat your fill before they begin clearing the meal."

He glanced at their half empty trencher. "You took the choicest of meats," he complained with a chuckle.

"Serves you right for leaving me to fend for myself and paying more attention to my captain than me." She waved her hand for a servant to bring another platter of meat. Once it had been placed in front of her, she began filling the trencher. She pushed it before him. "Eat. I would not wish for you to expire from hunger."

"'Twould take far more than an empty belly to take me down," Wymar boasted.

She perused him for a moment until a small smile lit her face. "If you say so," Ceridwen said again before she took up her chalice.

He grunted a response and began eating. Conversations swirled around them but his attention stayed upon the beautiful woman next to him. No one would recognize her in her finery from the warrior of earlier dressed in chainmail. She was fascinating and her unusual demeanor set her apart from the other women he knew in his past. 'Twas what most likely held his interest. She was far more appealing than any other lady he had ever met before.

He gulped hard when her lips parted and Wymar watched her tongue run across her lips before she took another sip of her wine. No longer able to resist the need to touch her, Wymar reached over to place his hand over her own, urging Ceridwen to move the cup closer to his own mouth. He watched her intently and saw the way her eyes widened in surprise when he placed his lips in the same spot on her chalice that her lips had just touched. He swore the wine tasted better than what was in his own cup.

A gasp escaped her. "What are you doing?" she said in a frantic whisper whilst her chest rose and fell as though she had lost her ability to breathe.

"What do you think?"

"Such a gesture is meant for lovers," she said quietly before she set her cup down with a shaking hand. She turned away from him to observe the room.

"You cannot hide from me, Ceridwen, nor ignore this invisible connection that pulls us together," he proclaimed just as softly. Her eyes seemed brighter than usual when she faced him once more.

Leaning forward, her words almost broke Wymar's vow to behave as a gentleman. "We are *not* lovers," she murmured in his ear so no other could overhear their conversation.

He gave a small chuckle. "Mayhap not as yet but who knows what the future may hold for us."

A laugh escaped her. "There is no *us*, Norwood, and you best get used to the idea that there never will be."

He ran a finger down her cheek and her eyes widened in surprise. "We shall see…"

Ceridwen continued to stare upon him until she gave a heavy sigh. "There is nothing to see, Norwood," she proclaimed. "I have responsibilities once I return home to Norwich."

"I suppose that means getting married and raising a family as any dutiful daughter would be expected to do." Wymar took a sip of his wine, but it tasted sour on his tone as he thought of some unknown man claiming the fair maiden as his own.

A snort left her. *"Dutiful…* if I had been dutiful, I would have adhered to my father's dictate and never left Norwich in the first place but aye… I am expected to marry… someone."

"Then your sire has not pledged a particular knight for you to wed? Someone of noble birth and with enough coins to fill his coffers so that you need not worry for the rest of your days?" he asked whilst waiting for her answer. Was she already spoken for?

Another laugh that sounded strained left her lips. "Oh, he has someone in mind, but I refuse to marry the lout. Better to remain unwed than to marry someone of that caliber. Besides, I care not how much the man I marry has in his coffers, only that we can find a common accord. I have enough of my own wealth to see me through all the rest of my days. If I am lucky once I wed, I will learn to care for the man."

"Mayhap you will find someone who might win your favor," he said wondering if somehow she might consider his suit if he had his title and lands restored to him. *God's Blood!* Where had such a thought come from? He watched as one delicate brow lifted and a small smile crept across those lips he would love to kiss.

"Like you?" she inquired in a breathy whisper.

A roguish grin slipped across his mouth. "We shall see..." he repeated his words from but moments ago.

"Ceridwen..." Her captain's voice saying her name as if in warning penetrated the moment Wymar and the lady had been sharing.

She sat back in her place at the table to distance herself from him. Wymar could not miss the brief flash of disappointment that their banter had been interrupted.

"I confess to still wanting to know what you were discussing earlier with my captain," she said, avoiding his eyes as she changed the subject. "I expected you both to burst out into a brawl at any moment. I have not seen Arthur frown in such a fierce manner in many a year. What did you say to him?" She took a piece of meat and began to chew as she waited for his answer. She swallowed but continued to watch him intently. "Well?"

"He is concerned for you. Since he is your captain I would expect nothing less of the man."

"He is very protective of me and has seen to my well-being for many a year now. 'Twas not his choice to go to war and yet he followed me all the same."

"You must trust him if he sleeps at the entrance of your tent," he stated with a sideways glance at Arthur. Maybe there was more to this than just captain to his lady. "Or is he your lover?" he burst out but immediately regretted his words the instant they left his mouth. Had they not just been talking about her needing to wed? Surely if the captain was her chosen, she would have said as much. Besides, he was certain she was still a maiden. There was an innocence about her in many ways even though she also appeared experienced considering the way she flirted with him.

Her cup rattled upon the table and her lips pressed together to apparently calm herself before she spoke. "How dare you ask me such a question," she fumed.

"'Tis a natural assumption…"

"…and none of your damned business!"

"'Tis no reason to be so defensive," Wymar said watching her lips press together. "As you just stated, 'tis none of my business who you take to your bed."

"You filthy minded cur! I should call you out for speaking to me thusly." Her low tone held a warning that Wymar could not miss.

"I am at your leisure if you feel you can best me, my lady." Seeing Ceridwen angry made something stir within him but such a feeling had nothing to do with fighting with a blade of steel but more with what was growing between his legs.

"On the morrow then, with the rising of the sun." She drained her cup and rose. She started to leave but changed her mind and turned back toward him. Hands resting upon the edge of the table, she peered down upon him with the fiercest scowl he had ever seen upon a woman.

"Somehow I was expecting more of you then to speak to me as you have. Although I should not have to clarify anything to you, my captain sleeping at the entrance to my tent was only a means of keeping me safe. What a disappointment you turned out to be."

Turning upon her heels, she marched up the stairs with Arthur following in her wake. Laugher rang out in the tavern as men began making wagers on who would be the winner of the battle of wills between Wymar and Ceridwen. He scowled at his brothers whilst they, too, placed their bets. He only prayed he would be able to save face come the morn.

CHAPTER FOURTEEN

He had to be the biggest fool in all of Christendom! Wymar left his tent, tracing his way on foot back to the inn. He should have gone after her immediately instead of waiting for hours to offer some form of an apology but instead he had allowed her to storm off in a huff. It did not truly matter to him if her captain was her lover, but he supposed he should not have voiced his thoughts aloud whilst they supped. 'Twas apparent he spent too much time in the company of men of late than to remember his manners in front of a woman.

He had held such high hopes for their evening together and he ended up making a mess of things by insulting her. Such had not been his intention. How sharing a trencher with her this night had turned into a duel in the morn was still beyond his ability to comprehend. On some level, he enjoyed verbally sparing with her and looked forward to seeing how accomplished she was with a sword in hand. Considering the amount of boasting she did by saying she could beat him would prove interesting if nothing else.

You are still a fool! he repeated inside his head. She had astounded him by appearing in her finery. He should have been complimenting her on how beautiful she looked, not asking questions that offended her. Now what was he doing? He was actually going back to the inn in the middle of the night in a feeble attempt to make the situation up to her. He would be lucky if her captain would let him pass so he could utter a few brief words of remorse for his actions.

Reaching the inn, he stared at the building determining if he could in truth go through with his plan to see her. He still had enough wits about him to know this was a bad idea. If he were wise, he would turn around and seek some form of solace in his own bed. That would have been the smart choice to make. Waking her up in the middle of the eve just so he could relieve his own guilty conscience over the idea that he had hurt her feelings was another stupid move on his part. He should go back to his tent. Instead, Wymar found himself entering the empty tavern common room and making his way up the stairs.

Since he had tossed the innkeeper a coin earlier to learn which room was Ceridwen's, Wymar knew where he was going as he made his way down the dimly lit passageway. He expected to see Arthur sleeping outside Ceridwen's door and frowned in concern. Mayhap he was right in his thinking and they would be abed together. There was only one way to find out and he gave a small knock upon the door. He almost prayed she would not respond. He could then slink away and no one the wiser.

"Arthur?" Her whispered voice was muffled by the barrier standing between them.

"Nay… 'tis not your captain." That she asked if Arthur was the one knocking showed promise since it meant he was not already inside, but why the man was not guarding her was beyond his ken!

"One moment."

Silence met his ear when he pressed it upon the wooden door. He did not have long to wait before the portal was thrust open causing Wymar to stumble to catch his footing. He took in Ceridwen in all her glory… loose flowing hair, the delicately-shaped mounds of her breasts peaking above her night clothes, a robe hastily thrown about her shoulders she was still attempting to set into place, along with her sword firmly gripped in her hand.

"Are we under attack?" she asked in a shaky whisper.

"Nay." He dared not say anything further whilst his eyes roamed over every inch of her creamy exposed skin. By God, his hands were trembling to touch such perfection. His mouth went dry.

She moved past him to peer out into the corridor before she came back to his side. "Are you drunk?"

"Nay, not yet, but the night is still young."

"Still young? Why, the cock will crow with the rising of the sun before long."

"I have lost track of the time."

"I have wine. Would you care for a cup?"

"If 'tis not too much trouble and will not inconvenience you," he managed to say before she closed her chamber door and went to pour him a goblet of wine. She held out the cup to him and he at last took a gulp of the heady brew. Watching her move about the room, he realized how aware of her he was. This was indeed a stupid and foolish idea he had concocted. He should not be here with her half-undressed.

She went to throw a log upon the fire and paid no attention when an ember jumped out from the hearth to land on the hem of her robe. Wymar quickly made his way across the room. Setting down his goblet upon the mantel, he kicked the ember back into place with his boot before kneeling down. Quickly, he put out the spark that was about to catch fire and continued his inspection to ensure no other part of the sheer linen would be engulfed in flames.

"You must needs be more careful, Ceridwen," he murmured when he stood before her but she only watched him with wary eyes.

"What are you doing here, Wymar? I thought we agreed to settle your insults come the morn. To be honest, I am in no mood to further spar with you with what little remains of the night."

"I came to offer my apology."

She gave a half snort, half laugh before folding her arms across her chest. Her action only drew his full attention to the neckline of her shift that was dangerously close to showing him a full view of the bounty that belonged to her. 'Twas apparent she had no notion of what she did to tempt him to reach for her. He was only a man after all.

"Apologize? You? I find that hard to believe. Are you trying to get out of fighting me come the morn?"

He gave a short chuckle. "Nay, I would not deprive you of giving me a sound thrashing if you are able. I am actually looking forward to it."

"Then why not settle this between us with the rising of the sun?"

"Because I wished to make right the wrong I did to you earlier this eve. 'Twas something I felt needed to be said."

"And the morn would not suffice?"

"Nay. Not when my conscience would not let me sleep until I did so. I am sorry for waking you and for my words earlier this eve." He went to stand before her and took her hands. Raising them to his lips, he placed a kiss upon her fingertips. "Forgive me…"

Her hands shook whilst his mouth lingered above her knuckles. He tightened his grip upon her hands and swore a zing of tiny currents raced up his arms when he did so. A breathy gasp escaped her lips and he knew for certain she was just as affected as he was being this close to one another.

"Y-you sh-should not be here," she stammered trying to pull her quaking limbs from his grasp.

"Tell me you do not feel this connection between us, *ma cherie*." The husky tone of his voice surprised not only himself but Ceridwen as well as he watched her eyes widen. He straightened but did not let go. Stepping closer, her mouth opened—to attempt to form some sort of a sharp retort he supposed—but it appeared as though she was having difficulty thinking of what to say next.

"You are trying to distract me," she answered lifting her chin and giving her hair a defiant toss as if to clear her vision.

"Nay. I am attempting to persuade you to admit there is something between us that is far more important than a battle of wits or what we think to accomplish upon a field of honor."

"I know not what you speak of," she huffed.

He took hold of her waist and brought her even closer. "Then why is your pulse racing with our nearness?"

She moved her arms until she pushed at his chest. 'Twas a feeble effort at best for he budged not even an inch. Her hands continued lingering upon his tunic before she began fingering the fabric. "I know not what you speak of," she repeated again before dropping her gaze.

He lifted her chin to stare into her aquamarine eyes and became lost. "Aye, you do," he said and lowered his mouth to meet hers.

'Twas at first a gentle kiss. An exploration... Searching... as though they were looking deep within themselves to find the answers she refused to admit aloud. But the moment her arms snaked their way up across his back to take hold of him, everything changed. Their kiss became possessive... demanding... a yearning for...

Something snapped into place as though this was what Wymar had been missing from his life all these years. He had not even realized until this very moment he craved something beyond monies, prestige, his title and lands restored, or even the Empress's favor. He needed a woman who would meet him head on and fight alongside him if needed. That woman was the one he held in his arms.

'Twas as though he were a starving man and only Ceridwen could satisfy the craving within him. 'Twas not until they stumbled into her bed that he realized they had been moving at all. His manhood roared to life whilst Wymar felt every inch of the womanly curves lying intimately next to him.

She opened her eyes as the reality of their situation reached her. With her chest heaving, she disengaged herself and flung herself from his arms, moving with lightning speed to stand near her sword. Clasping her robe about her, she nodded toward the door. "You must needs leave," she gasped, reaching for the goblet of wine she had offered him a while ago. She gulped the liquid down and pointed to the door once more. "Now, Wymar!"

"Listen to me, Ceridwen," he began.

"Nay, I will listen no more to anything you have to say. You apologize and then attempt to make me your whore by bedding me to prove your accusations of me were true from earlier this eve. I will be damned if you shall have what belongs only to the man who shall one day be my husband," she yelled.

"Ceridwen, 'twas not like that," he answered trying to plead his case once more.

In answer, she took hold of her sword and pointed the weapon in his direction. "We shall settle this between us on the morrow. Get out!"

Wymar held up his hands, not wishing to further irritate the lady. With a courtly bow, he left the room without another word and went to seek his slumber. But despite all his efforts to take his rest, the memory of the kiss they had shared would keep him awake for most of what remained of the night.

CHAPTER FIFTEEN

CERIDWEN HAD LITTLE to no sleep. Tossing and turning all night upon her bed, her only thoughts had been on that bastard Norwood. How could he have belittled her as he had done in front of the entire common room was beyond her ken. And then for him to come to her room in the middle of the night… Damn his soul to hell!

She had dressed this morn in her regular attire and had wasted little time saying her morning prayers before she made her way outside of the inn. She was surprised to see several men who were still in the process of making wagers. She had hoped this spectacle would have been between the two of them. She frowned as she watched the crowd continue to grow in size. Coins passed hands with most of the men calling for Norwood to be the winner and to put Ceridwen in her place.

But she was used to such taunts and they had never deterred her from her sword play in the past, nor had they spoiled her performance. They would not affect her today. Or so she hoped. Hearing the rumblings of some of the men toward the back of the crowd calling her a whore was nearly enough to bring tears to her eyes but she would not give them the satisfaction of letting them believe she was weak.

She continued to wait for Norwood to make an appearance and was at last rewarded by him appearing before the men. He waved his hand in greeting looking like he had already won their match and was planning to shout his victory for the entire world to hear.

"Shall we begin?" he asked when he at last casually strolled up to her, looking as casually at ease as though he was out for a pleasant walk about town.

"Unless you wish to publicly apologize before all these men and say that you were in the wrong, then aye. This should not take long."

"Your confidence will be your undoing someday, my lady."

She chuckled as she withdrew her sword from the scabbard strapped to her side. "My confidence is what has earned me my reputation of being an expert swordswoman.

"Let us put such a statement to the test but not to the death, if you agree."

"Aye, I agree if nothing else than to hold my winning over your head," Ceridwen said whilst taking up her stance.

"You have not won yet, my lady."

"We could settle this now by you claiming that I shall be your champion and you shall be mine," she mocked knowing he would never agree to such a proposition. 'Twas his manly pride that was now at stake after all.

"I think not."

"You cannot say I did not give you the opportunity. Let us begin, Knight of Darkness," she called out for all to hear.

Wymar began to circle her as he, too, pulled his sword from his scabbard. He began to assess her and Ceridwen made every effort to not appear uncomfortable when his eyes caressed her body from head to toe. "I can see for myself you have spent many hours practicing with your blade," he stated. "You hold yourself correctly to begin combat with your enemy."

"Will you stand there all day talking like some old woman, Norwood, or should you like to concede so we may continue the journey to reunite with our Empress?"

He threw back his head and laughed. "And deprive you of rubbing your victory in my face if you are so lucky to actually win our match?

Hardly."

Before she could make a sharp retort, Norwood's blade rang out flashing from the sunlight of the new day as it hit steel. Ceridwen was prepared when their blades made contact but was still surprised, and for a second left off guard, from the sheer strength of this warrior's arm. Time and time again their blades met but Ceridwen was quick on her feet and good at deflecting and getting out of the way of most of the blows. Her smaller frame gave her an advantage of being more agile but there could be no doubt he was stronger. She did not have the upper body strength to hold steady against him for long. But she did her best whilst he attacked her without mercy and she parried her sword just as fiercely. The crowd cheered them on but they continued to hack at each other with their blades as though they were completely alone.

"Concede, Ceridwen," Norwood ordered when they came face to face as their blades met yet again.

"Never!" Her voice echoed in the morning air even whilst she attempted to take in deep breaths of air, forced to acknowledged that she was more winded than he.

"You shall never win, my dear."

"I am not your *dear*!"

Norwood continued teasing her. 'Twas as though he was enjoying this endeavor as if 'twas nothing more than a game to him. "Even now I can see you tire. As much as you do not wish it, you must needs admit you are no match for a man of my strength."

He was right that the longer the fight went on, the more his greater strength worked to his advantage, overpowering her as she grew weary. But just because she knew that was no reason for her to say it aloud. She wouldn't give him the satisfaction.

She swung her blade in a mighty arc causing him to step back. "You bloody bastard."

"I hate to disappoint you, my lady, but I am indeed a nobleman by birth and rearing even if my family title has been stripped from me." He grinned. She seethed. They continued with their swordplay as though there was no one watching their display nor were they willing to concede defeat to the other.

They were so focused on their match that they were unaware of the sound of horses coming upon them. 'Twas not until the sound of a trumpet blaring in the morning air that they became aware of who was actually approaching. They broke apart, as Ceridwen attempted to hide the way her breathing was labored as she struggled to take in air. Those in the crowd began to fall to their knees and Ceridwen and Norwood followed suit.

"Lady Ceridwen…" The tone of the voice was stern and laced with disappointment. "You are a long way from home."

Ceridwen knew she would be paying for her disobedience. "My Empress," she replied holding out her sword with bowed head. "I offer you my sword for I am ever in your service."

"You have a strange way of showing it," Empress Matilda declared. She dismounted from her horse and came forward. The crowd pushed back as their Empress made her way to stand before Ceridwen and Norwood.

"I but wished to prove my worth to you in the best way I knew," Ceridwen replied, praying her voice sounded humble enough to satisfy her queen.

"Whilst I applaud your efforts to remain a part of my army, you would have better served me by obeying my words and staying at your estate. Think you I gave such orders without a reason?" the Empress asked.

"Nay, Your Majesty."

"Then I shall assume you thought my words were of no worth."

Ceridwen bowed her head even lower, not daring to look her queen in the eye. "Never would I think such a thing, my Empress. I am yours to command."

"We shall see," the Empress replied. Ceridwen only knew the queen's attention left her when she addressed another. "Who are you?"

"Wymar Norwood, originally of Brockenhurst, Your Majesty."

Silence. 'Twas indeed deafening enough that Ceridwen raised her head but an inch to see for herself the Empress's mood. The woman was not pleased.

"Both of you follow me inside so we might have a word in private," the Empress ordered. "Bring whoever else is in your party with you."

With the Empress leading the way, Ceridwen, Wymar, and the rest of their men followed along as if they were going to end up in a pillory. Mayhap 'twas best they were heading back into the inn for at least being inside would offer a meager relief from having the whole army witness the chastising Ceridwen knew was coming. Already the Empress's guards stood at the door to bar any who thought to follow inside.

Wymar leaned down to whisper in her ear. "Admit you would have lost, Ceridwen."

"I shall do no such thing!" she hissed. "If you recall, I was still on my feet with my sword in hand. The fight was not over yet."

"Silence," Matilda called out, "unless you are bidden to speak."

Put in their places, the Empress took a seat and waited whilst those in attendance once more took a knee. The only sound heard in the room was the crackling of the fire set in the hearth. Ceridwen felt as though the flames were licking at her boots.

"You have put me in an awkward position, Lady Ceridwen," the Empress began. "When rumor reached me there was a woman in my army fighting as a man, I had dared to hope that I would not find you here. But I suppose I should not have been surprised to see you this far from home. You always were a rebel, even as a child."

"But—" Ceridwen began only to halt any further words she may have spoken when the Empress raised her hand to silence her.

"I shall get back to you in a moment Lady Ceridwen," the Queen said. "Norwood... I have heard of you and your service to my cause. They call you Knight of Darkness, do they not?"

"So I have heard, my Empress," Wymar replied with a bowed head.

"Your reputation has served you well for I have indeed heard of all you have done in my name. Such a name strikes fear in the eyes of our enemies, or so I have been told by my advisors. Are these your brothers?"

"Aye, Your Majesty, along with our friend, Lord Richard Grancourt."

The Empress nodded her approval. "You men must have done an exceptional job of fighting on my behalf if I have knowledge of the names your fellow knights have begun to call you. Brothers all, in spirit if not in blood, and knights I shall claim as my own champions. That is... if you all swear to pledge your fealty to me," the Empress said whilst waiting for their answer.

"We would follow you to the ends of this earth and to our last dying breath, my Queen," Wymar answered as he once more bowed his head.

"We shall pray the situation does not call for such an end for you." The Empress reached out her hand and a lightweight ceremonial sword was placed in her palm. She stepped before Wymar who kneeled in front of her and tapped him on each of his shoulders. "Rise, Lord Wymar Norwood of Brockenhurst. For your service, I restore your title and lands to you and your family. Those who stole your estate have been already been vanquished and your people only await your return."

Wymar sunk to the floor, reached for the hem of her gown and kissed the fabric. "You are most gracious, My Queen."

"Now... back to Lady Ceridwen." The Empress returned to her

chair.

"I swore my fealty to you several years ago, Your Grace. I shall gladly do so again if this will please you." Ceridwen bowed her head in the hopes that this submission would be enough to appease the Empress.

"What would have pleased me would have been for you to have done as you were told in the first place. Have you no ken what is happening on your lands? The lands I wanted you to stay and guard in my name?"

"My father! Is he unwell?" she asked with furrowed brow, a cold chill moving down her spine as she recalled the horrible dream she'd had the night before they'd left the camp at Lincoln.

"I am uncertain as to his health. I wish I could tell you more as to his well-being but I cannot. What I do know is a runner arrived just this morn and has come to inform me that your estate has been seized by supporters of my cousin Stephen. That is all I have learned at this time."

Ceridwen felt faint for the first time in her life. Worry, regret, and thoughts of what she should or should not have done consumed her. She rose from her place on the floor and began to head toward the door. "I must go to my father at once!"

"Not so fast for I have not dismissed you," the Queen commanded, whilst Ceridwen returned to stand before her Queen. "Lord Wymar… before your return to Brockenhurst, I must needs ask a favor of you."

"I am yours to command, Your Majesty."

"First, I need both of your brothers for a scouting mission of grave importance. Their discretion is required, and I will send them off posthaste."

"And the second?" Wymar inquired without any hesitation in his words. One would have thought that he cared not that he would be separated from his siblings. Mayhap they were not as close as Ceridwen was led to believe in her brief encounters with them.

"I must needs first ask what you and Lady Ceridwen were fighting over. Do you bear each other ill will?" the Empress inquired with a raised brow.

Wymar's gaze briefly went to the lady in question. "Nay, my Empress. We are not enemies but were merely exercising for the benefit of the men. It was a simple wager where the outcome had yet to be determined."

"I see." The Empress continued to stare at them whilst drumming her fingers on the arm of the chair. "Lady Ceridwen... is this a fair description of the reasons behind your... sword play? Would you agree that you also bear no animosity toward Lord Wymar?" she asked, waiting for her answer.

"The score is settled, my Empress," Ceridwen whispered, "and I bear no resentment toward Lord Wymar."

"Since neither of you proclaim you are enemies, then I need not worry over my next request of you, Lord Wymar. See to it that Lady Ceridwen returns home and assist in any means necessary in securing her lands once more. I shall offer you extra forces to take back the castle. If you do this for me, you shall be handsomely rewarded."

Wymar bowed low even whilst Ceridwen was fuming inside, not that she would show any outward appearance to the queen of her anger. She felt as though she were being treated like some insolent child who was incapable of listening to her elders and who needed to be watched over by a minder lest she wander into trouble on her own.

Their audience with the queen over, they watched as she left the inn with her retainers following closely behind.

Ceridwen made for the stairs and Wymar halted her progress by taking hold of her hand. "Get your things whilst I find out details of the men the Empress will provide us. Meet me in the stable in an hour's time."

Ceridwen was uncertain if the look he gave her was concern for the welfare of her father or smug satisfaction that he had some kind of hold or power over her. Whatever the case may be, she had little time to mull over *Lord* Wymar. Her father needed her. 'Twas time she went home.

CHAPTER SIXTEEN

WYMAR'S PATIENCE WAS stretched to his limit as he waited for Ceridwen in the stables. Surely the woman had little to pack. What could be taking her so long?

He busied himself by saddling his horse, but by the time he had finished, there was still no sign of the woman. He continued to keep himself occupied by saddling Ceridwen's steed whilst she took her sweet time getting ready to depart. Still in shock that his title and lands had been restored, all he wished to do was head south to his home. But nay, even that was denied him. Yet how could he gainsay his queen after she bestowed his title once more upon him? Aye... he could do no less than what she requested but still... what would become of his brothers and what mission would they be undertaking for their queen? When he had imagined getting his lands restored to him, he had thought that he and his brothers would return there together, starting the next chapter of their lives in the home that should have been theirs all along. But none of this was going as he had expected.

The stable doors finally opened and the vision before Wymar felt as though he had conjured her up from his dreams. Gowned in the same blue dress as last eve, she was just as beautiful this morn. Mayhap even more so in the light of day. Wymar lost any thought of berating her for her tardiness. Nay... there was something about her that drew her to him like a moth to a flame. He could not doubt such a fact.

No woman before Ceridwen had ever held his interest. He had bedded his share, but he had forgotten those women as soon as they left his bed. What point would there have been in remembering them? No woman of noble birth would dare become interested in anything permanent with him when he led the life of a mercenary. Any woman of sense wanted a title, a gentleman of wealth, a man with an estate that could sustain her for her lifetime and the lifetime of her children. Yet from Ceridwen's own lips she had stated that she cared little for something that meant everything to most women looking for a husband. Perchance this was because she had her own wealth and an estate she would inherit one day.

As she began to make her way across the stable, light from above shone down upon her, making her appear as though she was heaven sent... an angel from above come to earth to tempt men... or mayhap one man in particular. Wymar had to admit something stirred deep within him whenever she came near. He was lost.

She sank into a curtsey. "My lord," she murmured before standing upright to stare into his eyes. She held out her hand and he willingly took it, bowing low before placing a chaste kiss upon her knuckles.

"My Lady Ceridwen," he said. "You look enchanting this morn."

"Better than when I was dressed as a man ready to beat you at our swordplay?" she teased lightly.

He pulled her closer and she gasped. "Can I admit something to you alone?"

"By all means. What is your secret you wish to impart?" she asked as a small smile turned up at the corners of her mouth.

"You are a woman of many talents," he admitted honestly. "Whether you dress in hose and tunic or in gowns and jewels, any man would be a fool to not appreciate a woman of such worth."

Her mouth opened into a silent O of disbelief. "You surprise me, Norwood."

"How so?" he asked concerned he had offended her once more.

"You spout nonsense about who might be in my bed one moment and then turn around and give me a compliment that would have any maiden swoon over. Who is the real Lord Wymar and the Knight of Darkness, I wonder?"

Wymar shrugged. "I am one and the same and can appreciate talent when I see it."

She gave a short nod of her head. "Then I will admit to you that I was impressed with your sword fighting. You kept me alert and made me give my best. 'Tis a talent I can appreciate," she admitted.

"My thanks, my lady," Wymar said before continuing. "I did not like knowing I had disappointed you, not when I had been admiring you so. I know not of any other woman who would so openly oppose the Empress and then go to war on her behalf. You are a rare gem worth treasuring."

Her eyes narrowed. "I am not some woman who wishes to be locked up in a tower to be admired and let out only to impress others," she fumed.

"You misunderstand my words, Ceridwen. I only meant any man would be a fool who did not wish you to fight by his side for any cause they both felt worthy enough to die for." He raised her hand once more to his lips and he felt the tension lessen between them.

"You just may be redeemable after all, Wymar," she said in a gentle tone that gave him hope they could possibly have a future together.

"I am at your service, my lady," he said placing a hand over his heart.

She gave a merry laugh. "As I am at your disposal, by the Empress's demand," she vowed whilst a look of what appeared disbelief etched itself across her visage. It appeared as though she had resolved herself that they must needs continue to travel together.

"Who would ever think such a thing would come between us?"

"No one in their right mind, my lord," she answered before going to her horse and pulling on the reins. "Shall we?"

He nodded his head and led his own horse out into the sunlight. Ceridwen's men waited near their horses, as did his brothers and Richard. Handing his reins to Turb, he made his way to his siblings. He took time to clasp them both into a fierce embrace, not caring who looked on at this open display of affection.

Theobald smacked Wymar on the arm. "I guess you have the better assignment," he said giving a slight nod in Ceridwen's direction. "Care to trade places?"

A scowl swept across Wymar's features. "You do not wish to tread there, brother, lest you anger me. That never turns out well."

Theobald's laughter rang out. "The company of a beautiful woman for days might very well be worth a good thrashing."

"Not if you value your life, brother," Wymar warned.

Theobald threw up his hands in defeat. "I yield to the better man… for now."

"Do you know what your mission is as yet?" Wymar asked, changing the subject.

"We accompany the Empress for now. She has declared she will let us know what she requires of us when she is ready to impart such wisdom," Reynard said not to be left out of the conversation.

Wymar ruffled his younger brother's hair as though he was just a small lad before Reynard swatted his hand away. "You best take care of one another in my absence."

Reynard briefly looked worried. "We were supposed to stay together," he said with a grim expression, "as a family."

Wymar grabbed hold of Reynard's arm and again gave him another fierce embrace. "I promise we will soon be together again. Have no fear."

"Aye, at Brockenhurst! I cannot wait until we can return to our ancestorial stronghold once more," Theobald answered with a grin.

"'Twill be a cause for celebration once we are all reunited," Reynard said. "I can barely remember the place since we last set foot there."

"There will be plenty of time to become reacquainted with our home, brothers. I have been told the keep still stands, which is a blessing," Wymar replied as he gazed upon them both. "Just stay alive until we are all together again."

Richard interrupted the trio. "You all best do as Wymar dictates or you will answer to me. I have not traipsed myself across the whole of England to lose one of you." He shook his gloved fist at the men before turning to Wymar. "I will continue to watch your back, my lord, and have already split the company as you ordered. Half will travel with us and the other half with your brothers."

Wymar nodded. There was nothing left to say until the brothers were reunited at some later point in time. "Godspeed," he said before turning away and mounting his horse.

With a wave of his hand, Wymar put his horse into motion. The course of his life had just altered and he began to realize that for good or bad, he would never be the same.

CHAPTER SEVENTEEN

They rode until the sun was low on the horizon whilst the sky was awash with vivid shades of orange and pink as the day came to a close. For Ceridwen, time passed all too swiftly and she was uncertain where her future would lie. She could not deny the attraction she had for Wymar. He was her equal in many ways, and he was superior to most men of her acquaintance who would never allow her to speak her mind, let alone spar with her upon the field to save her honor. But with that said, there was no doubt left her in mind of who was in charge of this small contingent of an army making its way southwest to Norwich. Ceridwen was none too pleased that any sense of leadership of the group she used to command now fell to Norwood. Although she would not admit it aloud, she could at least acknowledge to herself that Wymar was a born leader, commanding respect instead of demanding it from the men who willingly followed him. That did not make it easy to give up all sense of control, though.

Arthur had at one point given her a silent *I told you so* look. No words were necessary to voice his displeasure that another now took charge of their company. Norwood, for the most part, ignored her and rode ahead of the group. Scouts were occasionally sent ahead to ensure no one lurked within the trees to ambush them. With Norwood in charge, they were making good time and Ceridwen should be thrilled that she would soon reach Norwich. But everything about their travel was seemingly going all too smoothly, and she kept waiting for something to go terribly wrong with each curve of the road they traveled upon.

She was worried about her father and what awaited her when she returned to Norwich. Empress Matilda had said that her father's estate had been seized. She had no doubt that Sperling was the one who had done it. Was he holding her father captive, planning to force her to trade her hand in marriage in exchange for his safety? She could only hope that was not the case. She had no wish to commit her life to such a vile man, especially after how he had treated her. He was a traitor to their Empress. Surely she and her father, working together, could find some way to throw Ratcliff and his men from their gates.

A thatch of tawny colored hair caught her attention and she swore her limbs began to tremble just thinking of him. Aye, 'twas no wonder Norwood was so confident he could bend her to his will. He knew how to make her want him in the most carnal way, imagining their bodies coming together in every conceivable way, even though she had no experience with lovemaking to give clear form to her thoughts. Wymar was her first real kiss—she had told a falsehood when she had claimed that she had been kissed before. The ones she had experienced in her youth had been from inexperienced boys who but gave a quick peck to her lips. At times during the day, she began to hope Wymar would be the last man to kiss her. She shook her head at her fanciful thoughts. Their kiss may have meant something to her but she had no idea of Wymar's thoughts on the matter. Ceridwen may just be one of many conquests in his mind.

The night would bring its own complications or so she began to assume. She had no doubt that Wymar would insist he stay close to her, and she could already see the altercation between him and her captain. Arthur would voice his displeasure but in the end Norwood would have his way... *his way*... with her perchance? God forbid he thought her willing to forsake her maidenhead for a meaningless romp with a mercenary.

Nay, that was not correct. He was a mercenary no longer but a lord once more. His title and land restored by their Empress only made Ceridwen want to question him more about where his home was or had been. In their brief time together, they never once spoken of where he once hailed or how he might long for home. For that matter, with his brothers gone, did he miss them? Did he feel alone in the world much like she had been feeling for months on end? She ran her hand across her eyes knowing she was getting sentimental and no such emotion had a place leaking its way into her heart.

Arthur's horse suddenly moved closer to her own causing Ceridwen to pull on the reins of Defiance. "What?" she said, returning her attention to the present.

"You appear lost in thought, my lady," Arthur declared, his brows crunched together.

"I have much on my mind," she murmured. A small smile lit her face when Wymar looked over his shoulder and caught her eye before he returned his attention to the road.

"By *Saint Michael's Wings*, my lady, you will be the death of me. You must keep your feelings to yourself or before you even know what is happening, you shall be ruined!" Arthur snarled.

Ceridwen pulled on her reins to bring her mare to a halt and watched her captain do the same. "You dare to voice your opinions of my future, and yet you have no say on how I shall run my life!" she fumed.

"How can you not see Norwood will bring you to ruin?"

"You have no right to—"

"I have every right!" Arthur shouted and several knights turned to watch them, especially one knight in particular. "You have been left in my care. I am the captain of your guard. Until your father releases me from my vow to protect you, then you continue to be under my protection and my responsibility! For once in your young life, listen to my words and heed them well."

"I have always listened to your council when your words held truth and sensible advice. But your warning now is unnecessary. Norwood will deliver us to Norwich without further loss of men and fulfill his oath to our Empress. He will then be free to return to his own estate and will forget all about me."

A snort left her captain. "You know nothing of men and their desires, little one. Norwood will never forget you, Ceridwen. How could he? You are a woman beyond compare but I refuse to see you lose your heart to a man of his ilk."

"Who said I am falling in love with him?" she asked, even whilst her heart beat a rapid staccato inside her chest, betraying her and the words she had just spoken.

Arthur heaved a sigh. "You are already halfway there, Ceridwen, from the looks the two of you share. You cannot in truth know if he is a man of honor."

"You know nothing of him and his character," she returned lifting her chin defiantly.

"And you think you do?"

"Aye… I believe I do. He is an honorable man."

"He lets you see that which he wants you to see. Men of his kind will never settle for one woman nor will they marry for love, Ceridwen. He will have the obligation to marry a woman of wealth who will fill his coffers and help him rebuild all that has been destroyed. You deserve better than what he can offer you."

"And who is to say I am not wealthy enough for him to wed?" she retaliated. She turned her ahead away from her captain, afraid she might say something she could regret.

"I am concerned that you will lose yourself to a man who will only seduce you and then leave, Ceridwen. Aye, I know you are a wealthy woman who stands to inherit Norwich but I wish for you to find the love of a good man. I do not want you to marry a man who will only think of the monies and land you bring with your union," he stated.

She returned her attention back to the rider leading their group.

'Twas as though Arthur had listened to every doubt Ceridwen had inside her head. "I stand by my words, Arthur. Norwood is a man of honor," she said softly.

"Just please remember your own self-worth, Ceridwen, and heed my words and counseling," he stated.

He continued to stare at her waiting for some form of answer. She could only nod her head to show that she had heard his advice. Arthur then kicked his horse into motion, leaving her doubting all that she had been feeling toward Wymar. Mayhap Arthur was right. Perchance there was no future for her and Norwood and she should just let the matter rest between them. His future waited for him in Brockenhurst whilst hers was in Norwich. She would marry one day but not for love. Such romantic notions were only for the bards who came to their hall to entertain them.

She flicked her reins to follow her captain, and whilst Wymar continued to look back upon her as they rode, she hardened her heart to any further feelings of love to a man who must one day desert her.

CHAPTER EIGHTEEN

They at last made camp for the eve. Wymar assigned several men to take turns on making the rounds to ensure their safety. No tents were erected for the night. 'Twas unusually warm and an eve under the stars would ensure they could break camp quickly come the morn.

He watched the woman who all but ignored him from across the campfire as she laughed with her men. She was upset with him but he could not understand what he had done to deserve her anger. He had thought that mayhap they had come to a common accord, and he wondered what her captain had said to her earlier in the day for this was when he noticed the subtle change in her looks toward him.

He stepped forward into the firelight and watched in dismay when her face fell before she turned away from him. 'Twas as though he had insulted her but he knew not when he might have done so. He had no doubt he would soon get to the bottom of what was going on inside her beautiful head. Time passed as the men continued their lighthearted conversation though Ceridwen no longer contributed to their discussions.

His patience at an end, he moved around the fire pit only for her captain to bar his way from the lady.

"Step aside, Chamberlayn," Wymar ordered. "I mean your lady no harm."

"You shall answer to me if you do," Arthur said with clenched teeth although he stepped aside to allow him to pass.

"Lady Ceridwen," Wymar said holding out his hand. "May I have a private word with you?"

Ignoring his outstretched limb, she rose on her own accord with head held high. "If I must."

They did not go far, only a short distance into the trees before Wymar whirled around so quickly Ceridwen bumped into him. She muttered an apology but still refused to look upon him.

"What ails you, woman?"

"Excuse me?" she gasped out.

"What have I done to earn your displeasure? You act as though I have done you some harm and yet I cannot fathom what has occurred between us since this morn that I've earned the snubbing you continue to give me."

"'Tis nothing. Your imagination is running away with you," she said and began to turn away.

He pulled on her arm and she stumbled into his embrace. He could feel every breath she took and knew she was feeling something for him. Anger? Desire? What?

"I imagine nothing, including the fact that there is something between us that we should not deny."

She pushed on his chest but he refused to let her go. "And what shall this so-called connection gain me but a babe in my belly and a man who shall desert us? I am required to marry a man who will build a life with me in Norwich, as my father wishes. I do not have the luxury as some might to be frivolous with a meager dalliance that will gain me nothing but sorrow." Her last words caught in her throat and Wymar could only ponder where all this pent-up resentment was coming from.

He traced her cheek with his thumb and the wetness from the tear escaping her eye gave proof that she, too, felt something for him although she refused to admit it aloud.

"Ceridwen…" he said softly. "I know not what shall become of us but can we at least for the moment be friends?"

A sound escaped her as though it was wretched from a pit of despair. *"Friends?* We cannot be just friends, Norwood."

"Why ever not?" he asked. He had thought that mayhap if he put their relationship on friendly terms they could work through the rest in due course.

"You truly do not know why?" she asked whilst tears now streamed down her cheeks.

"Tell me," he whispered in encouragement that he would at last hear her heart's desire.

"Because I am drawn to you, Wymar, for all the good it will do me. The feelings you bring out in me are ones I have never felt for any other man who has crossed my path. I am constantly left confused and uncertain due to these emotions you have stirred within me. Desire. Yearning. An ache in my heart that longs for you to put an end to my misery. But I do not know how to handle or act upon these feelings for if I do, what will that leave me? Alone and having to deal with the consequences of my foolish actions after a brief dalliance with you. That is why we cannot be mere friends, you bloody cur!" Her voice carried into the night and Wymar stepped back in shock to hear such a confession.

"Ceridwen, I—" he stumbled to figure out the right words to say. He couldn't think of how to express how he felt about the woman who was waiting for him to also confess his feelings. In many ways, his own emotions mirrored hers as though he was already on the way to learning he could someday fall in love with her.

Before he could respond, a sob escaped her. "As I thought. I am nothing to you. A woman you would ruin so you could conquer another heart and leave them without another word come the morn. Arthur was right about you. I should have listened to the voice inside my own head and my first impression of you back at the inn. You are a disappointment and I should have never given you my very first kiss.

You are not worthy of such a gift."

She turned and fled, leaving Wymar still reeling from her admission of the strength of her feelings for him. Confusion tore at him as he attempted to figure out how to soothe the hurt he had unknowingly thrust upon the woman. He cared for her. There was no doubt of that, but he was hardly in the position to offer her marriage. He did not know what awaited him back at Brockenhurst. And knowing how much her home and her father meant to her, he could not ask her to leave them behind.

He made his way back to the camp only to find Ceridwen curled up in a blanket near the fire. Her back was turned away from the flames but Wymar could still feel her tears and heartache far into the night. He was a fool to dally with this woman's affections. He would return her to Norwich and make his way back home. She was lost to him and this time he was not going to be able to charm his way back into her life. Mayhap 'twas for the best.

He grabbed his bedroll on the opposite end of the fire even as Arthur came to stand next to his lady guarding her throughout the night. Ice formed around Wymar's heart and he vowed he would never let sentiment guide him again.

CHAPTER NINETEEN

SPERLING WATCHED IN satisfaction as the battering ram shattered what remained of the keep door at Norwich. They had finally broken through the last of their defenses. Knights swarmed inside the keep even whilst he heard a man shouting to yield the day. 'Twas obvious those seeking shelter inside the keep had seen enough bloodshed given they had not many left to defend the land. Bodies outside in the bailey were scattered everywhere but Sperling barely gave them a thought as he rushed inside and strode confidently into the great hall.

Ceridwen's father stood proudly near the hearth. His blood-soaked tunic gave testimony to those in the king's army he had slain prior to seeking what he assumed would be safety within the keep. The man swayed when Sperling neared. Lord Hamon was either injured or just taken aback that Sperling had successfully led the attack on his castle.

"Sperling," Hamon shouted. "What the bloody hell is the meaning of this invasion? Why are you with Stephen's men?"

"'Tis obvious, is it not?" Sperling waited but a moment before he continued. "Hamon Ward of Norwich, I hereby claim Norwich Castle in the name of His Majesty King Stephen and strip you of your title. I also sentence you to death for the traitor you have become by favoring the false queen!" Sperling grinned as he delivered Lord Hamon's sentence.

"How dare you invade my home? *You* are the traitor to our true queen! What have you done with my daughter?" he shouted as two knights took him into custody.

"Your daughter is no longer your concern. She will no doubt return before long and she will swear her fealty to the rightful king *and* to me before I take her to my bed. I have Stephen's favor now and no longer need her as my wife in order to secure the lands. She will make a lovely whore, will she not?" Sperling laughed when Hamon lunged for him. He still intended to marry Ceridwen, for he had no wish for their sons to be illegitimate, but there was no need to tell Hamon that. Not when there was such pleasure to be found in baiting him.

"I will see you in hell first," Hamon warned.

"Keep a place warm for me then since you will get to the fiery pits much sooner than I ever will." Sperling came up to the hearth and sat in the overly large chair reserved for the lord of the keep. He gave a wave of his hand. "Take him away and see that his head is placed on a pike outside my gates. 'Twill be a welcoming gift for Ceridwen upon her return."

As Sperling watched them wrestle getting the man out the front door of the keep, he clapped his hands with a fair amount of gratification that all was going according to his grand plans. Now, to only await his wife's arrival to Norwich. He would use her in every way he could think of to ensure she knew her new role in life… to see only to his pleasure.

CHAPTER TWENTY

CERIDWEN LOST COUNT of the days they continued their journey south. At times she swore she could detect the scent of the salty ocean breeze in the air and she became homesick. At others, the odor of smoke caused her to wonder where the smell was coming from. She only wanted to see her father and have him wrap her in his embrace and tell her everything would work out as it should. She should have never left Norwich. She should have listened to his council. She could not change her foolish decision to fight for the Empress's cause but Ceridwen would beg his forgiveness as soon as she entered their hall. She was so close to home now and wanted to throw caution to the wind and race Defiance the remaining way to the castle. But that would be another foolish act on her part considering she knew not what awaited her return.

Regret consumed her along with the thought of never seeing Wymar again. She caught his stare before he turned away and knew he, too, was thinking of their short time together. A heavy sigh escaped her, and she swore her heart would never be the same again. Her Knight of Darkness had left an impression on her heart that would be hard to erase, even though they could never be together.

"'Tis for the best, Ceridwen," Arthur exclaimed coming abreast of her horse.

"Aye, I know."

"You shall find another and he will be worthy of your love," he continued, staring ahead to the road before them.

"Nay, I will not. Love is for fools. Better to wed for monies and land than to let such a stupid emotion as love dictate how your life will be led."

"Do not be so rash and appear so sad, my lady. You will find love one day."

She turned her face to her captain, willing the tears to not creep from her eyes. "I will never allow love to rule my heart." Her breath hitched at her vow and she took a moment to regret what could have been with Wymar. She almost laughed at the irony. She had no idea if she even really had Wymar's affection to begin with.

"You do not mean that, Ceridwen."

"Were you not the one who said I should be wary of Norwood?"

Arthur frowned before answering. "Aye."

"Were you not the one who said he was not to be trusted with my heart?"

"Aye, but—"

"There are no *buts*, Arthur. You have known me all my life. I have heeded your council and have seen the wisdom of your words. If Norwood had even given a hint of his affection for me, I would have thrown caution to the wind and we would not be having this conversation. Since he did not, then it stands to reason that you were right in your assumptions of him. Let the matter rest. We will go on as we did before we left Norwich. Once we have secured Norwich once again, I will wed as my father dictates. I will say no more on the subject. Now please leave me in peace so I may suffer in silence."

She put her heels to the side of her steed who trotted off to leave Arthur behind. She rode up to Thomas and Symond who gave her wary smiles.

"I swear if the two of you plan on berating me for anything other than the foul weather, I will leave you behind in the dust as I have done to my captain."

The two men sputtered before they began talking about all their plans once they returned home. Home… Ceridwen could barely contain her excitement to see her lands and father again. She still had fear of what she would find, but she couldn't believe that Sperling could have truly managed to capture the entire estate. Surely her father was safe in the keep. She and the others would end the siege and drive Ratcliff and the others away. She felt sure of that.

The rode in silence for several more miles and just when she caught a glimpse of the rooftop of her keep through the trees, a scout who was one of her men came galloping back to their group. Instead of reporting to her, he made his way straight to Wymar who held up his hand to halt their progress whilst he listened to what the man learned. Inwardly, Ceridwen fumed that her own knight had not reported his findings to her directly. It did not help matters that she could not make out any part of the conversation. All she could tell was that Wymar did not seem pleased. She would not sit silently whilst her future awaited her.

Kicking Defiance into another trot, she rode up to Wymar and waited for him to notice her whilst he continued issuing orders to make camp.

"I will see what game we can hunt to fill our empty stomachs," Richard said.

"Nay," Wymar replied before rubbing the back of his neck. "No fires. They may alert those standing guard at the castle that we are close."

Ceridwen interrupted them. "They will already know we are here, Norwood. You cannot hide an army this size so close to the keep."

His brow rose as if he noticed her for the first time. "Go back to the rear of the company and stay with your captain and men."

"What is going on at Norwich that you are not telling me?" she said leaning over to take his arm. 'Twas a mistake to touch him for tiny currents of fire raced up her arm at their contact. She jumped back as though she had been burned.

"'Tis nothing to concern yourself with," he answered before dismounting from his horse.

"Nothing to concern myself with? Why, your braying ass!" she shouted pointing in the direction of the castle. "That is my home and my people, if something that insignificant may have escaped your notice."

Wymar swore beneath his breath before he came around toward her horse. "Get down," he ordered."

"Not before you tell me what is going on," she said flipping her hair from her face.

He pulled the reins from her grip. "Get down from this horse, Ceridwen. I will not tell you again."

"Make me!" she shouted.

"Fine. You want to act like a spoiled child, then I shall treat you as one."

Before she knew what was happening, Ceridwen was pulled from the saddle and thrown over Wymar's shoulder as though she weighed nothing. She saw Arthur coming to her aid but Norwood ordered him to stand down, and for some reason, he complied. Hitting her fists against Wymar's back only made her hands sore because he wore his chainmail.

"Put me down, Norwood!"

He continued on foot until he came upon a small clearing where he did just that. Tossing her upon a bed of moss, she stared up at him in confusion whilst her heart raced and betrayed her.

"What are you not telling me, Wymar?" she asked although she had the notion she would not like his answer.

"Ceridwen, I do not know how to tell you this," he began until he came to sit down beside her. He took her hands that began to shake.

"Oh God," she cried out. "Just tell me!"

He did not waste any more words but told her of the situation. "Norwich has been taken. The village sacked. There is nothing left to the fields for the coming winter. Those who fought against Stephen's army have been left to rot where they were slain."

Her lips quivered. "No, please tell me some of my people have been spared."

He rubbed her hands to try to get some warmth into them but nothing could break through the chill running down her spine.

"'Tis hard to say," Wymar continued. "The scout dared not get too close in order to avoid being seen. His only words were that the way across the drawbridge was… ghastly."

"How so?"

"'Tis war, Ceridwen. You are certainly aware what happens during a siege and what becomes of those closest to those they serve."

"Are you trying to tell me they have been beheaded?"

"Aye, I am afraid so."

"And my father?" she asked with tear-filled eyes.

"The reason I sent one of your own men to scout ahead is because he would be familiar with the workings of Norwich and those he served. He confirmed my worst fears. I am so sorry, my lady." Wymar hung his head with his words.

A low wail escaped her parted lips. "No!" she screamed and jumped from the ground even whilst Wymar called out her name, begging her to stop.

She ran as fast as her feet would carry her, jumped upon her horse before anyone could stop her, and galloped to the edges of the forest. She slid from the saddle to peer upon the keep all the while holding onto the trunk of a tree for support.

She was close enough to see them all and 'twas a sight she would never forget. One could not go back after seeing your father's head sitting on a pike along with his most trusted knights. She fell to the ground as a cry of anguish sprang forth from the very depth of her soul. She only realized she was no longer alone when she felt Wymar's arms go around her, pulling her into his embrace.

"My lord… how may I help her?" Arthur choked out. His tone held his own sorrow of what he, too, had witnessed. Ceridwen barely heard Arthur come upon them whilst she was clinging to Wymar.

"She will need time, Chamberlayn. I will keep her safe," Wymar vowed, dismissing him. Arthur quietly left.

Wymar muttered words of comfort and somewhere they registered into Ceridwen's broken heart. They could not take away the pain or the scars that would be left behind but somehow, they erased a small part of what she had lost. Regret once more consumed her for not being there for her father and people. She cried in earnest of what would never be far into the night. When she found some form of solace from her despair by falling asleep, she was safely wrapped in the arms of her knight.

CHAPTER TWENTY-ONE

THE NIGHT WAS still, almost too still. Not a sound disturbed the forest, causing Wymar to continue searching the dark for enemies that would attack. But all was quiet and he began to relax for the first time since Ceridwen had fallen into his arms in despair. Her cries of anguish over the loss of her father had torn at his heart, breaking down the barriers he had erected to protect it for the past several days. He had no idea where their relationship was going, if he could call what was between them some sort of bond. He only knew he needed her in his life.

She had clung to him in her sleep, wrapping herself around him so closely that it felt as though he had a second skin. At times she would cry out her for her father and he would soothe her with words of comfort until she calmed again. At other times, she would murmur out his name as if they were lovers and Wymar would pull up every bit of strength within him to not make her his in every way.

She stirred again and he pulled more of the blanket around her when he felt her shiver from the cold. *Cold... God's Blood...* how could she be cold when having this woman this close to him was causing him to burn? Aye... he wanted her more than any other woman he had ever desired but now was not the time to give in to this constant craving for her. He needed her as much as she needed him, but protecting her was far more important than slaking his lusts. He leaned his head back to stare up into the stars. When had he become so drawn to her? Mayhap when she first revealed herself as a woman instead of the knight he had thought her to be.

"Kiss me…"

Wymar smiled as he pulled her closer and her hand wound its way around his neck. She was dreaming again and flashes of memory of their all-too-brief encounters swiftly ran through his mind. Ceridwen was a fiery vixen one moment and a calm, determined woman the next. He gave a small chuckle, thinking of the woman he was becoming to know.

"Wymar… kiss me… please…" she whispered into the night.

He gave a heavy sigh and restrained himself in fulfilling her demand. He could not take advantage of her plea whilst she slumbered, much to his dismay. She would never forgive him and he no longer wished to have disagreements driving them apart. He was tired of the fighting for what was right, tired from the years of trying to restore his family name, and tired of trying to figure out this complicated woman who tore at his heart. He might as well confess his feeling for her come the morn. He cared for her. That much was true but he was unsure if he was truly capable of loving anyone. She deserved better. She deserved someone who could stay with her, give her the future that she wanted.

Her captain's words echoed in his mind. Aye, she deserved better than what Wymar could offer her. He had no idea what awaited him at this own home, only that he must return there. And he still had the matter of taking back the castle for Ceridwen and his queen. There was still much to do before he could ever begin to think of offering for the woman who unknowingly owned his heart.

"Why will you not kiss me, Wymar?"

He stole a look at the woman in his arms and realized she had been watching him and was very much awake. Wymar could only assume her profound grief was the driving force for her request. She required some form of comfort from him. But surely he could give her the comfort she needed without crossing any lines. As if to contradict his thoughts, she swiftly moved to sit in his lap causing a part of him to spring to life at her nearness. Wymar swore he could feel the very heat of her through their garments.

"Ceridwen, you need your rest. Go back to sleep," he urged as he attempted to pull her from his lap. Instead, she pulled herself even closer and he nearly unmanned himself to feel her entire body intimately claim his own.

"Always telling me what to do," she teased. "Can you not throw caution to the wind and just *feel* for a change? You do not always have to be in control, Wymar."

A low moan caught in his throat. "I will not have you hate me come the morn, Ceridwen. You have no idea how much I want you at this moment. And yet, I will not take advantage of you during your grief and give in to my desires to claim you."

She looked around where he had taken her to slumber only to realize they were very much alone. "If you wished for us to remain chaste, then you should have picked a better spot where we would be close to the others, Norwood," she said with a laugh.

"We thought it best, out of respect, to allow you some privacy in order to grieve," he whispered.

"*We?*" she asked.

"Chamberlayn and I discussed it and reached the decision, along with the rest of your men," he answered.

"'Twas considerate of you all," she murmured. "Allow me to thank you for that consideration." She leaned down and softly blew into his ear and he shivered. "I want you."

"You do not know what you are asking of me," he said in a husky whisper. "I am only a man and am barely holding on to the remaining shreds of my vow to keep you safe as it is."

"I am always safe with you, Wymar. Safe to make this decision for myself. And I know what I want. Make me yours in every way. Show me the way to the heavens so that I can relive this one moment for the rest of my life. I promise I will ask nothing more of you than that."

"Ceridwen…" her name lingered in the space between them and he watched her smile.

"I love when I hear my name pass your lips. Kiss me, Wymar. Touch me. Teach me about pleasure, and make me yours. We belong only to each other at least for this one eve. We will not worry about what the morrow may bring. Let us bring the darkness that surrounds our lives into the light so that for just this one moment in time we might know the meaning of love."

She bent forward and their mouths were but a heartbeat away before she claimed him. One touch and any bit of chivalry left Wymar as he took what she so willingly offered. He had been starving for her and as she opened her mouth and plunged her tongue to dance with his own, Wymar lost control. The kiss became possessive as though they each wished to live this one moment without regret.

Ceridwen pulled back, her chest heaving as though trying to catch her breath. She gazed down upon him before reaching for his tunic and pulling it from his body. Exposed to the night air, goosebumps raced across his skin before her fingers skimmed his feverish flesh. A low moan escaped her before he pulled her from his lap and stood. Holding out his hand, he helped her rise and began untying the laces in the front of her gown. Once finished, he pulled the garment off along with her underclothing, tossing them to the ground. She had no time to react when he turned her and tugged her back against him, his chest pressed along her back. Reaching around her body, his teased the nipples of her breasts and kissed her neck.

"You had me at a disadvantage, but turnabout is fair play. Tell me to stop this instant if you have changed your mind. If we continue on, I may not have the will to stop." He groaned at the thought of not being able to continue. Still waiting for her answer, Wymar turned his lady around to again face him.

Her hand cupped his cheek before moving once more down his

chest before she began removing his hose and braies. When they both stood naked to the elements, she once more wound her arms around his neck and pressed her body into his.

"I am yours, Wymar, just as you belong to me for this night alone."

They were all the words he needed and he pulled her into his body and kissed her as he had never done before. Picking her up, he laid her down upon their discarded clothing. His hands stroked her body and left no part of her skin untouched. His hand lowered to the very center of her being and he could tell she was ready for him. As much as he wanted to plunge into her softness without any more delay, he refrained. For the first time in his life he cared more about the woman beneath him and her needs than he cared for his own. Was this love?

Slowly, his lips left a trail down her body. He lavished sweet kisses on her breasts, sucking the nipples until they puckered inside his mouth even whilst his fingers stroked her softness. Ceridwen began to come alive, as he had never seen her before, which only drove him further to give her as much pleasure as she could take.

Further down her body did his lips travel, his tongue wet on her burning flesh. When he neared the space between her legs, he felt her tug his hair and he looked up to see her staring at him in confusion.

"What is this you do, Wymar?" she said with a breathy whisper.

"Teaching you, my sweet. Be a good student and enjoy."

"But—"

"As you said, Ceridwen... just *feel* and let yourself go with the moment," he urged and went down to feast upon his treasure.

The first moment his tongue touched her center, she bucked in surprise. It did not take her long before she truly lost herself in the pleasure she was receiving from him. She said his name over and over again, which only encouraged Wymar to continue lavishing his attentions on this woman who was on the brink of ecstasy. Her hips rose and a sound tore from her lips as she reached her climax. It was the most beautiful sound he had ever heard.

His manhood was throbbing for its own release, but her needs still had to come first. He had no wish to frighten or overwhelm her, particularly for her first time. If that meant taking a pause, then they would. If it meant stopping altogether before things went any further… then so be it. She had already given him a gift far greater than any maidenhead. Wymar waited for Ceridwen's breathing to return to normal. He kissed his way back up her body and was surprised with the overwhelming emotions coursing through his own. Aye… she had broken down the last of his walls and he cared not that he had not found his own release. He pulled her closer and caressed her hair as she snuggled into his chest.

How long he held her, he did not know. But he was well aware he was half asleep when he felt her hand moving down his chest, skimming her fingertips over his own nipples and teasing the hair as she made her way toward the very essence of him. He held his breath in anticipation of what she had planned for him but he was unprepared when she wrapped her hand around his manhood. He hissed in surprise and she stopped.

Raising her head from his chest, she peered at him. "Is it not permissible to touch you?"

"You may, although I may not last long under your tender administrations."

"I do not understand," she said as she once more began to move her hand up and down his shaft.

God's Bones he wanted to be inside her, he thought as she continued her play. He could stand her exquisite torture no longer and he placed his hand over her own to stop what she was doing.

"Cease, Ceridwen. I can stand it no more," he said with clenched teeth.

"But there is more for you to teach me?" she asked.

"Aye, but not tonight. I will not take you here on the forest floor after all you have been through."

"But we may not have any more time together, Wymar. It must be tonight because the morrow is not promised."

He was confused at her words but as she tightened her grip upon him, he moved so she was now beneath him. "Are you sure?"

She nodded. "Aye. Teach me. Make me yours in every way."

He could not bring himself to argue any further. His lady's wish was his command. Taking her legs, he wrapped them around his hips and placed his manhood at the very heat of her. Bending forward, he placed his manhood at her core until he found the barrier he knew he would find. Aye, she was a maiden but after this eve she would be his forevermore.

"I am sorry this will hurt you, my love," he whispered before kissing her lips and plunging further inside to completely fill her womanhood.

Her cry was muffled with his kiss and he resolved himself to remain still whilst she grew accustomed to his size and the fullness of him inside her where nothing had ever been before. When he felt her move, he began also. Slowly at first until their rhythm fell into one that was as old as time itself. He ravished her lips for they were now as one, never to be the same ever again.

As he at last neared his own release, Wymar knew Ceridwen was almost there as well. He whispered in her ear. "Come with me, my sweet, and we shall see the heavens' stars together this time."

He drove into her faster and faster until her hips rose and she cried out. 'Twas still the sweetest of sounds and Wymar drove himself one last time into her heat and flooded her with his seed. Time stood still. Their breathing slowed as they stared into each other eyes and returned to earth together.

Wymar rolled over but continued to face his lady-love. Aye, love her he did, if the passion that filled his heart was any indication what the emotion was truly about. He caressed her hair before placing another kiss upon her rosy red lips.

"You are now mine, Lady Ceridwen Ward. Until the end of time itself, we will now only belong to one another." He sealed his vow with another kiss before bringing her close into his embrace. He reached for a nearby blanket and pulled it over them. "Sleep well, my lady."

"And you, Wymar."

He closed his eyes and finally slept and when he dreamed, he dreamed of a woman with aquamarine eyes who forever and always would hold his heart in her hands.

CHAPTER TWENTY-TWO

CERIDWEN'S EYES BEGAN to flutter open. She squinted before raising her hand to cover them when rays of sunshine flashed into her face. The smell of smoke in the distance was not as strong as the day before but was still a grim reminder of a home that was no longer belonging to her family. Pulling the blanket up to her chin, a slight smile broke across her face as she remembered the eve before. She rolled onto her back and reached for Wymar only to realize he was no longer sleeping by her side.

She panicked for an instant before she heard the camp coming to life in the distance. Reaching for her garments, she quickly dressed and tried not to think about no longer being a maiden. 'Twas not as though Wymar had not given her every opportunity to halt their lovemaking before they had reached the point of no return. But she had had no wish to turn back. She'd wanted him, pure and simple. She *still* wanted him, and she knew she always would. She would no longer deny what she felt in her heart for this man, even if in the end she could hold no claim to him as her own. She gave a heavy sigh of what her future might hold without Wymar in her life.

As she continued dressing, she remembered when she had woken up from the nightmare her life had become. All she could sense was Wymar holding her safely in his arms and fighting off the demons tormenting her mind. With her father now gone, Wymar unknowingly offered her the sense of stability she was craving. Arms of steel keeping her safe, along with loving words calming her worst fears. She felt protected with him. At the time it only seemed natural when she had asked for his kiss. She chuckled. Obviously, he had been lost in his own thoughts, for what man would not react to such a heartfelt plea as the one she had given three times?

Her hands ran down her gown to smooth out the wrinkles but lingered on her stomach. What if there was a babe after their coupling? She shook her head refusing to think on that now. She would deal with such an outcome if the situation came to fruition. She would only remember the joy of how wonderful their time together had been. *So, this was what all the bards talked about when they came to entertain us in our halls*, she thought. If this was love, then she would cherish their time together for as long as it would last.

And if he left come the morrow, then so be it. She would always have yester eve… a perfect memory of one night together when duty and responsibility were not at the forefront of their minds. She would not hold him back from continuing on with his duty to his land and people just as she must needs find a way to wrestle her land back from the enemies who killed her father.

She finished putting on her boots and stood tall with a new determination to reclaim her land. Picking up their discarded blankets, she began heading toward the men. Her eyes searched for Wymar but there was no sign of him. His squire, Turbert, was nearby shuffling his feet in the dirt as was his man Richard.

Some of the men stared at her with frowns marring their visages. Wondering what could be wrong, she turned to find Arthur glaring at her as though he knew what had occurred between her and Wymar the night before.

"Where is he?" she began before continuing on as she pulled Arthur to the side to afford some bit of privacy, "and why are his men looking upon me as if they want to place a dagger in my back?"

"You have missed much this morn whilst you continued your slumber," Arthur said not gazing upon her. "Several of Wymar's men are at odds having to remain behind when—"

"He is gone?" she asked. She began to panic at the thought that Wymar had left her without even saying farewell. "He has departed for his own home before I have even reclaimed mine?"

"Nay, I never said he left for his lands, my lady."

"Then where the bloody hell has Norwood gone so early in the morn?" she demanded.

Arthur nodded in the direction of Norwich. "He went to scout out the area near the castle in the hope that he could possibly negotiate the return of your estate."

"Negotiate? With the mindless cur that laid siege to my home and murdered its people? He should know you do not negotiate with men of their ilk."

"Aye, he should but he would not listen to our advice. Norwood hoped to find a way to have Norwich returned to you without any more bloodshed," Arthur answered whilst raking his hand through his hair. "You will not like who that murderous mongrel is that laid siege to Norwich."

Ceridwen's eyes narrowed, but she couldn't deny that she was already certain of the truth. There was only one man who could have committed that terrible deed. "It was Ratcliff, was it not?"

"Aye, my lady. It was."

"The bastard!" she snapped pacing across the forest floor. "Why did Norwood not wait for me or take reinforcements? Most of our men are sitting here waiting for instructions, or so it seems."

"Norwood had no intention of allowing you to step anywhere near the gates of Norwich once he learned who had taken the castle."

"He had no right to make such a decision for me."

Arthur's brow rose. "Norwood claimed he did but if it makes you feel any better, he also refused for his man Grancourt to accompany him."

A growl of frustration burst from his lips. "Please tell me that fool did not go there alone."

"He took only a small contingent of men. As I mentioned, he would not listen to anyone's council much to our dismay. No one could talk any sense to him. He felt 'twas better to deal with the situation with a small group, although why he thought he would be able to negotiate with Ratcliff was beyond our comprehension."

"The fool!" Ceridwen fumed. "Where is my saddle bag? I need to change from this infernal gown. I have the feeling we are going on a rescue mission."

Arthur followed behind and motioned for Symond and Thomas to join them whilst Ceridwen gathered her belongings. The men stood guard whilst she went behind some shrubbery and began to change. Once attired in tunic and hose once more, she shoved her gown into her bag and turned to voice her plans. Richard had joined them.

"He was an idiot to leave behind such a number of reinforcements who could have watched his back," she said to Richard, who nodded.

"Aye. I said much of the same thing, not that he would listen. I fear the worst since they have not returned."

"How will we know where they have taken him, my lady, if he has been captured?" asked Symond.

Ceridwen strapped the belt around her waist and placed her sword within the scabbard. "Ratcliff and Norwood have history. If apprehended, I have no doubt the minute Norwood was brought before the new... *lord*..." she said with disgust and held back a smirk when Thomas spat on the ground, "he will be taken into custody. That is if they have not already killed him."

Richard stepped forward. "If 'tis any consolation, his head is not sitting on a pike outside the gate to add to the others," he said, and Ceridwen blanched at the thought. "My apologies, my lady."

Ceridwen gulped but waved him off. "No, you are right. 'Tis something to keep in mind. Ratcliff is the biggest arse in all of Christendom, but he will also want his ego stroked, knowing he has seized his biggest rival. If he killed him, he would have posted his head where everyone could see it. But… I think it very likely that Norwood is still alive. Ratcliff will want the opportunity to gloat over the fact that he has imprisoned Norwood," she reasoned, whilst fingering the hilt of her sword. "Aye… he will keep him alive if only to torture him further. Knowing this, Ratcliff shall place Norwood in the dungeons beneath the keep."

"Then how are we to get him out?" exclaimed a small voice coming from behind the trees.

Thomas went and grabbed a handful of Turbert's tunic and brought him forward into the group. "I see we have a spy amongst us, Lady Ceridwen," he proclaimed.

"I want to help," Turbert said crossing his arms over his chest. "Lord Wymar is my master, after all. 'Tis my job to watch over him."

Symond tsked disapprovingly. "Off with you, boy, before you get yourself killed."

Ceridwen stepped forward. "Let him stay. He may be of some use." She watched as the young lad puffed up his chest. She turned back to the men.

"We have the advantage of knowing the castle and its layout better than Ratcliff ever could. He may know the basics of where the kitchens, halls and bedchambers are located but he has no knowledge of the underground passage that leads to the bowels of the castle."

Arthur nodded. "Aye, she speaks the truth. Only those in the family, and their most trusted friends, are ever told of the escape method to avoid capture by the enemy."

"Why, then, did Lord Hamon not make use of it?" Thomas asked with a frown of displeasure.

Ceridwen sighed. "I can only assume that something kept him from making his way there. Mayhap the way was barred, or he was attempting to protect the remainder of his people. I may never know for certain. As much as I may wish my sire was still among the living, I cannot dwell on what I cannot change. We must needs concentrate on rescuing Norwood without further casualties."

"What do you have in mind?" Richard asked.

"First, I will create a diversion at the front gates," Ceridwen began while Arthur fiercely scowled in her direction. Her captain was about to voice his displeasure until she held up her hand to silence any protest that was about to spew from his mouth. She continued to explain to the men her idea to rescue Wymar. She would not lose him too!

CHAPTER TWENTY-THREE

WYMAR HELD HIS breath as the leather straps of a whip slashed across his already abused back. He would not give them the satisfaction of seeing him break his resistance. He silently vowed to remain level headed no matter how much they tortured him. But while he would not cry out, he could not deny the toll on his body. His arms had gone numb after being stretched above his head for the past several days... or was it a se'nnight? Time seemed to have no meaning when you were being held a prisoner in a place where there was no daylight.

He had been a fool to think he could march up the gates of the castle once a parlay was agreed upon and bargain with a man who hated him. Of course, he had not known who had taken over Norwich at the time. Perhaps if he had, he would have been more cautious. His only thought had been to somehow manage to regain control of Ceridwen's home no matter what he had to do to obtain it for her. He should have listened to Richard and taken more of his men with him but at the time he had thought this would only lead to another siege and more loss of life. Norwich could not afford to lose any more of its people. So instead, he took a small group with him.

It had been a plan doomed to fail from the start. He had barely entered the great hall before he realized, moments too late, that it had been a trap all along. The parlay they agreed upon was nothing but a ruse to get Wymar and his men into the keep as they began fighting for their very lives. Guards swiftly overtook them and Wymar witnessed several of his men fall to their doom. His nose was surely broken. His sword had been wrenched from his hand but at least Wymar had the satisfaction of having killed several of Stephen's men before he was overtaken. Even his dagger hidden in his boot was found and confiscated. He had no knowledge what had become of his men who had survived the initial conflict. Wymar had the notion they had already met their untimely demise.

His face a bloody mess, he was thrown on the floor to kneel before the very man who had ordered the killing of Ceridwen's father. Or perhaps he had committed the act himself. Wymar would not be surprised to learn he could be that cruel. Ratcliff offered him a wicked smirk but with a wave of his hand, Wymar found himself knocked unconscious. He awoke to his worst nightmare. A plaything for a vengeful man bent to break another's will to live.

Another slash across his back brought him back to the reality of what his life had become. He could feel the blood trickling down his bruised back. He had lost count of how many lashes he had received. Five? Ten? If this continued, Wymar had no doubt he would indeed break. There was only so much a man could take before he would beg for death.

"Hold!" a voice in the dimly lit dungeon called out even as Wymar raised his head in defiance. He would prove to his tormentors that he could still rise above the pain they inflicted on his battered body. "Cut him down."

His legs gave out when the ropes that were connected to a metal loop in the ceiling were cut. Falling to the floor, blood rushed to his arms whilst he attempted to catch his breath.

Ratcliff knelt down in front of Wymar and smiled slyly.

"My, how the Knight of Darkness has fallen. Look at you now," Ratcliff sneered, pulling at Wymar's hair so he had no choice but to look directly into the face of his enemy. "I have heard of your exploits at Lincoln, but you've gone from a champion knight for that bitch you call a queen to nothing more than a plaything for my amusement. Did you honestly think Lady Ceridwen would want some weak sword hand over someone who has the rightful king's favor? If you do, then you are indeed sadly mistaken and a bigger fool than I already thought you to be."

"You lie, Ratcliff. Ceridwen would never stoop so low as to bed someone who executed her father, not to mention a traitor to the Empress Matilda."

Laughter echoed off the walls of Wymar's prison but that was nothing compared to the pain of Ratcliff's fist smashing into Wymar's face. The bastard shook his hand to ease the pain and smirked again.

"How little you know the woman. You were both so overly confident by just striding up to my gates expecting me to bow down to your every whim. But she at least saw reason, realizing that I would not bargain away your release so easily. And I certainly did not allow her to think that Norwich would be turned over to her at such a small sacrifice on her part." He wrung his hands together obviously enjoying this moment to hold over Wymar's head. "Do you know that she offered to marry me to save your sorry hide? Why, even now, she awaits me in my bedchamber. I cannot wait until I at last have that tiresome bitch beneath me."

Wymar spit out a mouthful of blood and glared at Ratcliff. "When I finally get out of here, 'twill give me the greatest pleasure to kill you."

"That is a strong statement for someone who is a prisoner in my dungeon."

"I will get free," Wymar vowed.

Ratcliff stood and stretched, peering down upon Wymar who could not miss the hatred flashing across the man's face. He took up an iron brand from the flames of a nearby fire and held it out so that Wymar could see the design.

"Do you see this? 'Tis my personal brand. I like to mark all my prisoners in case they escape. And in the off chance you do get yourself free from here, you will always be branded as my property."

He dug the scorching iron into Wymar's shoulder. The sizzling sound and smell of burning flesh almost made Wymar retch, but he held his composure as best as he could through the pain. When all was said and done, Ratcliff threw the iron rod aside and walked toward the doorway chuckling.

"I think I will go attend my bride. 'Tis not polite to keep a lady waiting. I wonder if knowing I am bedding the fair virgin you thought to have for yourself will finally break your spirits? I will enjoy telling you all the details of taking her upon my next visit," Ratcliff declared as he once more headed toward the stairs. "Throw him into the pit. Mayhap that will cool his temper."

"Ceridwen!" he shouted her name as if she could in truth hear him whilst his arms were taken in a death grip.

Wymar struggled but in the end it was useless. The sound of metal bars squeaking in protest as they were opened alerted him of what was in store for him next. He was then falling and landing with a splash into God only knew what. The smell alone was enough to wake him even as the bars high above were slammed shut.

"Enjoy your stay," the guard taunted before he spat into the pit for good measure and left. There was no reason to stand guard. Given the depth of his newfound cell, Wymar was not going anywhere.

He scrambled over some of the debris to get himself above the water. Something scurried across his boots and Wymar kicked the animal aside. Looking above, he saw the meager bit of light from a torch fade away before he was plunged into total darkness.

Thoughts of Ceridwen sacrificing herself for his sorry hide drained the remaining bit of hope Wymar had been holding on to. He could not erase the vision of her in bed with Ratcliff. The thought tortured him and twisted his guts into knots. He needed some kind of a miracle in order to save the woman he had come to care for. Unsure if he was worthy to receive such a gift from the heavens, he bowed his head and began to pray.

CHAPTER TWENTY-FOUR

WYMAR SHIVERED IN the dark. There was no doubt in his mind he was going to die in this God forsaken pit. How long had he been here, waiting for death? Hours? Days? 'Twas no way to tell whether 'twas day or night... not with the darkness of this cesspit from hell. No one had come to offer him even a meager bit of food, not that he could have stomached it even if they had. The stench of his prison surely must be permanently burned into his skin, to be carried with him forever even if he were to ever see the light of day again. He was sick, his body on fire most likely from the infected wounds on his back and wrists. He would not think of the brand also ingrained into his shoulder. He had given up hope hours ago... or mayhap 'twas days.

God had abandoned him. Praying to a higher being had been useless but still he had to at least make the effort to somehow fight for his freedom but 'twas mostly for Ceridwen. Thoughts of her bedding Ratcliff continued to twist his soul in agony.

A light appeared or mayhap 'twas a vision for he swore it took shape in the form of his lady-love.

"Wymar..."

"Ceridwen..." he managed to whisper between his cracked, parched lips. He stretched his hand forward with what little strength he had left but she disappeared from view.

"My Lord Wymar," a voice called from above and Wymar tilted his head back yet covered his eyes from the brightness of the torch.

"Turb?" Was that really his voice sounding as weak as a newborn kitten?

"Aye, my lord. We have come to save you."

At last, he thought before leaning his head back against the slimy wall. He barely heard the hinges squeaking as the bars above were opened and a rope thrown down. Too weak to make any effort to grab at the lifeline that had been tossed to him, he at last made out a form descending from above.

"Thank the Lord, we have found you, Wymar," Richard declared. "Can you climb up onto my back?"

"Aye," he said but failed in his attempt to get any kind of a firm hold on his friend.

"Arthur!" Richard called up quietly. "Attach the other rope and get down here. We are going to have to pull him up together."

Wymar swore he lost consciousness several times before he was hoisted out of that pit. The rope that had been secured around him was taken off and several men began to carry him from the dungeon.

"Ceridwen… where is she?" he whispered, taking hold of Arthur's arm with what little strength he had left.

A grunt came from Arthur. "Ceridwen knows how to take care of herself. You are free. That was her main concern."

Freedom! Aye! He was free of that pit from hell. Wymar looked around at the men who had come to save him. He swore he gained strength see both his men and Ceridwen's after his ordeal as they made their way through several passageways. He would look forward to the next victory once they in turn rescued Ceridwen.

⁂

THIS IDEA OF hers had been just as insane as Wymar's had been. She had been positive that if she showed up at the keep, 'twould provide the distraction needed and give their men enough time to free Wymar. The hardest part for her had been to walk across the drawbridge and not look at the men who had served her father. She had almost lost her nerve when her sire's sightless eyes stared upon her when she passed.

How could she have known the depths that Ratcliff would sink in order to own her? He had already claimed her land in the name of the usurper. Ratcliff's plan to marry Ceridwen would ensure the remaining servants of the castle, the knights who guarded its walls, and the serfs who tilled the fields would fall into line with its new master. Her sacrifice of being captured was worth the outcome if Wymar would be set free. But Ratcliff had locked her in her bedchamber for the past three days without her seeing that Wymar yet lived. She was glad she had another plan in place and could only pray that her men were now underground making their way to Wymar. Or even better... that he had already been rescued.

Ordered to dress like the woman she was, a servant who had not been at Norwich previously had helped her change from her hose and tunic before she took the garments away. The woman had been the only person she had seen since that first brief encounter with Ratcliff. The isolation and not knowing what was going on around her would be her undoing. She had never been one to sit idly by with needle and thread and 'twas as though Ratcliff knew that locking her away in a room would drive her mad.

She took a look around the room and a sob tore at her throat knowing this had been the last place she had had a conversation with her sire. Memories of their speech together filled her head and she wondered if Ratcliff had thoroughly searched the room. He would have done all he could to remove anything in view that could be used as a weapon, but perchance something still remained. Did she dare hope...

She went over to a rounded window seat set in the castle wall and sat. Pushing aside one of the cushions, she began wiggling one of the stones and a smile of satisfaction lit her face when one came loose. The jingle of keys alerted her that someone was about to enter so she quickly reached inside the hideaway and pulled out her mother's jeweled dagger. Thrusting the blade into her boot, she quickly replaced the cushion and pushed open the wooden shutter to appear occupied with the outside scenery. She had just taken an indifferent stance when the intruder entered.

"I have sent for a priest," Ratcliff announced whilst he shut the door and locked it.

Ceridwen turned, her brow lifting at his words. "You agreed to allow me to see that Norwood still lived. If you expect me to hold up my end of the bargain by cooperating with your demands, then bring him to me." Making such a vow to this scum had been no problem in Ceridwen's mind. If her men were able to free Wymar, then she was one step closer to her own freedom. She cared not that he had called for a priest for she would never utter vows to this cur. However, she kept her guard up. If she knew nothing else about the man standing before her, she knew Ratcliff could not be trusted. She highly doubted he would keep his word to show Wymar to her.

He came forward, taking a lock of her hair and twisting its golden lengths around his fingers until she had no choice but to step closer as he continued winding her hair.

"And you also promised me a sampling of what you have to offer come our wedding night. Let us start with a kiss," he urged grabbing her waist and bringing them chest-to-chest. His hand let go of her hair as he began to fondle her backside.

As he started to lean forward, Ceridwen turned her head aside and his lips fell to her cheek instead. "Bring Wymar to me so that I know you have not killed the man. Only then will there be reason to call a priest," she let the lie fall from her lips.

"What is that bastard to you anyway? If your father yet lived, he would have never consented to you wedding a mercenary. He is not nobility and sells his sword arm to the highest bidder," he spat.

She pulled away from his embrace but there was only so far she could go in a room where he held the key to her release. A smile cracked her lips. "Did you not hear the news? Mayhap you and your traitorous friends were too busy fleeing the battlefield after learning your false king had been captured."

He grabbed her arm, yanking her closer. "Stephen is the rightful ruler."

She smirked. "Even now, the Empress makes her way to London to be crowned Queen."

"'Twill never happen," he said dismissively. "Now what was that you were saying about other news?"

"First... Stephen even now most likely resides in the dungeon of Bristol Castle. He is the Empress's prisoner. And even more importantly, Empress Matilda restored *Lord* Wymar's title along with his lands. He is more than worthy to become my husband. At least he did not choose to kill innocent people in order to win the day."

"Bah! Any title restored to him by your so-called queen is worthless. In the end you will be mine..."

"...as long as Wymar yet lives. Otherwise, you may take this body, but I will never truly belong to you," she said pulling her arm free. "And I will *never* swear vows to you."

A laugh escaped him. "Do you honestly think I care whether you willingly go to the altar or not? You are a mere woman and are mine for the taking. If such a title as being the lady of these lands means so little to you, I can easily make you my whore."

"Show me Wymar is alive and I will submit to you," she said hiding her shaking hands behind her. God, how would she ever allow Ratcliff to touch her after all that she had shared with Norwood? But she knew her conversation with Ratcliff was but a ploy to give her men more time to rescue the man she truly loved. She would never give herself to the traitor standing in front of her.

"Willingly? I find that hard to believe given our past together," Ratcliff muttered but came to stand before her. "Swear it upon your very soul, Ceridwen."

"Let go of me!"

"Swear it to me," he urged.

"Aye. I swear it," she growled out, knowing with all her heart that Wymar was already free. She struggled against Ratcliff as he once again pulled her roughly into his arms.

"You are not giving me any kind of proof you speak the truth when you recoil from my touch. If you are so eager to barter your freedom for his safety, submit to me by showing me with a kiss," he said before lowering his head.

She stilled in his arms, but knew she would never find any sort of pleasure with this man, especially when he forcefully thrust his tongue into her mouth. He made an attempt to urge her participation but while she didn't fight against him, she gave very little effort to prove she was enjoying his attention.

He pulled his lips from hers and frowned. "That was pitiful, Ceridwen. You will have to do better than that, my dear," he said watching her carefully.

"What did you expect, Ratcliff?" she said quietly before lowering her eyes for appearances' sake. She did not wish for him to see the anger resting dormant just beneath the civility she showed him.

He took her chin between his fingers forcing her to look at him. "I suppose I should not expect much from a virgin who has not been taught how to pleasure a man. But we will have many years ahead of us for you to learn what I like. I will summon you once I bring the prisoner up from the pit."

"You put him in that disgusting pit?" she fumed, taking a step forward. She reached for him as though she would like nothing more than to strangle the very breath from him. She lowered her hand when her sanity returned.

"Tsk, tsk, my dearest lady. You would not wish to test this small courtesy I bestow upon you, would you?" he asked. His sarcastic tone tore at Ceridwen's nerves. "Answer me!"

"Nay, Ratcliff," she said keeping her anger in check.

"Say my first name. I would like to hear it said sweetly for my benefit."

Ceridwen swore inside her head before she lowered her eyes and conjured up the strength to appease him. "Sperling."

He laughed and clapped his hands. "Now that was not too difficult was it, my lady? I shall bring Norwood up. Consider this gesture of good faith between us as an early wedding gift."

He put the key to the door and left, locking the portal before she heard his footsteps fading down the passageway. Her knees buckled and she fell to the floor. If all went according to plan, Ratcliff would find only an empty pit. Only then would Ceridwen plan her next move to be rid of her enemy. Setting Wymar free was her main concern. The rest she prayed would eventually fall into place as fate dictated. Only time would tell if she would end up on the winning side.

CHAPTER TWENTY-FIVE

Sperling led the way down the spiraling steps deep into Norwich's bowels. Torch held high, he thought of the enormous pleasure he was going to take in flaunting Ceridwen in his arms before his prisoner. They reached the area where the pit was located only to see that the bars were open.

A growl of rage echoed in the chamber when he saw the pit empty. How the devil had he escaped? Wymar barely had the ability to move after all they had put him through. He must have had help.

"Who checked on him last and when?" Sperling shouted to the men surrounding the hole in the floor.

"'Two days… Mayhap, three. We have been celebrating our victory," one knight said from the rear of the group. "There was no place for him to go considering the depth of his cell."

Several knights nodded their heads. Sperling came to the man who had spoken and took him by his tunic before throwing him into the pit.

"See if you can get yourself out of there and enjoy your new quarters," he shouted down before looking at the others standing nearby. "Anyone else care to join him? No? Then search the passageways and find him. He could not have gone far," Sperling ordered before making his way back above.

That bitch must have known Wymar had somehow escaped and that is why she'd agreed to his proposal. There was no way she would meekly say her vows before a priest now… but 'twas no matter. She still belonged to him whether he made her his wife or not. Either way, Ceridwen would be in his bed and there was no reason not to take what he wanted from her!

His footsteps echoed throughout the great hall and he took the turret stairs two at a time until he reached the fourth floor of the keep. He took the brass key from a guard standing near the door and shoved it into the lock. Thrusting open the door, he slammed it shut and put the bolt into place.

The lady turned from the window as though she had not moved since he left her but a short while ago. A smile passed across her lips before she quickly covered up her apparent amusement knowing Ratcliff had failed.

"You knew!" he accused before taking her in his arms and shaking her.

"How could I know anything going on outside of the walls of my bedchamber, Ratcliff? I am but a prisoner here." She looked around him toward the closed portal. "Why do you not bring Norwood before me? Have you lost him?"

He raised his arm and slapped her across her cheek with all his strength, leaving the beginnings of a red imprint on her smooth creamy skin. "You bloody bitch from hell!"

She looked dazed when her eyes finally met his and still she had that same regal, disdainful look upon her as if she were better than him. "I will assume by your actions and the fact you are alone that you could not bring Norwood to me. Is he dead or alive, I wonder?" she asked whilst lifting her chin in clear defiance.

"Hopefully dead after we got done torturing him," he spat and watched when the color drained from her face. So… she cared for the bastard just as he thought but 'twas of no matter. He would take her maidenhead from her and receive the satisfaction of knowing that he was the first to have her.

Grabbing a hold of her arm, he tossed her onto the bed and quickly jumped upon her when she tried to scamper away.

"You have been a pain in my arse from the moment I first came to your gates but today I will get my revenge. At last, I will have something that Norwood will never be able to have for you can only be a virgin once!"

The sound of her gown ripping when he tore at the linen was nothing compared to the smile of contempt she tossed at him. "Then you have lost even that treasure, Ratcliff, for Wymar has taken that pleasure from you as well. Why, even now, I may be carrying his child within me."

Disgust and rage coursed through him and he got off the bed. Her hand went to her stomach causing Sperling to inwardly seethe. He would in no way bed her if there was a possibility that she carried his enemy's child. When she birthed a babe, he would need to know for certain that 'twas his. Otherwise, he would suffocate the bastard before it could take its first breath. He made his way to the door.

He looked back whilst she held the fabric of her gown together. "Enjoy your brief moment of victory, Ceridwen. We shall see how smug you are once I have Norwood's head on a pike outside my gates."

"Those gates belong to me, Ratcliff."

"Not any longer."

"We shall see!" she bellowed as though from the depths of her soul.

He slammed the door, locked it, but held onto the key. No sense taking further chances where that woman was concerned.

<hr />

THROBBING PAIN DROVE Wymar from his slumber as it slashed its way across his back. 'Twas a reminder of the lash that had been slicing open his flesh whilst imprisoned. Opening one eye, he saw he was in a tent and gave a heavy sigh of relief. He was grateful to those who had risked their lives to save him. He tried to rise but only fell back down on his stomach, the softness of the pallet a welcome reprieve after spending God only knew how many days in that disgusting pit.

A noise at the entrance to his tent alerted him that someone was about to enter and it took every ounce of effort on his part to rise to a sitting position. His head swirled at being upright and Turbert ran to steady him.

"Easy, my lord," he said, taking Wymar's arm to hold him in place. "You have had a difficult few days."

"D-days?" he croaked. "Bring me wine." Turbert went to a table and poured a cup even as Richard filled the entrance to the tent. After his squire helped him take a drink, Wymar gave him a nod and Turbert took his leave.

"Where is Ceridwen?" he asked attempting to rise.

Richard came to him. "Where do you think you are going? Sit back down, you fool. You do neither yourself nor her any good if you open your wounds again. *God's Blood*, you were nearly at death's door!"

"I may have passed that threshold a time or two. I swear the Devil was about to take me down to hell, if I was not there already when they threw me into that pit."

Richard helped him take another drink before taking the cup away. "Aye, we thought we lost you there a time or two. We did not risk our lives to save you, however, only to lose you once we got you back to camp."

"You have not answered my question. Where is Ceridwen?"

Richard ran his hand through his hair clearly frustrated. "Still inside Norwich. Much like you, she did not listen to reason. You may have ended up in the dungeon but she had the feeling she would be held in one of the upper floors of the keep. What information we have been able to gather confirms this to be the truth. It meant that when we liberated you, we were not able to get to her to free her as well."

"What of the other men who went with me?" Wymar asked, taking a sip of the wine.

"Most perished once you entered the great hall as you probably already surmised. Several were in the dungeon and even now are thankfully back in our camp."

Wymar nodded. At least some were spared, the brave souls. "And Ratcliff?"

Richard sat on a stool. "He has been lording his position over everyone, much as we expected. A tyrant who is in complete control with no one to gainsay him. We have had no word from Lady Ceridwen, but we have received reports from the servants that confirm she is still inside."

"*Bloody hell!*" Wymar attempted to stand but only fell back down upon the pallet. "I am as weak as a babe. How long have I been in and out of consciousness?"

"A se'nnight…" Richard answered.

"That long?" Wymar said in dismay.

"…mayhap more. Honestly, we lost count of the time whilst we did everything in our power to keep you alive to fight another day."

"I owe you my life, along with the others."

"You owe me nothing. We have been watching each other's back for how many years now? I am certain we both have repaid such a life debt more than a time or two."

"We must needs get to Ceridwen and rescue her," Wymar said and stood on wobbly legs with his friend's assistance.

Richard gave a small laugh. "You must know your lady knew she would need our help for her to escape Ratcliff's plan for her. She did not go into this plan blind. She got his promise of her safety before she entered the keep, but she knew better than to believe he would keep his word. The bastard is a traitor, after all."

A weak grin formed for the first time on Wymar's lips. "Had I known who I would be dealing with, I, too, would have planned for him to belie his promise. Her plan for my escape worked well. Now, I still must do all in my power to see her out of Ratcliff's hands."

"As resourceful as the lady is, she has come up with something to stall until we can get to her."

"But can the castle afford another siege?"

Richard shrugged. "Who is to say? There were not many who survived from the last one. Any men left inside would be loyal to Stephen."

"Traitors, every one of them," Wymar spat.

"I agree and hence not worth worrying over if they should perish considering they have already betrayed our Empress."

"Let us make plans for an attack," Wymar said, slowly making his way to a table where maps of the area were already laid out for his perusal.

"You are still recovering and 'twill be days, if not weeks, before you are able to lift a sword," Richard grumbled.

"I suppose that bastard Ratcliff still has mine," Wymar cursed thinking of his father's sword in the hands of his enemy, "but that does not mean I cannot see to the planning of laying another siege. I will get my lady out from underneath Ratcliff's control if 'tis the last thing I do."

As men began to fill the tent, Wymar sought out Ceridwen's captain to better understand the interior of the keep. They may not have started out as friends but now they had a common accord to rescue Ceridwen.

CHAPTER TWENTY-SIX

Ceridwen listened to the muffled sound of a battering ram, knowing her rescue was imminent. She had etched out a brief plan to her captain and Richard to lay another siege to Norwich once they had Wymar securely away. Her hope had been that Ratcliff would be so preoccupied with what was happening at the barbican gate, that he might forget about her whilst she waited to make her escape. But breaking down the defenses of Norwich was taking far longer that she had thought it would. She was restless and tired. Tired of being held hostage inside this chamber with nothing to do but worry about what Ratcliff might do next. At least a fortnight had passed, mayhap more. He had already assaulted her mind on a daily basis with taunts of Wymar's death. What more could he do?

Tears threatened to leak from her eyes when memories of his verbal abuse continued to wreak havoc with her mind. Ratcliff left no detail untouched as he described how his men had tortured Norwood. His laugh when he told her how he had branded the man with his mark had been pure evil and still Ceridwen held on to the smallest reserve of hope that Wymar still lived.

But could a man live through such torment if what Ratcliff said was true? What terrified her even more than anything else would be if Ratcliff finally lost what little reserve he had left within him and took her physically. She was unsure why he had not done so already. Heaven knew how often he threatened her. Mayhap he waited to ensure she did not carry Wymar's child. She liked the thought of that, since it meant that with their lovemaking, Wymar had saved her yet again. Ratcliff could torment her mind all he liked. Ceridwen thought she could handle such an assault. But to submit to his touch? She shivered at the thought. She would only be able to fight him off for so long before her strength gave out. Unless the opportunity presented itself to use the knife she had managed to keep hidden and she stabbed the rat bastard. *That* would give her immense pleasure!

But she could not rely on that plan when 'twas just as likely that he would get the knife away from her as that she would be able to stab him. 'Twas the one weakness, as a woman, that she could not overcome. With a sword in her hand, she could stand valiantly against any foe, but in close-quarters combat, none of the advantage was on her side. Pinned down by a man much larger than her, how long could she hold him off from taking her? Several days ago, Ratcliff had come to her chamber, his actions growing bolder as each day ran into the next. He had come upon her so quickly, she had no time to even try to take hold of the dagger she continued to keep in her boot. He had grabbed hold of her before running his hand under her gown to stroke her leg. But a well-aimed and unexpected punch to his belly had earned Ceridwen her freedom, though he still had continued to torment her mind.

Once Ratcliff had caught his breath, he once more forced his weight upon her so she could in no way miss his erect manhood straining at the fabric of his hose. "As soon those traitors who dare attack my gate have been killed, I will finally take you, my pet. Then I will have my revenge on you both. You can then ponder whether 'tis my seed or Norwood's that shall fill your belly." His sneer and laughter as he left her had echoed inside her head for days. She had been numb ever since. She surmised that this was the reason why Ratcliff delayed in taking her. Thoughts of possibly having Wymar's babe brought her a small amount of comfort.

Lucky enough for her, the siege outside her gates prevented any priest Ratcliff might summon from entering Norwich, thus prohibiting any ideas of a legal marriage taking place. She did not see how a marriage between herself and Ratcliff would benefit him at this point, but she did not spend too much time worrying over it. His reasoning mattered little to her. 'Twas apparent, however, that Norwich's own priest had been killed in the previous siege and she briefly mourned his loss and the other people of Norwich who perished in the last siege.

Now she prayed her army of knights would soon break through the keep door. She would not think of Wymar and what they had once shared. Time alone in this chamber had caused her to realize that they both had an obligation to their people once this was all over. She must see to Norwich just as Wymar must see himself homeward bound.

A key sliding into the lock alerted Ceridwen that the time was upon her to confront her enemy. But to her shock, when the door swung silently open, a young lad poked his head inside.

"Turbert?" she was surprised to see the boy of all people.

"Lady Ceridwen," he said with a small bow as he entered the room.

"What are you doing here? You are the last person I expected to come through the door."

"'Tis not obvious?" he smirked. "We have come to rescue you."

"We?"

The door swung wider and her eyes drank in the sight of the man who seemed to fill every room he entered with his presence. "Aye, *we*. You did not think we would leave you to fight this alone, did you?" Wymar asked holding out his hand and not waiting for her answer. "We must hurry, my lady."

"But how did you enter the castle?" she asked looking him over. As wonderful as 'twas to gaze upon him again, she was forced to admit that he did not look well. His face was ashen and beads of sweat had formed on his brow.

"The same way you sent the men to rescue me. How else?" Wymar said with a grin. "Ratcliff is too busy trying to defend the keep after the front gate fell—without much success, I might add—to look to the cellars for a weakness in his defenses… again."

She placed her hand upon his shoulder and he flinched in pain. "You are hurt," she surmised.

"'Tis nothing…"

Turbert stepped forward. "He should be back at camp recovering but would not listen."

Wymar gave the boy a shove. "And you must needs learn to keep your mouth shut so as not to worry the lady."

Turbert ducked his head. "Aye, my lord."

Wymar took her hand and raised it to his lips. "We must away whilst Richard and Arthur continue their assault at the keep door. If we are lucky, we can make it back down to the tunnels with Ratcliff none the wiser."

Ensuring the way was clear, they entered the passageway with Ceridwen leading the way. After all, this was her home and she knew the keep better than anyone. When Wymar was about to turn left, Ceridwen pulled his arm and watched him wince again. "Not that way," she urged nodding in the opposite direction. "The stairs at the end of this passageway lead down to the kitchens. We can access the dungeons from there," she said quietly.

They had only gone down two flights of stairs when their path was barred by a knight making his way up. Surprise registered on his face but before he could call for aid, Ceridwen leapt forward with her dagger and ended his life. She turned back to see how Wymar was progressing with the stairs. Sweat beaded on his upper lip now.

"Take this," she ordered, handing him the dagger and taking his sword.

"Give me back my sword, Ceridwen," he grumbled. "I can handle my own weapon."

"Clearly you cannot, given that you look like you are about to fall over. If you pass out, there is no way I can carry your weight and I highly doubt your squire will be of much use either," she fumed wondering why Arthur was not in Turbert's place since he was more than capable of coming to her aid.

They had just made it into the kitchen when all hell exploded. With the keep door breached, men flooded through the entryway and into the great hall. The sound of steel against steel echoed throughout the room. Ratcliff stood near the hearth with his sword raised to defend himself even whilst his army took on Ceridwen's and Wymar's knights.

Seeing her opportunity, she turned to Turbert. "Keep your master safe," she ordered. Slashing at her gown to allow herself freer movement, she paid no heed when Wymar called her name. Raising her sword, she jumped into the fray, killing one enemy after another in order to get to Ratcliff.

The sound of the dying filled the room and still she pressed forward until she cut down the final man who stood in her way.

"Ratcliff!" she called out pointing her sword in his direction. "Let us finish this between us!"

Surprise registered momentarily upon his face before a wicked smile plastered itself upon his face. "So be it. Let the better man win."

The force of when his sword met her own caused Ceridwen's arm to quake. She had been foolish to take his blow head-on rather than deflecting the blade to the side as she usually did. She was too emotional, which her sword master would have told her was the worst way to fight. But she had not become an expert swordswoman overnight and now was not the time to show any signs of weakness. This was her moment of revenge. She would restore her home and make Ratcliff pay with his life for what he had done to her father and her people.

Marshaling her mental strength, she focused on the fight. Again and again, her sword swung forward even whilst Ratcliff parried with his own. A smile of satisfaction crept across her lips when she saw several places where she had drawn blood. The wounds were not deep but they outraged Ratcliff when her blade met his skin.

Her arm began to quiver in exhaustion and she did all within her power to find the strength to continue onward. She ducked, narrowly missing the blade aimed at her head but her feet flew out from under her in the process when she slipped on the blood of the fallen.

Ratcliff grabbed her braided hair and pulled her back into his chest. "Now I will have you at my leisure and your lover can watch whilst I take you in your own hall for all to witness my dominance over you."

Before she could respond, a sickening smack sounded close enough that the air rushed from Ratcliff's lungs. He loosened his grip and Ceridwen looked to see her mother's dagger protruding from his forehead. His eyes rolled in his head and Ratcliff pitched backwards to stare upwards with sightless eyes.

Ceridwen turned toward the kitchen to see Wymar hunched over from his efforts to save her. With a nod in his direction, she pulled herself from the floor and continued to fight for her home until the remaining enemy surrendered.

CHAPTER TWENTY-SEVEN

Days quickly fled, and almost before he knew it, another fortnight had passed. Wymar took this time to heal whilst Ceridwen saw to the running of Norwich. The dead had been laid to rest and a new priest who came to reside at the castle blessed the graves, including those who had been their enemy. Wymar was unsure he would have been as generous as the new lady of the hall. But Ceridwen had sworn she would not pass judgment over them and left the matter to a higher being.

She had been avoiding him again and he knew not why. He had questioned Arthur on more than one occasion. Ceridwen's captain had only grunted a half response telling Wymar that when the lady was ready she would reveal all. In the meantime, Wymar tried to summon up a fair amount of patience. He was uncertain if another day could go by without them having speech together.

A soft knock sounded at his chamber door and he went and opened it. Her blonde hair left unbraided, Ceridwen was dressed in a dark blue gown with her white undertunic coming to points at her wrists. Jewels of some worth hung around her throat and a large diamond came to rest just above her breasts. She was lovely and was hardly recognizable from the young lord he once thought her to be.

"May I disturb you, my lord?" she asked with a regal tilt of her head.

"Of course, my lady," he answered swinging the door wide for her to enter, "although I hardly think given our past that we should stand on such formality."

Was that the slightest flinch he detected in her demeanor? He hoped such was not the case but could not easily dismiss what he knew he saw. She was troubled, that much was certain, and he could only await what she planned to tell him of what was tormenting her mind.

He waved his arm toward the room to show she was welcome. A faint hint of flowery fragrance drifted and assaulted his senses as she strode by and he closed the door. She went to the window, opened the shutter, and stared at the view of the ocean.

Silence. 'Twas deafening whilst he waited for her to tell him what was on her mind. She continued to keep her back toward him. He waited and watched her take several breaths. He knew 'twas up to her to begin this conversation. Whatever she was about to tell him was of grave import. She turned and he took notice of the streaks of tears running down her face. He took but one step in her direction, aching to comfort her in whatever way she would allow, before she raised her hand to stop him.

"Please," she said before continuing. "If you touch me, I will never have the ability to say what needs to be spoken."

"Very well," he murmured holding his hands behind his back whilst watching her carefully. She appeared as skittish as a newborn colt. She at last moved from the window. Taking a seat near the hearth, she beckoned him to take the chair opposite her.

She stared at the flames for several minutes before she spoke. "Are you feeling better?" she asked, twisting her hands in her skirt as if that could hide the way that they trembled.

Oh, how he wanted to reach for her but something inside told him that would be a mistake. So… she apparently wanted to keep their conversation casual, filled with small talk. *Will she reference the weather next?* he mused. He leaned back into the chair instead of reaching out for her hand. His effort to remain indifferent tore at his guts. "Well enough to at last travel to Brockenhurst."

He watched her nod whilst a small smile lit her features. "Yes, 'tis that matter that I wished to discuss. We both know 'tis well past time for you to return home and put your estate back in order," she declared as though she were saying farewell.

"And to find out the whereabouts of my brothers," he added.

"Aye, of course. Mayhap they will be in London attending our Empress as she prepares for her coronation."

"Perchance."

"'Tis on the way, is it not?" she asked whilst smoothing the linen of her gown. "Your home, that is."

"Aye, farther to the west." He watched as another tear escaped down her cheek. He knew what she was not saying. She was indeed somehow trying to bid him farewell. "You could come with me," he offered as though he could change her mind.

A sob caught in her throat before she finally turned to face him. "I cannot."

"Because of your duties here at Norwich?" Wymar watched her nod. "Certainly, your captain is more than capable of watching over things until the land heals and crops can be planted again."

"That is not the only reason why I cannot go, Norwood," she murmured so softly he needed to lean forward to hear her words. He rested his arms on his thighs, close enough to reach out to touch her if she would let him.

"What other reason could there be? I thought you and I had come to an understanding that night in the forest. Was I mistaken?" he asked, afraid of her answer.

"You know that is not the reason why I cannot accompany you."

"Then what is? Do you honestly think I could ever forget you after such a night?"

"I will never forget you, Wymar, but you must needs find yourself a wife who will be worthy of becoming the lady of your hall. Not someone who feels soiled by another."

She cast her eyes downward and suddenly Wymar guessed the truth of the matter. "Ratcliff? Did he touch you?" he asked, wondering what that bastard had done to his lady. If the man were not already dead, Wymar would have taken great pleasure in torturing him for such an insult.

"Nay, not physically as you and I shared, but 'twas still bad enough to leave a foul memory I cannot yet seem to shake. 'Tis the mental abuse that still consumes me, especially having to listen to the joy in his voice whilst he constantly described my father's death. He wore me down day after day by telling me what he would do to me once we were wed. His patience was beginning to wear thin because he began touching me more often, although he did not go so far as…"

Her words fell off when she placed her elbows on her legs and covered her face. Her crying tore at his soul and made him want to vent his fury on the gutless bastard who had caused it, but Ratcliff was beyond his punishment now. And besides, now was not the time to let his anger over what could not be changed interfere with how he still felt for this woman.

"Ceridwen… whatever happened with him does not make any difference about my feelings for you," he said honestly.

"But it matters to me!" she shouted with such a hopeless tone the sound tore at his own heart. "I cannot be with you, or any other man for that matter right now, until I can find myself again. I have never been a weak woman and always stood up to right a wrong. But that vile piece of fodder got the better of me by tormenting my mind! Every breath I take, every waking moment, every nightmare I have replays in my head as though he did in fact physically take me. Sometimes I feel as though I will go mad if someone so much as touches me." She stood, squaring her shoulders as though making an attempt to get herself back in control. He rose from his chair. His audience with the Lady of Norwich was almost at an end.

"You need time to heal, my lady," he said and his heart cracked to see the anguish reflected in her magnificent blue-green eyes. A physical wound he could help heal, but how did one go about fixing a problem inside another person's head?

"And I cannot expect you to wait for someone who may take years to let go of what someone took away from her."

"My offer for you to join me in Brockenhurst still stands whenever you may be ready," he said walking her toward the door.

Ceridwen turned back to face him. Hesitantly, she reached out and cupped his cheek. He felt her hand trembling as she rubbed her thumb across his skin. "You shall always own a piece of my heart, Wymar. For all time will I treasure that one moment when I was allowed to love."

Before he could give any response, she quickly pulled open the door and left, taking with her what was left of his heart. Come the morn, he departed with his army, never once looking back at the castle and what could have been.

CHAPTER TWENTY-EIGHT

London
April, 1141

WYMAR SAT IN the dimly lit tavern, a cool mug of ale in his hands. Earlier this day, his meeting with the Empress had not gone according to plan. With the usurper Stephen held at Bristol Castle, Matilda was petitioning the bishops of Westminster to crown her as Queen of England. So far, she had failed in her quest to win the crown but she still continued to push the issue along, ensuring her subjects bowed to her will. Wymar was no exception. Still…

Her edict left a sour taste in his mouth but what else could he do but obey her command? She had restored his title and his lands. With such an obligation, Wymar knew he must needs wed and produce an heir, as she had commanded. What he had not expected was for the Empress to have already picked out his bride.

Still reeling from Ceridwen's rejection, how could he have known that his queen would be sending a bride for him to wed in the coming months? He was told to expect her. Nothing more. Even her name was denied him. She was just some nameless woman who would bear his children but who would never own his heart. It had already been given to a lady he would never see again.

His heart screamed that this would be a betrayal to the woman he loved, yet how could he reject the Empress's demands? He was once more thrust into a situation he had no control over. He did not care for what was expected of him, but he would, as always, obey the demands of his sovereign. Bitter darkness once more glazed over his heart. He swore he would never let the light in again.

He raised the mug once more to his lips and swallowed hard. *God's blood!* When had Ceridwen woven such a spell around him? He had found that he could think of little else but her since he left Norwich. No doubt the Empress had plans for Ceridwen as well. As a noblewoman, she, too, would be expected to wed and leave the running of the estate to her new husband. With Norwich's location to the east, in an area of great strategic importance, Wymar had no doubt that Stephen's loyal supporters would make every attempt to once more claim the land in his name. His brow furrowed whilst his mind ran amuck. 'Twas hard enough to imagine the woman he had come to care for being tormented by that scum Ratcliff, let alone she would have to give up her body to some other faceless man. Or worse yet, face another siege at her gates.

Wymar swore he could even now feel her trembling hand upon his cheek. He muttered a curse beneath his breath and prayed Ratcliff was burning in hell for what he had done to Ceridwen and her people. At least Wymar had the satisfaction of being able to save her. There was pleasure in knowing that 'twas by his hand that Ratcliff had died, but that pleasure was not enough to compensate for the grief he felt at the knowledge that Ceridwen's spirit had been broken. To see her so afraid to reach out and touch him after all they had shared tore at his soul. But there had been naught he could do to ease her before he had departed. And now that he was gone, 'twas very unlikely their paths would ever cross again. Besides… what hope was there of any kind of a relationship with the Lady of Norwich when Wymar was now expected to wed another?

The door to the tavern opened, bringing a ray of light into the otherwise dreary dwelling. Richard and Wymar's brothers entered. He pulled Theobald into his arms to give him a fierce hug and copied the gesture with Reynard and Richard. Together again… at least for a while. How he missed his siblings and Richard. He motioned to a serving maid and called for more ale whilst the men took a seat.

"How fare thee, brothers?" he asked, wanting them to fill the conversation so his mind did not wander to a situation he could not change.

Theobald took a gulp of his drink all the while eyeing the pretty maid who had served them. He tore his gaze from the girl whose smile promised him much… as long as he had enough coin for her time. Wymar chuckled before Theo continued. "The Empress has me awaiting her orders on her next steps to gain the crown. Londoners are not pleased with her latest dictates. There are times I feel she thinks of me as one of her knights she can trust, but without details of her intentions, mayhaps 'tis just wishful thinking on my part. Perchance she will one day confide in me and bestow upon me the privilege of knowing such particulars but that time is not yet upon us."

Wymar nodded, thinking his brother may receive the gift of land of his own for his service to their queen. "Mayhap a title and lands will also be given as reward for your services to her," he said and smiled for the first time in what seemed like days. As pleased as he would be to have his brothers back with him at Brockenhurst, he would rejoice at any opportunity given to them to build a fortune and a legacy of their own.

Theobald placed his tankard down and reached over to pinch the bottom of a pretty maid who giggled in delight. "Such a reward would require me to wed some noblewoman, would it not? I think I would rather just enjoy a life of leisure if the Empress releases me from her service one day. I will rejoice that you at the very least, brother, have been rewarded our ancestral home."

Wymar nodded, then turned his attention to his lifelong friend. "What of you, Richard?"

"She sends me on a mission of grave import but alas, like Theobald, I have as yet to learn of where or when I am to travel or my duties once I arrive. I could certainly use a well-deserved rest instead of traipsing further along English soil," he laughed before taking a drink from his tankard.

Wymar joined in. "You? Rest? Most likely not for long."

"Aye, you are probably right on that account. I cannot stay idle in one place for any length of time. I get restless for some action," Richard said with another grin.

Wymar chuckled at his friend's words before looking across the table. "And what of you, young Reynard? Does our Empress have plans for you as well or will you return home with me?"

Reynard shrugged. "I am still in her service but like Theo and Richard I am in the dark on what her immediate plans are for me. I am, however, to head to Brockenhurst to witness your marriage when the time comes."

Wymar's smile faded from his visage at Reynard's words whilst watching his youngest brother's forlorn face. Thoughts of his forthcoming marriage to some unknown woman made Wymar uneasy. He had yet to become accustomed to the notion that his bride would not be the fair Ceridwen. "Do not be too disappointed, Reynard. I am certain she has your best interest at heart."

Richard leaned forward to rest his elbows on the table before he turned his attention toward Wymar. "Like the plans she has for you?"

Wymar took a sip of his drink before he answered. "So, you, too, have heard. I am still attempting to come to terms with the situation for what it is. 'Tis an inconvenience, for certain, and yet 'tis nothing more than fulfilling my duty to gain my title and lands. I have always known that 'twould be my duty to father heirs who can one day carry on in my stead. As for the wife who will carry them… I am at the command of the Empress and cannot gainsay her."

Richard swore beneath his breath. "Marriage to someone who you do not even know is not doing you any favors, Wymar."

Wymar shrugged. "Marriage of convenience is nothing new. 'Tis done all the time for the advantage of gaining lands and monies. Does it matter who I wed if I cannot have the woman who I care the most about?"

"You could petition the Empress to change her mind," Reynard said with a frown.

"The Empress is too busy trying to be crowned Queen of England to be bothered with having her orders disobeyed," Wymar muttered. "Nay, I will obey her just as I have faithfully followed her all these years. I will pray I can at the very least find some common accord with this woman, whoever she may be. There is no further need to try to persuade our Empress when she has made her directives clear. I will wed before the end of summer and will not look back at what could have been."

The men fell silent, each lost in their thoughts until Wymar raised his cup. "To my brothers… two who share my same blood and one the brother of my heart."

Tankards clanking together, the men drained their cups before slamming them upon the table. He resolved to enjoy this moment while it lasted. He could sense 'twould be some time before they were once more all together again.

CHAPTER TWENTY-NINE

June, Norwich Castle

CERIDWEN RACED DEFIANCE through the fields and toward the ocean beach. She needed to get away from the castle, the responsibility of its people, and the missive she had received from the Empress that contained nothing but depressing news.

Plans had not gone well in London for her Empress. All her efforts to be crowned Queen of England had ended in disaster. Even without the missive confirming Ceridwen's worst fears, word had spread to Norwich that Stephen's wife, Matilda of Boulogne, had raised an army on her husband's behalf. They had arrived at the Thames and threatened the city of London. Even the people of London had risen up in opposition to the Empress who had displeased them with the imposition of taxes and the favoritism she showed to her followers in the West Country. Before the Empress's coronation could take place, Londoners had stormed out of the city to attack Westminster. Such an act caused the Empress to flee, her plans in complete disarray.

Even now, Ceridwen had no knowledge of who exactly was protecting the Empress until she and her army could regroup and form their next course of action. She only knew that she was not to be included in the Empress's plans. She had other directives for Ceridwen and although she had wished such news would be put off a bit longer, 'twas clear that her time as the mistress of Norwich was running out.

'Twas not until she reached the shore that she at last pulled on the reins and slid from the saddle. She knew her horse would stay where she left her whilst Ceridwen ran to the water's edge. Fury filled her soul. Anger for the lingering memories of Ratcliff that continued to haunt her dreams no matter how hard she tried to rid herself of the thought of him. Anger for that damn missive. Anger with herself that she could not change where the course of her life would lead. She had thought given her service to the Empress that she would allow Ceridwen to run Norwich since she was the last surviving member of her family.

But the Empress made it clear that Ceridwen was only a woman and therefore unable to be the castle's mistress. Somehow this did not sit right with Ceridwen. If the Empress could do everything within her power to take control of running the whole country, then surely Ceridwen was more than capable of running this keep and lands. She muttered a curse, knowing that however much she might dislike the idea, she must needs obey her Empress's commands.

The sound of a thundering horse over the crashing waves caused her to glance behind her but she calmed seeing Arthur had followed her. Arthur... faithful to her with every breath he took. She should release him from his duty and reward him handsomely for his devoted service. Then he would have enough monies to buy his own land and find a wife to live out the rest of his life in the comfort of his own hall.

She turned back toward the ocean, waiting for some sense of peace to fill her. But she felt nothing, much like she had felt nothing since she last espied Wymar leaving through her gates. If he had only taken a moment to look back upon the keep, he would have seen her watching him from the highest point on the battlement walls. Waiting for some sign that he might stay even though she knew he could not. She had willed him to turn around so she might have one last look upon his face but grimly watched such hope fade when he at last left her vision.

She sighed and waited for Arthur to speak, knowing he had much on his mind.

"You knew this day would come, my lady," he began as he, too, faced toward the ocean to stare out at the horizon.

"But I am more than capable of seeing to Norwich. I do not need some steward dictating how the place should be run until my husband, whoever he may be, decides what to do with the estate," she fumed. She swore her whole body shook with fury.

"There she is," Arthur said with a small laugh.

She turned a quizzical brow to him when she looked up at him. "Who?"

"The young woman with the fiery spirit who has been missing of late. *That* is who."

Ceridwen managed a weak smile. "She has been gone a while now. I do not know if she shall ever return."

"She will… given time."

"But how much time do I really have?" she asked, lifting her fist heavenbound. "Time to ensure Norwich is secure before this steward shows up to run the place in my name whilst I must needs go marry some *man* who will expect me to bow down to his every whim?"

"Not every man is Ratcliff, Ceridwen."

"Do not dare mention his name to me!" she ordered.

"Mayhap 'tis best we discuss him now. I may not be the person you would most prefer to have this talk with, but since your lady mother has been gone many a year and you have no one else to confess what that scum did to you, I am here and willing to listen. I can assume what happened given your aversion to being touched."

He laid his hand upon her back ever so gently in a soft caress and although she at first flinched, she realized that the comfort Arthur offered her was nothing more than providing solace to her troubled soul.

"He never went so far as to touch me in *that* way although it seemed he was growing closer to it. He certainly grew bolder as each day passed into the next." She did not mention how the thought of her possibly carrying Wymar's child was the only thing that deterred Ratcliff from going further in his desire to take her. She had flung the notion into his face often enough. If only that had turned out to be true! When her monthly courses started, another bout of sadness had filled her knowing she did not carry the last part of Wymar with her. Of course, the fact that there would be no baby simplified things in many ways. If she had been unmarried and with child, this would have only brought further complications into her life. But still, she mourned for what could have been.

Arthur heaved a sigh of relief. "Then we can be thankful you were not violated in such a way."

"But how will I stand a husband who I do not know…" she looked up at him with tears filling her eyes, waiting to spill over, "touching me… in that way?"

He lifted her chin so she would look him square in the eye. "You are Lady Ceridwen Ward of Norwich. You will manage your wifely duties the way you have done everything in your life: with courage to handle any difficult situation that may be pressed upon you; with valor, for this has been engrained into your very soul since the time of your birth; with determination to return to some semblance of a normal life, for this is what your parents would have wished for you; and with all the love that you can give, if you are so blessed, to your children who will one day carry on your legacy."

She nodded to show that she had taken in his words, even if she wasn't certain she was willing to accept them as yet. Still, she was grateful for the comfort from this man who had watched her back for many a year now. She gave him a hug before putting some space again between them. "You must think highly of the paragon of virtue that you think I am."

"Aye, that I do, my lady. I only pray that eventually you will see that although you have been hurt, time will heal your heart so you may learn to live your life again."

"And this man I am to marry?" she asked as though God had forsaken her in her desire to remain unwed.

"Mayhap you will even come to care for him. The Empress would not send you to marry a nobleman who is not worthy of you. Did she give you his name?"

"Nay! She told me nothing in this missive, only that before the end of summer she will send a retinue to take me west to my new home. At least she has given me through the summer to see the fields are ready to be harvested in the fall for the coming winter."

"Mayhap all will work out as it should," Arthur suggested.

A snort escaped her. "I highly doubt such will be the case but I am glad you think so."

"Time, Ceridwen… everything takes time."

That night in her chamber as she stared at the ceiling, she was overwhelmed once more with fear for the unknown. She closed her eyes and at last dreamed. For the first time in a long while, 'twas a pleasant dream of a man with tawny colored hair who loved her in a forest glade and blue-grey eyes she could lose herself in. She was in love again and loved in return. And with the dawning of the new day, she awoke smiling.

CHAPTER THIRTY

August, Brockenhurst

WYMAR CAME IN from the fields. For months he had been restoring Brockenhurst so that one day the estate would be returned to its former glory. Upon his return, he quickly learned that many of the outbuildings had been destroyed. Rebuilding them all would take time, but at least the keep was still intact. Overseeing the land to ensure everything was ready for the coming winter had become a daily ritual for him. The years since he had last set foot on his birthright seemingly faded away, and Wymar could almost envision the stone walls that would again be erected to surround the place and keep him and his family safe one day.

A runner from the keep had informed him a wagon approached and he assumed that his future bride had at last arrived. He would need to clean himself before he received her. He had no desire for her first impression of him to be reeking of his horse.

He had been on edge for the past two fortnights torn between wondering whom the Empress would send for his wife and reminding himself that it did not matter since this was a union for convenience only. A way for his bloodline to continue long after he was gone from this earth. 'Twas no matter who the Empress had chosen to be his bride. This mystery woman would never find a place in his heart for that space had already been claimed by a blonde shieldmaiden whom Wymar still could not forget. He would perform his duty as his future wife would perform hers... to sire an heir and that was all. He could then say he had obeyed his Empress.

Theobald had somehow managed to send a brief missive that he was following the Empress when she fled London to Oxford. Reynard but recently returned home which would seem to confirm that the time for Wymar's marriage was fast approaching. Other news was fleeting and only caused Wymar to worry if his brother yet lived. Knowing Stephen was still proclaimed king did not sit well with Wymar but there was little he could do on that matter. His fighting days for the Empress were at an end until and unless perchance she called for his aid again. For now, he would obey her command and hold this estate in her name. 'Twas all that was expected of him, and he would do no more than that.

A servant had already seen that a bath awaited him in his chamber and as he stripped off his garments and sunk into the steaming hot water, thoughts of that golden-haired vixen once again entered his mind. He hated to admit how much he continued to have thoughts of the blue-green eyed beauty. On some level, he knew she still cared for him, but did she love him as he loved her? Or had all of that changed in those terrible weeks that she had been held captive? Mayhap she even blamed him for his part in her dilemma. If he had not been so foolish as to get himself captured in the first place, then Ceridwen would have had no need to sacrifice herself to see to his rescue. Aye, they both had been fools in their endeavors to save one another but he could not dwell on the past. He prayed his lady was well and time was healing the mental abuse that had been inflicted upon her.

His lady… Aye, he still thought of her as somehow belonging to him but that was purely a hopeless fantasy on his part. No doubt she would also soon be required to wed. Mayhap the Empress had a groom in mind for her already. Wymar scowled at the thought of some unknown man making Ceridwen his wife. As much as he wished otherwise, the reality of their situation meant he could in no way claim the woman as *his*.

A growl of frustration filled the room, and Wymar rose from his bath. Drying off, he waved away Turbert, who stood nearby, and dismissed the boy. Wymar was more than capable of dressing himself and he would see to the lad soon to ensure he was kept busy in his other duties as his squire. He chose a blue tunic and leather jerkin. Hose and boots came next, and he took a ceremonial dress sword and placed it in his belt. He might as well look the part of a wealthy nobleman for his new bride when he greeted her.

He took his time descending the turret stairs in order to delay the inevitable, even if only for a few moments more. As he entered his hall, he noticed a woman with long black flowing hair standing in front of his hearth. Her attendants were also near as they stretched their hands toward the fire to warm them.

"Welcome, my lady," Wymar said hoping the sound of his voice had a welcoming quality that did not echo as grimly as he felt. She turned and he was surprised to see who stood before him.

Richard's sister, Lady Beatrix, stretched out her hands to take his and turned her cheek toward him. He dutifully placed a chaste kiss there before he returned the gesture to the other side of her face.

"Wymar... 'tis so good to see you. It has been so long since I have been to Brockenhurst that I just knew I had to come once I learned you had reclaimed your birthright," she exclaimed, her eyes dancing in delight whilst she examined him with an affectionate gaze. "You are looking exceptionally well, my lord."

"As are you, my lady," he answered holding her at arm's length and looking behind her. "Richard has not traveled with you?"

"Nay. He still attends to matters for the Empress or so his missive informed us once it reached us. He has been missed at home, however, since he went gallivanting across the countryside with you. My parents are especially reluctant to see him disappear again for months on end."

"'Twas hardly as though we were on a journey of leisure, my

dear," Wymar answered. Beatrix had always been a beautiful woman in his opinion, but she was his friend's sister making her off-limits as far as he had been concerned. The way she was gazing upon him made him ponder if she was thinking of their relationship as more than that. *God forbid...* that was all he needed.

She gave a casual wave of her hand. "Aye... attending to the Empress's business with all that such a duty entails, I suppose. We must needs all appease her and obey her commands. I see Brockenhurst once more thrives under your care, my lord," she said whilst her gaze continued to take in his appearance along with his hall.

His brow furrowed whilst he searched her face. Her words about the Empress and obeying her commands had his stomach sinking. Was she talking about... *God's Wounds!* The Empress would not make him marry a woman who was more like a sister to him, would she?

He stepped back from the woman before him even as she stepped forward to keep him close to her side. "You have been sent by the Empress Matilda?" he inquired, lifting his brow whilst his question lingered in the space between them. Her visage transformed quickly before him: one moment showing appreciation at how he appeared, he supposed, and the next moment, there was a frown furrowing her brow. She recovered swiftly.

She gave a laugh before answering. "Aye, our Empress has sent me to you," she said before her gaze traveled to her ladies who also appeared just as surprised at her statement. "Why else would I be here without Richard?"

She frowned at her ladies and Wymar questioned to himself if such a look was a brief silent warning to her attendants to play along with her ruse. But Beatrix once more quickly transformed her features and turned a smiling face in his direction.

"I cannot believe she would send you as my bride," he said voicing his doubts aloud.

Her eyes widened in surprise before a laugh escaped her perfectly formed lips. She stepped forward, causing a flowery sent to invade his senses. Her fingers began running down the edges of his jerkin. "Why ever not, Wymar?" she asked letting all formality drop between them. "We are more than compatible, both from noble houses. My dowry alone will see you well established even if you were not in need of the monies I would bring with our union. You must have known that I have held a certain affection for you for many a year."

"But you are like a sister," he insisted with a raised voice. How the bloody hell had he gotten himself into such a mess?

"Nevertheless, I am here because I care for you, Wymar, and, of course, at the Empress's command. We do wish to stay in her good graces, do we not?"

"Aye, we must obey at all costs," he muttered between clenched teeth. The last thing he needed was to have his title and lands stripped from him again by an angry monarch. But still… Beatrix of all women would cause him much anguish if she were to become his bride. Why Richard had not sent a runner with such information so as to warn him was beyond Wymar's understanding. Unless he had no such knowledge of the forthcoming union whilst he went about the Empress's business?

Beatrix seemed relieved by his answer before she gave a yawn. "We are tired from our travels, Wymar. Do you suppose…"

He ran a hand through his hair, then motioned for a servant. "Have chambers readied for Lady Beatrix and her attendants," he ordered before giving the lady a short bow. "I will see you at the evening meal."

"I look forward to many such meals together," she whispered before turning her head to one side.

He bent forward and placed a chaste kiss upon her cheek. 'Twas not as though he had not performed such a task many a time in the past but now 'twas a different situation. Beatrix… his soon to be wife… *God's Wounds!* What a farce his life had become.

CHAPTER THIRTY-ONE

CERIDWEN'S SERVANT FINISHED tying a purple ribbon throughout her braided hair. Sitting still this long had been pure torture but she had to make herself presentable. The Empress's messenger had arrived, and she had kept him waiting long enough. With his appearance, she knew she would be leaving Norwich, perhaps never to set foot on the estate again. But after overseeing the progress the serfs in the fields had made, she smelled of horse and God only knew what else. She certainly could not receive the Empress's appointed man smelling like a stable hand.

"Ye look beautiful, milady," Agnes said interrupting her thoughts. Agnes patted her hair one last time whilst inspecting her work. "Just like yer mother."

Mother... She had not thought on her dame for many a year, having lost her long ago to an illness when Ceridwen had been little more than a babe. But she knew that her mother and father had shared a great love, and she had learned much of the woman from her father's stories. She supposed there was some comfort in knowing that her parents were at least together now. "Do you really think so?" she asked before standing and smoothing out the fabric of her gown. She was nervous. She would finally be heading to her soon to be husband, or so she had been told.

"Aye, ye be the spittin' image of her," the servant replied with a smile of encouragement.

"Thank you, Agnes," Ceridwen replied before heading toward the door. There was no point in putting off the inevitable. She was to wed. Period. Did it truly matter whom the groom would be if she could not have the man she loved?

The passageway felt colder than normal as though 'twas a premonition of how her life would now be. Each step down the winding turret brought her closer to her fate. Her heart began hammering inside her chest as if 'twould explode. Before she came into view of the great hall, she took a deep breath to calm her fears and raised her head. She would in no way let the new steward intimidate her. She knew her worth even though she felt like a pawn in a game she could not win.

Descending the last step, she began making her way toward the hearth where the gentleman sat. The chair faced the fire so his features were obscured but his black hair fell in wavy lengths to his shoulders. He lifted a tankard to his lips and Ceridwen noted the fine cut of his tunic. He was obviously wealthy enough to see himself well attired. He must have been lost in thought for he did not hear her approach.

"I am glad to see my servants have seen to your needs, good sir," she began offering this slight bit of hospitality even though she wished him to be on the other side of the kingdom.

"My apologies for not hearing you, my lady," he said quickly, putting his tankard down and turning to face her. Blue eyes twinkled back at her in amusement before he gave her a courtly bow. "'Tis good to see you again, Lady Ceridwen."

"Good heavens, Sir Richard. You are the last person I expected to receive in my hall. Is their aught amiss with Wymar? I mean… Lord Norwood," she said whilst she began shaking with the thoughts of the wellbeing of her former lover. Though she might try to deny it, she was still in love with the man. Even when another man took her to wife, she knew she could never forget her feelings for Wymar.

"Wymar is fine as far as I know. Last I saw of my friend he was in London although he was to make his way home come the morn. Shall we take our ease, my lady? I must admit 'tis been some time since I have had the luxury of a fire and a cup of ale to enjoy," Richard replied whilst waving to the chair opposite him.

Ceridwen nodded and took her place beside the hearth whilst a servant readily thrust a goblet of wine into her hand. 'Twas as though the woman knew she would need sustenance to get through the conversation. *Good heavens!* The Empress did not expect her to wed with Norwood's friend, did she? She made every attempt to calm her nerves before she spoke. "What brings you to Norwich, Sir Richard?" She took a sip of her wine awaiting his answer.

His brow furrowed before he replied. "You did not receive the Empress's message?"

Her wine almost spewed across the space between them. She began choking before air once more returned to her lungs. "I am waiting for the steward who will oversee my lands…" she began.

"…and to be taken to your future husband," he finished taking another sip of his drink.

"But why are *you* here then?"

He hid a smirk beneath his tankard before placing it down. Amusement rushed across his visage. "I would think the reason for my presence would be obvious, my lady. I am here to ensure your lands are taken care of in Wymar's name before we travel to Brockenhurst for your wedding. Did not the Empress inform you that you are to be my friend's bride?" 'Twas obvious from his twinkling eyes that Richard already knew her answer.

Shaking hands placed the goblet upon a nearby table but still it rattled upon the wood until she steadied it. Beads of sweat formed on her upper lip, and she swore she felt faint. *Wymar? To be her husband?* she mused whilst the room spun before her eyes. All these months spent agonizing over whom the Empress may have chosen as her husband were for naught! She could not be happier.

Richard reached over to take one of her hands. "I see this all comes as a surprise… a pleasant one, I hope," he asked whilst rubbing the back of her hand with his thumb.

Ceridwen's attention returned to the man before her. "Aye, I cannot complain about the Empress's choice in a husband for me, yet I am not pleased on her delivery of such information. She could have informed me months ago. 'Twould have given me peace of mind instead of endless hours worrying over whom she might have chosen."

Richard chuckled before releasing her hand and taking up his tankard once more. "Our Empress does as she pleases and at her whim. Who are we to gainsay her on her approach to such matters? Besides, she has had a difficult time of late whilst attempting to gain control of England."

"Aye, you have that aright," Ceridwen whispered whilst thoughts of being with Wymar once more filled her heart with joy.

Richard took up his tankard again. "Do you have someone in mind that you can trust with the upkeeping of Norwich? Although I know you were expecting some stranger to take over the running of the estate, the Empress made it clear that you were more than capable of appointing someone you were already familiar with who lives here. I am certain Wymar will be more than agreeable to anyone you might name to watch over the estate."

Ceridwen was once more surprised at Richard's words. She did not have to think overly hard on the matter. "Aye. My guardsman Arthur is more than capable of becoming steward of Norwich. He was my father's right-hand man for many a year whilst he also watched my back. He would be perfect for such a responsibility, and there is no one I would trust more."

"Then you can tell him the good news that his status has been elevated. You will no longer need to have him as a guardsman once you arrive at Brockenhurst. Wymar will always ensure your safety," Richard said whilst draining his cup.

Ceridwen nodded and could hardly wait to tell Arthur of his good fortune. "We shall ride out come the morn so I may show you the land. In the meantime, I will have a chamber readied for you." She motioned for a servant and conveyed her instructions to the woman who hurried off to do her bidding.

"I will appreciate the comfort of a bed and good food for a change instead of traveling on the open road. I will admit I have tired of the ground to sleep upon."

"I will show you to your bedchamber personally," Ceridwen said before standing. Taking Richard's arm, he escorted her through the great hall and up the turret stairs all the while speaking of Brockenhurst.

"My own estate is near to your new home. You will love it there, Lady Ceridwen. The forest is so thick you sometimes wonder how a castle was built without using all the trees for its lumber," he boasted.

"I am sure I will love making my home," Ceridwen said as a small smile lit her features. They continued down the passageway before she halted at his chamber. "When do we leave?"

"A fortnight," Richard said whilst opening the door. "You can be ready by then?"

"Of course. I have been packing for several se'nnights now. There has been no reason to delay the inevitable. I knew not how much time I would have to ready myself, so I ensured all was taken care of. I have some instructions I will need to convey to Arthur, but then I would be most happy for us to be on our way."

"Good!" Richard said with a broad smile. "I am certain Wymar will be just as glad to welcome you to your new home as you have welcomed me to Norwich."

"D-does he k-know I am to be his b-bride?" she stammered.

"Nay. 'Tis to be a surprise as the Empress instructed," he replied before giving Ceridwen a low bow. "I will see you at the evening meal. I look forward to seeing what you have made of the place since your father's passing."

Ceridwen nodded and returned to her chamber. She twirled around in happiness. She could not wait to see the look on Wymar's face once she arrived at her new home!

CHAPTER THIRTY-TWO

Wymar leaned an elbow upon the blanket as he watched Beatrix and her ladies stroll by the lake. It had been a peaceful day of leisure, allowing Wymar time to contemplate the woman who claimed to have been chosen by the Empress as his bride. The past fortnight had given him plenty of opportunity to watch Beatrix and determine she had told him a falsehood. What he still did not know was why she would lie about something of such import. If he wed Beatrix, contrary to the Empress's wishes, Wymar would be subject to Empress Matilda's wrath. His land and title could once more be stripped from him. Beatrix's falsehood made no sense.

He had always known the younger woman had held a certain amount of affection for him but he had never contemplated that her feelings were this strong. Had he known, he'd have sought a way to gently discourage her. She was Richard's younger sister, and he would never allow their friendship to be tested by falling for the girl. Besides that, while she was pretty enough, she was too used to getting her way, and her pouting whenever she was thwarted put him more in mind of a child than a woman. She simply did not have the inner strength and maturity to appeal to him.

Nor did she have wisdom enough to see when her advances were unwelcome. He had done his best to maintain distance between them, but she was getting bolder as each day passed into the next. A touch here… a whispered word there… 'Twas as though she wanted to provoke him to pounce on her and ruin her reputation so entirely that he would have no other recourse than to wed her. But he would not be fooled into such a game, and she knew not who she played with when she tried to wrap Wymar around her finger as she did with her parents.

Hence, his insistence on having her ladies with her today on their outing, along with a few of his knights. She had planned this little diversion herself, knowing of this hidden gem on his property from previous visits. What she had not planned was Wymar's insisting that others attend as well. Her pout would not sway him nor her batting eyelids. He was no fool!

As he sat, his mind wandered to the other question pressing on him. If Beatrix wasn't his bride, who, then, was? Doubtless, she would be arriving soon, which meant he needed to settle this matter between Beatrix and himself posthaste. 'Twould be a disaster for his true bride to arrive with another woman attempting to claim him as her own.

Reynard concluded a conversation he'd been having with one of Lady Beatrix's ladies at the water's edge and came to sit next to him, a satisfied smirk plastered on his face. "She's a beauty, that one is," he said nodding to the woman as she waved to him. He returned the gesture and watched her blush. "Pretty as a spring rose."

Wymar chuckled. "And always looking for a new conquest so be careful with that one, brother," he warned. "She is searching for a husband, and I am not certain she cares whether you are titled or not."

Beatrix and the women gathered together, then giggled whilst the men standing behind Wymar began shuffling their feet. *"God's Bones,"* one cursed even as the men began muttering with him.

"They care not which one of us shows them attention."

"My wife would strangle me if she found out another had her eye on me."

"Do you think one of them would be up to… a…" One of the knight's words faded away as he apparently contemplated the women before them until another man elbowed him in the gut.

"Shut up, you fool, before they get any more stupid ideas in their pretty little heads."

Wymar chuckled although the look Beatrix bestowed upon him practically sizzled in the air between them. He gulped, understanding the men's plight. "Go ready the horses. I think we have had enough for one day. Let us head back to the castle and mayhap spend some time training. 'Twill be far more pleasant than how we have spent the day thus far, doing nothing but gazing at women who have plans I have no intention of partaking in."

The men took off as though fire had been licking at their boots. Wymar observed his brother's attention return to the woman with whom he had been speaking before.

"She *is* pretty," Reynard whispered before heaving a sigh.

Wymar gave him a playful nudge. "Better to think with your head instead of what is between your legs, brother," he teased as he watched his men lead the women to their horses. He stood and picked up the blanket. "I never did ask why the Empress dismissed you. Did you do something wrong?"

A snort escaped Reynard's lips. "Nothing of the sort. 'Tis only a temporary visit. I am to return to her service after you have wed. I cannot believe she would send Lady Beatrix for your bride. Such an outcome is unsettling," he said with a frown crinkling his forehead.

"The lady and I must needs have speech together. I cannot believe the Empress has sent Beatrix for my bride. I believe Beatrix has spoken a falsehood. The connection does not make any sense, at least inside my own head."

"'Tis best you have that conversation soon, Wymar. She is set on having you and has made that perfectly clear to anyone who would care to listen. She even plans the ceremony for two days hence. She acts as though she is already the mistress of Brockenhurst."

Wymar rubbed the back of his neck. "Do you think I do not already know this? She is getting more demanding with each day that passes into the next. Perchance I best speak with her as soon as we return to the castle."

"If you ask me, you should have had speech with her the moment she set foot upon the grounds and proclaimed her intentions. You cannot marry her! She is like our sister."

"I repeat… do you think I do not already know this? There is no way I can take her to wife." Wymar grumbled a curse beneath his breath. "Let us away. The sooner I get this over with the better."

Wymar went to his horse, his brother all but forgotten. He flinched when a woman's gentle touch caressed his back. He did not need to turn around to know who was behind him. "What is it you want, Beatrix? We have had enough of laying around doing nothing and must needs return to the keep."

She pressed herself into him and Wymar whirled around taking her by the arms and holding her back. Her eyes widened in surprise most likely from the force with which he held her until he gentled his grip. "Whatever is wrong, my love?" Her whisper held a seductive tone as though they had already shared a bed.

"I am not your love," Wymar muttered returning to checking the leather straps of his saddle.

She placed her hand on his arm, rubbing the fabric of his tunic. "But I will be your wife in just a matter of days. Are you not happy we are at last to wed?"

He sighed, finished tightening the cinch, and once more turned to face her. "Beatrix…" he began as he watched her face light up with a smile. "We must needs talk privately when we return to the castle."

"Of course, my love." She gave him a seductive grin before leaning forward to place a kiss upon his cheek. "I am yours to command."

She gave him no time to reply for she left him to mount her horse. Her laughter rang out in the forest as though she had not a care in the world. Wymar had the feeling she would not be laughing after they had their long overdue conversation.

CHAPTER THIRTY-THREE

CERIDWEN SAT IN awe as she took in the beauty before her. Richard had been so descriptive of the home he had visited for most of his youth that she had surely thought he had jested with her. But now, after coming out of the dense forest to see the castle sitting off in the distance, she understood his words to be correct.

To be sure, she could see that there was work aplenty to be done. The stone walls surrounding the keep were still in need of repair from the siege that befell it years ago. Richard had told her that Wymar had been in the process of repairing most of the inner buildings but at the very least the keep was livable with minor repairs still needed. And oh, but it was wonderful. The keep itself rose majestically at least six stories tall and Ceridwen could not wait to inspect every inch of the castle she would now call home. Her eyes traveled to the upper level of the keep where knights walked the parapets high above and four round turrets were situated at each corner along the battlements.

"I told you that you would like it, my lady," Richard declared when he moved his steed next to her.

She turned in the saddle to face Wymar's friend and gave him a bright smile. "Aye... you did indeed, Sir Richard. 'Tis just as magnificent as you described, mayhap more so." She leaned an elbow on the pommel of the saddle to take a moment unto herself to continue her assessment of her future life that awaited her.

"The place still needs a lot of work, but I doubt not that Wymar will eventually see his home restored to all its former glory, even if it takes years," Richard stated.

"I am certain the place will be glorious," she murmured.

"And was I not also correct when I thought you would enjoy the view more from a saddle than the wagon the Empress sent for you?"

Ceridwen looked behind her. The wagon she was supposed to reside in had been quite lavish with fluffy goose feathered pillows, blankets, and silk overhangings to keep the sun from her face. The Empress had indeed ensured Ceridwen had every imaginable comfort for her long journey to her new home. 'Twas what any woman would wish to arrive in, and it befitted her station in life. But such a mode of transportation was not for her. She gave a brief glance down at her attire, knowing Wymar would not care if she arrived riding Defiance and wearing the clothes of a young knight that she had originally met him in. She had plenty of gowns packed in her trunk to change into when she took her rightful place at Wymar's side as his lady.

She gave a short nod to Symond and Thomas before returning her attention back toward her future. Her future with Wymar. "'Tis a good thing I did not accept the wager you proposed. My purse would be much lighter if I had done so," she said with humor laced in her tone.

Richard chuckled. "'Twas a sure bet but I am a bit sorry for the loss of extra coin that would have lined my purse. The look on your face when you saw Brockenhurst was more than enough to know I was right. Shall we?" he asked waving his hand toward the castle in invitation.

"Aye," she said taking up the leather reins once more. "I am most anxious to see Wymar."

With a press of her heel into her horse's side, they were off. The closer she came to the remains of the barbican gate the more anxious she became. All she wanted to do was run to Wymar's side and leave the past behind them. A knight standing guard gave Richard a salute and waved their party forward.

Entering the outer bailey, she quickly slid from her saddle to the ground before tossing her reins to a stable lad who came forward to take her horse. "See that she is rubbed down and taken care of. My steed has served me well during our travels," she instructed whilst taking off her gloves and looping them into her belt.

Ceridwen and Richard had begun making their way toward the front steps when the front door opened. Reynard had a moment of surprise etched upon his face before he quickly recovered and offered her a wide smile and a bow.

"Lady Ceridwen. What a pleasure to see you again," the young man offered as he rose.

She gave a light laugh. "I would have thought Wymar would be expecting my arrival," she mused aloud, looking around Reynard to see if Wymar would also welcome her.

"My brother is in his solar... discussing business," he said. His eyes narrowed toward Richard. There was an expression on his face that she could not quite understand. It almost looked like... warning?

"I cannot wait to see him," Ceridwen replied. "Which floor? I am certain I can locate him on my own whilst you two discuss what you have missed with one another."

Richard chuckled. "Take the first turret once you enter the great hall on the left. Third floor. Fifth door on the right."

Ceridwen nodded her thanks and left the men.

"You dolt!" Reynard bellowed toward Richard. "There is much to be discussed. You do not know what you have—" That was all that she heard before her quick steps took her out of earshot.

Ceridwen gave them no further thought whilst she went in search of her betrothed. She could barely contain herself with thoughts of being held once more in Wymar's arms.

⁂

WYMAR POURED A chalice of wine and offered the cup to Beatrix. He was not looking forward to their conversation. The woman before him was the beloved sister of his best friend, and he had always viewed her as nearly a sister to himself, as well. He did not wish to hurt her feelings, but Wymar did not return her affection in the way that she clearly wished him to and it was time he made that clear. There would be no wedding. He could easily forgive the falsehood she told him about being his intended bride. She was young and used to getting whatever she wished. However, it was not his place to indulge her, particularly when following along with her plan would mean going against the Empress's dictates.

"Let us sit by the fire, Beatrix," he said waving toward one of the chairs near the hearth.

"You sound so serious, Wymar. Whatever you have to say, just say it," Beatrix coaxed as she slid her hand down the front of his tunic before taking a seat. "We have known each other for far too many years to not voice our minds freely and openly with one another."

"Very well." He watched her sip from her cup before placing it on a table next to her chair. He went to stand at the hearth, leaning an elbow on the mantle and staring into the flames to collect his thoughts. He might as well plunge right in. "You lied to me... Why?"

A sharp sound escaped her lips before she composed her face, making her eyes go wide and her expression go soft as though she were innocent. 'Twas an expression better suited to a child sneaking a sweet from the kitchen than a grown woman being confronted with a deliberate and damaging falsehood. "I have no idea what you are talking about, my love."

His patience snapped. Grabbing her arm, he gave her a reckless shake before he remembered himself. He stood tall to peer down upon her before taking the chair opposite the lady. "Do not play games with me, Beatrix. Generally, I have forgiven you much over the years, but you could have cost me all! You know very well the Empress did not send you to me so that we may wed. Why would you tell such a falsehood on a matter of such import? If we had in truth married, the Empress could have had my titles and lands stripped from me once more for having disobeyed her directives."

Beatrix had the decency to wince and appear apologetic at that. But her sparkling eyes told Wymar that she was not yet willing to give up. She still wished to convince him to marry her after all, even if it meant going against the Empress's wishes.

The smile that etched its way across her lips was that of a siren on the prowl for her mate. "You can hardly blame a girl for trying, Wymar," she all but purred. Her voice dripped like the sweetest nectar. "You have known me since I was a small child. Surely you must have been aware that I held hope that we would someday wed."

"I have never given you any indication that I shared those hopes, Beatrix. I have only thought of you as a sister," he fumed. "Never at any time have I thought of you as anything else!"

She shook her head whilst her laughter rang out in the room. "Given enough time, we could change that."

A low growl left him. "We could be waiting for the second coming and the way I feel for you would never change, Beatrix. You must cease pretending there has been any kind of grand romance between us. Up until recently, I was but a lowly mercenary waiting for the opportunity to prove my worth and possibly have my title and lands restored to me. I am certain you never gave me a moment's thought until I was once more landed nobility."

Her brow lifted at his words. "You are mistaken, Wymar. I have waited patiently for years whilst you ran about the countryside, hoping and praying for just such an opportunity as this," she declared waving her hand in the air. "Now, you are home. Your lands and title rightly restored. Now you must needs find yourself a wife. That wife should be the lady sitting here before you and none other."

A loud laugh escaped him. "I admire your audacity, my lady.

However, you forget the Empress has already chosen my bride who should be arriving any day. I cannot gainsay her choice for me even if I wanted to."

"We could run away together," she proposed as if this would solve the problem.

"And lose the favor of Empress Matilda when I have just regained all that had been lost? You must be out of your mind," Wymar snapped. He reached for his cup and downed the contents.

A soft sigh left her lips. "Must I repeat myself, Wymar? I am a woman who knows what she wants and will do all in my power to achieve what I desire. If we must go against the Empress's instructions, so be it."

He leaned his head back to stare upwards as though pleading to the heavens to give him strength. He pinched the bridge of his nose. "You are proving my point that you know nothing of what this would cost me even if I *did* want to have you as my wife, which I do not."

"'Tis only because we have been apart these many years," she coaxed before rising from her chair. She stood over him in indecision before she lowered herself into his lap. "You think of me as a child because you haven't had the chance to know me as a woman. We can change that now and forget all else."

"What are you doing?" Wymar asked sharply, holding on to the edges of the arms of his chair as if this could save him from whatever Beatrix planned to do next.

"'Tis obvious I must take the initiative to show you how well we would suit," she murmured before wrapping her arms around his neck.

"This proves absolutely nothing, Beatrix, and my only response is to think that your brother would kill me if he were to witness what was going on in this room," Wymar complained whilst she moved even closer into his body. He took hold of her arms and gave her a fierce shake to try to deter her.

A light laugh escaped her. "Let me worry about my brother, my darling, and I will show you exactly how affection will grow between us."

Trying to pry her arms from around him was no small task and, although Wymar should have expected it, he was still unprepared when she placed her lips upon his own.

He jerked in his chair even whilst she did her best to get him to give her some sort of a romantic response. Pushing her lips and rubbing them against his own got her no further in her endeavors. There was nothing passionate about this encounter between them. If anything, it only reaffirmed that kissing Beatrix was like kissing a sister. It was as if such an act was wrong not only in Wymar's mind but in the eyes of God Himself!

"Wymar! I am finally here," a familiar voice whispered across his soul when the door burst open in the woman's excitement.

Beatrix tore her lips from his and frowned at the beauty standing in the room. "Who the hell is she?" she demanded whilst Wymar hastily pushed Beatrix from his lap. Once she got her footing, she stomped her foot in protest at the interruption and crossed her arms over her heaving bosom. "Well? What is the meaning of this, Wymar?

Wymar ignored her and went to the lady he never thought to see again. "Ceridwen…" Her name hung in the room and her presence was as if God had answered his most heartfelt prayers. His husky tone all but conveyed how much he had missed this lady. How he had longed to see her in his home even though he had never thought such an occurrence would come to pass. Yet even as he felt lit up with joy to see her, her features went from excitement to what looked like disappointment, giving him pause.

"Wymar…" Ceridwen replied as she silently assessed the other woman in the room. A frown marred her perfect features, betraying how annoyed she truly was about the situation she had walked in to. "Am I interrupting something important?" Her words were laced with so much sarcasm even Wymar had to flinch at the tone. Honestly, could he blame Ceridwen for being upset with what she had come upon?

"Aye," Beatrix shouted.

"Nay!" Wymar interjected at the same time.

Ceridwen's gaze furiously turned toward Wymar. "Which is it? Because the lady does seem to appear as though she has some claim upon you."

"I am his betrothed," Beatrix announced, stepping forward and laying a hand upon Wymar's arm.

"Are you, now?" Ceridwen answered. An arched brow appeared before turning her gaze back toward Wymar again as she waited for his answer.

"Nay, she is not," he replied whilst disengaging Beatrix's hand.

She continued to stare upon them as though she needed to weigh who was right and who was wrong. Beatrix began to curse beneath her breath until he silenced her with a look that quickly clamped her mouth shut. He waited for Ceridwen to cause a scene as well. Most women would do so when the man they cared for was caught in the arms of another woman. But he knew this woman well. Ceridwen knew her worth. She should know that his feelings for her had not changed in a matter of only a couple of fortnights. Hopefully she knew in her heart that there was more to this story set before her than what met her eyes.

A stolen look in his direction and the slightest grin of her lips told Wymar much. She finally voiced what she had been thinking.

"For a moment I was concerned that you somehow forgot you were only supposed to have one betrothed. I must admit, Wymar, I am relieved such is not the case," Ceridwen said with a hint of humor in her tone that Wymar had not expected given the circumstances. "It appears introductions are in order. Will you introduce me to the lady?"

"This is Lady Beatrix Grancourt, Richard's sister," Wymar said as if announcing her name would explain everything.

"Richard's younger sister?" Ceridwen repeated with a slight chuckle. "And does your friend know you are dallying with her? Somehow, I do not think that would go over well with him."

"We were not dallying," Wymar replied.

"Mayhap you call what you were doing something else, but it certainly appeared as dallying to a casual observer," Ceridwen remarked before stepping forward and handing a parchment with the Empress's wax seal into Wymar's hand. "We have much to discuss once you have perused our Empress's message. I will leave you so that you may conclude your business with the lady."

"Ceridwen, wait," Wymar said as he watched her walk away from him.

She opened the door before replying over her shoulder. "I shall ask your brother to show me the bedchamber reserved for the lady of Brockenhurst. He is currently speaking with Richard, who accompanied me here. You may wish to have speech with him regarding his sister's... behavior."

Her words impacted more than one person left in her wake as she left the chamber. Wymar smiled for what felt like the first time in months. But 'twas the sudden weeping of the young woman he had known all her life that made Wymar reach out to comfort her the best he could. Beatrix sobbed whilst the reality of the situation finally revealed itself that she would not get what she truly desired.

CHAPTER THIRTY-FOUR

AFTER BEING SHOWN to her bedchamber, Ceridwen busied herself with unpacking her belongings, waving aside the servant who tried to take over the task. 'Twas not as though she had not performed this service a dozen times or more without anyone's aid. She gave a heavy sigh, feeling as if her days of being a soldier for the Empress had taken place years ago instead of months. Thoughts of Wymar raced through her mind: their time together... their time apart... their reunion which had not gone exactly how Ceridwen thought 'twould play out.

She had to admit, at least in the privacy of her own bedchamber, that she had felt the briefest glimmer of jealousy to see Lady Beatrix sitting on Wymar's lap, kissing him. Such a scene had been like a dagger to her heart, and yet she could not dismiss the look of unmistakable joy that flickered in Wymar's eyes when he saw her enter the chamber. His heart was hers. With that certainty to bolster her, Lady Beatrix would not get the best of her nor would she allow the young woman to stand between herself and the man she was commanded to wed.

Commanded... 'twas not so much a command as 'twas her heartfelt desire to take Wymar as her husband. She should have not been so foolish months ago when he offered for her, but she had not been in a good place in her mind. Until she had resolved her turmoil, she could not freely give herself to Wymar no matter how much she cared for him.

Aye! Cared for him she did. Yet, he must needs take care of the situation with Richard's sister and see to it that she no longer presented an obstacle to their marriage. After all, the Empress herself gave her blessing to the marriage between them. That in itself should be enough for the young woman to leave them in peace.

If Ceridwen thought long and hard about what she had witnessed, she could possibly understand the lengths Lady Beatrix might go to if she had held an affection for Wymar all her life. But this did not change the fact that Wymar and Ceridwen would wed, and she was not foolish enough to think Lady Beatrix would not have a place in their lives. The young lady was the beloved sister to Wymar's closest friend. They were bound to see the woman from time to time and 'twould be in their best interest if they could find a common accord.

A soft knock on her bedchamber door echoed in the room and Ceridwen bid whoever was on the other side of the portal to enter. She looked up, hoping to see Wymar, only to be disappointed. Agnes, who had traveled with her from Norwich, was there to assist Ceridwen with dressing for the evening meal. Either Wymar was too busy dealing with Lady Beatrix or he was not as happy to see Ceridwen as she had hoped.

There was no sense in delaying the inevitable. As the soon-to-be lady of the estate, there were certain expectations she must meet. Her responsibilities would be no different than if she had been allowed to stay at Norwich. The maid pulled out several garments that Ceridwen only recently put away, Agnes awaiting Ceridwen's approval on which gown she would don for the eve. She nodded to a garment the color of autumn leaves knowing the color would complement her. The servant carefully laid the dress upon the bed, put the rest of the gowns away, and then waited for Ceridwen to sit in order for her hair to be done.

Agnes began to weave her magic as she coiffed her hair, much like she had done the day Richard had arrived at Norwich with his news that she would wed Wymar. Multiple braids with a ribbon matching her gown had been interwoven into her golden tresses. Agnes then wound them all around her head as if like a crown. It looked pleasing enough and Ceridwen murmured her thanks. The gown came next and before she knew it, she was prepared to go down to the great hall. She was, however, unsure if she was to wait for Wymar to come and accompany her downstairs or if she was to go there on her own. Agnes gave her the answer she stood in need of.

"Lord Wymar asked ye to meet him in the great hall, milady. Do ye remember the way or would ye like me to show ye? I have been inspecting the passageways to get myself familiar with the keep," Agnes said.

So… she was to enter the lion's den without the reinforcement of her soon-to-be husband. So be it. "Nay, I do not need you to show me the way. I can find it," Ceridwen answered, and the servant bobbed a curtsey. "I never thanked you for agreeing to accompany me here to Brockenhurst, Agnes. It is nice to have someone with me who remembers my mother and all I left behind."

The woman's eyes widened momentarily before she gave a wide smile. "'Tis an honor to continue my service to ye, milady."

Ceridwen gave the woman a nod. "Thank you for the lovely job you did with my hair and getting me ready for the evening meal. I shall not need your assistance when I retire later so you may go and enjoy the rest of your eve to spend at your leisure."

Agnes beamed. "Thank ye, milady. That is very gracious of ye." She held open the door, waiting for Ceridwen to leave the bedchamber. Taking a deep breath, she squared her shoulders and mentally prepared herself to meet whatever ordeal that awaited her in the great hall.

She began her descent down one of the turrets. Conversations of those already seated in the hall reached her and she once more found the courage within herself to show these people that she was more than ready to become the mistress of Brockenhurst. When she stood on the last step and appeared at the entrance, all conversations diminished into a deafening quietness and but awaited the lord of the manor to say something to break the awkward silence.

Head held high, Ceridwen began making her way to the hearth where Wymar, Reynard, and Richard stood. She nodded whilst passing the many knights and ladies already seated at lower tables, and their speech began to grow louder the farther into the room she went. Once she stood before the three men, they bowed and she curtseyed until Wymar held out his hand for her to take. Her fingers trembled once they touched the warmth of his palm.

"My lady," Wymar began, "you are a vision beyond compare. May I be the first to formally welcome you to your new home?"

She arched a delicate brow thinking that this public greeting was overdue and should have been his initial response hours ago. But she would not push the matter, at least for now, in front of their people. "You are too kind, my lord. I look forward to the day when we can take our horses for a ride and see the rest of your lands."

He nodded before raising her hand to his lips. "Our lands," he murmured never taking those hypnotic blue-grey eyes from her.

"Aye, of course. Our lands," she repeated. Her nerves were on edge not knowing how their conversation would proceed during the evening meal. Had he spoken to Beatrix and set the young lady's mind at ease? If Ceridwen were in the younger woman's place, she would be distraught with grief knowing Wymar would never belong to her. Ceridwen had already gone through such an ordeal months ago, and she never wanted to be in such a position again.

"Shall we sup?" Wymar asked, tucking her hand into the crook of his elbow. His other hand was placed lightly on her waist whilst he pulled her close. Her heart flipped once more acknowledging her true feeling for her future husband.

Not waiting for her answer, he began escorting her to the raised dais reserved for the lord and lady of the keep. Once seated, Reynard took his place next to his brother whilst Richard sat to her left. With a wave of Wymar's hand, servants began bringing in platters of food for the hungry people waiting to sup. A trencher was placed between them, and Wymar began filling the plate with the choicest of meats. He waited for her to partake of the meal, yet she was still uncertain of all her unanswered questions that continued to run amuck inside her head. She was unsure if she could stomach any food until she had her answers.

She hesitated whilst her hand lingered near the trencher. Instead, she reached for her chalice and took a drink of the heady red wine that did nothing to calm her nerves. Ceridwen's stomach churned with the sensation of being in some sort of an eternal conflict of wanting to demand answers. But she also did not wish to appear as a shrew by daring to berate him for whatever his involvement was with Richard's sister. Ceridwen's eyes quickly swept the large great hall full of people. Beatrix was noticeably absent from any of the other tables Ceridwen could see causing her to once more ponder the poor girl's fate.

Wymar leaned over and his nearness was as intoxicating as the rush of memories of their very first kiss. "You will not eat, Ceridwen?" he asked whilst whispering in her ear. "You must be hungry after your journey."

She shivered with desire no matter how conflicted she felt. "Aye, I but awaited you to begin," she replied with nervous knots racing down her spine.

"Ladies first," he gently coaxed, causing her heart to flutter inside her chest.

Left with no alternative and not wishing to cause a scene, she began to nibble at the food set before her. She had not realized how famished she was until she began to eat. More wine was poured and was just as delicious as the meal she began to consume.

Wymar was preoccupied with a low conversation with Reynard leaving Ceridwen to gaze upon Richard. He appeared… uncomfortable to say the least. He cleared his throat, took hold of his own goblet before him and took a sip of his wine. He then turned to face her.

"My sincerest apologies for my sister, my lady," he said quietly. "I pray you do not think too unkindly of her. My parents have spoiled her to the point where she has but to crook her finger and her demands have always been met."

Ceridwen reached for her chalice and also took a sip before replying. "I have yet to have speech with Wymar regarding her," she murmured, "so I am unsure how to reply."

"'Twas not how I envisioned you being reunited with my friend."

A gruntled response escaped her. "Nor I." She glanced at Wymar who was still in a deep conversation with Reynard. "Have they always been close?"

"Of course... they are brothers," Richard declared.

She swatted his arm knowing he mistook her meaning on purpose as an excuse to change the subject. "You must know I did not mean Reynard."

He gazed upon her sheepishly before turning his focus to the food. He began pushing it around on his trencher but never brought any of the meat up to his mouth to eat. Clearly uncomfortable, Richard at last set the fork down to answer her. "Beatrix has been like a sister to the Norwoods. Anything more is a product of her own imagination. She can be very... determined."

"I see." Ceridwen sighed, pondering how to proceed. She did not wish to insult Richard but she could not let Beatrix come between her and the man she was to marry soon. "Should I be concerned as to her future motives where Wymar is concerned?"

Richard at last took a bite of his food and washed it down with a large gulp of wine. "I have had speech with her. She is distressed and at the moment inconsolable. This explains her absence and why she is not at the evening meal. But I am certain she will see reason in time."

"Mayhap I should talk to her," Ceridwen suggested.

His brow rose. "Such a talk may not go over well but I thank you for the offer to ease her distress."

"I hear woman to woman discussions can be helpful, though I have little experience with them myself. I have never had another woman close enough to confide in."

Richard nodded and continued to consume his meal. Ceridwen turned her attention to Wymar when she felt his hand rest upon her arm. He appeared concerned and she assumed he had listened in on most of her conversation with his friend.

"You heard?" she asked.

"Aye." He gave her arm a gentle squeeze. "You are kind to offer to have speech with Lady Beatrix."

Ceridwen shrugged. "It was only a suggestion. Given the despair the young woman projected earlier, I can understand her plight… at least to a point. I do not wish to be the cause of bad feelings between you and a woman you consider a beloved sister."

"As I said, you are most kind," Wymar replied, taking a sip of his wine. His eyes never left hers.

"That *is* all she is to you, is she not?" She watched his brow lift as though in disbelief before she continued. "You must know I need to ask. I do not wish our marriage to begin with a lie nor with a woman who will become an obstacle to our happiness. I will not tolerate your mistress under my roof."

Wymar set his cup down and leaned forward so their conversation was not overheard. "Beatrix is *not* my mistress nor have I ever had the slightest inclination to make her so. Richard would have called me out years ago for such an offence."

"As long as she is aware that nothing further is between you then I will be satisfied," she said whilst a small part of her was still concerned. "I am not foolish enough to believe that we will never see her again considering she is like family to you and your brothers. But I do not want her to continue to believe she has a hold over your heart."

His finger traced down her cheek. "I assure you, Ceridwen, there is only one woman who has ever held my heart and I am staring at her now. I have never brought a woman home as a possible bride because none before you ever held my interest to do so."

"You mean when your parents yet lived and still held ownership over the land?" she asked softly. They had never discussed his youth and Ceridwen was curious how he came to be a champion knight for the Empress.

"Aye. My mother died giving birth to Reynard, so we were raised solely by our father. His death at the hands of the usurper's men still weighs heavily on my mind even after all these years. His allegiance to the Empress is why our lands were stripped from us. He died protecting myself and my brothers during the siege. When the three of us made our escape, I vowed that day to keep us together. I hired out my hand to the highest bidder in those early days but finally came to lead a number of men for the Empress. Somewhere along the way, my reputation grew until I was known as the Knight of Darkness. I suppose such a name fit given the rage I felt back in those days. Those were indeed dark times."

"I am so sorry for all you have been through in your past, Wymar. It could not have been easy having your brothers under your care whilst plunging yourself into numerous battles."

He sat back in his chair and gazed about his hall. "I will admit 'twas not always easy, but I would not forsake the memory of my father's last wish that we remain together. Now, I have my title and lands restored to me once more," he said before turning his full attention back to Ceridwen. "I look forward to the years ahead as we once more make Brockenhurst a home."

Her own heart leapt at his words. There was indeed hope for their future. "Then you are pleased we are to wed and that the Empress sent me as your bride?"

His smile was broad before he reached over to lightly grip her chin so she had no choice but to keep her attention upon him. "God above could hear the joy in my heart when I saw you earlier. Your arrival was the answer to all my prayers. Aye, I am most pleased and hope you are the same."

"Aye. I am indeed pleased, Wymar."

"Good! Then we can begin anew and plan our wedding in the days to come. After reading the missive from the Empress, I have learned that her men will remain here to ensure the marriage takes place but she is demanding we wed posthaste. She needs her men to return as soon as they are able, including my brother. Things have not been going well for her of late in her quest for the crown."

"There have been rumors…"

He held up his hand. "We can discuss the Empress at a later date. This time belongs to you and I, and I plan to take full advantage of every moment we share together from this day forward." He bent forward and placed a light kiss upon her lips. His mouth lingered near her own whilst their breaths became as one. She kissed him again and sat back in her seat.

Her smile in response to such an intimate moment surely told the whole room how much in love she was with the lord of Brockenhurst. Aye… she, too, was more than pleased to take Wymar as her husband!

CHAPTER THIRTY-FIVE

THE DAY COULD not have gone any better as far as Wymar was concerned. He had risen early and with a light knock upon Ceridwen's door, he had told her to dress quickly to go riding. He was momentarily distracted to see her standing with the door only partially open. She held her robe together and he wished they were already wed so that he might wake with her with the rising of the sun. But there would be time for such mornings and evenings soon enough. Today, he would show her the estate of her new home.

'Twas just the two of them for their morning ride. He felt more than confident that Ceridwen was safe with him as her guard, particularly since she was more than capable of defending herself. He glanced over as she rode her white mare. Defiance had served her well and Wymar was pleased she had brought her horse with her and not left the animal at Norwich. The mare would be a good addition to their stable and they could possibly breed her with his own horse, Aries.

Ceridwen was beautiful this day with her blonde hair billowing in the breeze as their horses stretched their legs in a gallop across the strand of the beach. At last, she was the Ceridwen of old and the woman he remembered with a determined fire in her eyes knowing she was in charge of her own life and no longer weighed down by the memories of what Ratcliff had done to her. Thankful she was as happy as he was that they were to wed, they only awaited her gown to be finished before they would marry in Brockenhurst's chapel.

His slowed his horse and she did the same. The smile that lit her face spoke volumes. He had not seen her this carefree before and the look suited her. He prayed to God above to allow him every opportunity to make this woman happy for the rest of their days and far into eternity.

"You know me well, Wymar," she beamed at him whilst casting her gaze at the ocean waves. "This was just what I needed."

"Somehow I thought a ride might please you. Besides, 'twas going to be too fine a day to be cooped up inside the keep," he replied with a chuckle. "As you have seen, our lands stretch far from the coast and inland."

"'Tis no wonder the Empress wished for you to secure these lands in her name. Do you suppose she will call upon you again to fight for her cause?" she asked. 'Twas apparent her words voiced her innermost fears.

"Would you miss me?" he teased with a wink.

A laugh escaped her. "I would not dare admit such to you or you might become too conceited. Do you not think 'twould make it difficult for me to live with you?"

He reached over to take her gloved hand. "I wish to never be parted from you again, my lady."

"I would like nothing more than to live out our days quietly and without war or sieges at our gates," she murmured. "I have little faith that she would allow me to join her forces by your side should she call upon you again."

"Never again, Ceridwen," Wymar growled out. "I will not risk your life for anyone ever again. Besides… there may come a time when we have babes to see to. One of us must live to see to their upbringing."

She moved her horse closer. "Do not speak such things as if you might die in war and leave me alone. Quick, say a prayer so such a horrible event might not come to pass."

"You say one for me, my love," Wymar murmured whilst he watched her close her eyes and offer up a prayer on his behalf.

Opening her eyes, she once more turned her attention in his direction but he could see for himself that some of the joy he had witnessed but moments ago was gone. She gave him a small smile but it did not reach her aquamarine eyes. "Mayhap we should return home. There is much to do before we are to wed."

He nodded and as he turned his horse around toward home, he called out over his shoulder. "I shall race you. If you win, then you may tell me what you wish of me as your reward."

Her visage transformed once again to pure joy. "I accept your challenge, Wymar. Prepare yourself to lose!" She kicked her horse into motion as clumps of sand flew from behind her steed.

Wymar chuckled before flicking the reins. Aries quickly lessened the distance between them. The beach left behind, they raced through the village, their horses neck to neck, but when an old woman stepped out onto the path, Wymar pulled back on the reins allowing Ceridwen to race ahead. His opportunity to win was gone, although he in truth had held Aries back a bit in order to keep the race even before then. She was the first to reach the outer bailey after galloping through the barbican gate. She slid off Defiance with a satisfied grin.

"I won," she taunted whilst giving him a satisfied grin. "Declare you were at last bested by a woman!"

He grinned, jumping down from his own horse as he handed his reins to the stableboy. "You did not expect me to trample over that poor woman did you? You won only by default."

She came up to him, running her fingers over his leather jerkin. "Admit it, Wymar, you lost."

"And what does my lady expect as her prize?" he asked. His breath hitched as she stepped even closer. The heat of their bodies so close together caused a part of him to strain against his hose.

"A kiss."

"Now?" he said whilst his arms snaked around her waist bringing them chest to chest.

"Aye." A simple answer and a prize that he would never deny her... or himself.

He lowered his lips to hers in a gentle kiss before he stepped back in an effort to keep some form of control. He wished nothing more than to take her to his chamber and make her his in every way. She frowned upon him and placed her arms upon his shoulders.

"Really, Wymar... I know you can do better than that," she teased.

A moan escaped him when she all but threw herself into his arms, leaving him no choice but to give in to her demands for a kiss that would set her toes on fire. He left no doubt that this woman was his as his mouth slid across hers and his tongue began to dance with her own. 'Twas only the sound of a woman's gasp that tore the couple apart. Wymar and Ceridwen broke apart to witness Beatrix sobbing before she turned and ran into the keep.

"*By Saint Michael's Wings!*" Wymar swore even as he heard Ceridwen give a heavy sigh.

"Let me go to her," she suggested whilst she lovingly placed her hand upon his cheek.

"Are you certain?" he asked. "She can be... unpleasant at times when situations do not go her way."

"All the more reason for me to be the one to go to her," Ceridwen replied. "I believe this is something that must needs be settled between the two of us. Do not worry, Wymar. I have no doubt she will see reason."

"I will see you then at the evening meal," Wymar said. She nodded and he watched her retreating form until his lady entered the keep. He could only pray Ceridwen would be able to convince Beatrix that her future lay in another direction than with the lord of Brockenhurst.

CHAPTER THIRTY-SIX

CERIDWEN STEADIED HER nerves as she walked the passageway to where Beatrix's bedchamber was located. Ceridwen heard the woman's crying before she even reached the door. She could imagine what the poor young lady was going through: jealousy, hatred, and perhaps even fear of the unknown since she could no longer be sure where her life would lead. 'Twas obvious that Beatrix was in love with Wymar and likely had been her entire life, but Ceridwen held out hope that she and Beatrix could come to an accord that would allow their lives going forward to be, at the very least, amicable.

She knocked upon the wooden portal, pondering if Beatrix would even allow her entry into her chamber. The crying ceased and there was a long pause while Ceridwen supposed the young woman was making every attempt to compose herself. When the door at last opened, Beatrix had a welcoming smile upon her face. When she saw 'twas the soon-to-be new mistress of Brockenhurst, her face quickly fell.

Beatrix opened and closed her mouth several times before her brows drew together in a fierce frown. She at last found her voice that was filled with unsuppressed hostility. "I expected Wymar," she fumed whilst fingering the lace of her sleeve.

Ceridwen held her ground. "As you can see, I am here in his place."

Her eyes widened. "He sent you instead of coming himself to ensure I would be all right?"

"Nay. He did not send me," Ceridwen answered honestly. "I offered to come speak to you, so that we can settle what will come to pass in our future."

"*Our future?*" she sneered. "'Tis apparent I have no future here anymore."

"I disagree," Ceridwen replied in an attempt for Beatrix to see reason. "You are like family to the Norwoods. Why do you think this would change?"

"Because I desired to have Wymar as my husband," she bellowed before turning away from Ceridwen. "I hate you!"

Ceridwen gave a heavy sigh. She had known this conversation would not be an easy one. "I am certain you do," she stated whilst Beatrix looked over her shoulder at the woman who would obviously wed the man she loved. "May I come in?"

Beatrix gave a shrug. "If you must…"

"Thank you," Ceridwen said entering the bedchamber and shutting the door. The room contained several small, personalized objects scattered around the room to add to the lady's comfort. 'Twas either these personal effects stayed here whenever she visited or else she really had felt that her scheme to wed Wymar would come to pass, and she had brought them thinking this would be her permanent home.

Awkward silence sliced through the chamber until Beatrix made her way to a chair near the hearth. "You may as well sit," she said waving to the empty seat across from her. "I suppose you will not leave me in peace until you have had your say."

Ceridwen strode the length of the room and sat, taking a moment to search for the words to begin to heal the rift between them. "Lady Beatrix… you must know that none of this was meant to hurt you. Even if the Empress had not commanded Wymar and I to wed, we would have found a way to be together… or at least I would have prayed that would have come to pass in time."

"*Time*... If you had not arrived when you did, Wymar and I would even now be wed." The confidence she exuded would have felled a lesser woman but Ceridwen was not new to fighting for what she believed in... like her efforts to join the Empress's army.

Ceridwen placed her forearms upon her legs, leaning forward. "And if you had done so, what would that have cost you?" she asked waiting for the woman's answer.

Beatrix gave a short, disgruntled laugh. "Cost me? 'Twould have cost me nothing. I would have *gained* the man I have loved all my life as my husband." She gazed upon Ceridwen dressed in hose and tunic and all but turned up her nose at her appearance. She pointed her finger toward Ceridwen. "You do not know Wymar as I do nor will you ever be able to live up to his expectations of a proper wife, particularly if you continue to dress so bizarrely."

"You may not care for the way I dress but I assure you this is not the first time Wymar has seen me dressed thusly. I was the daughter of the Lord of Norwich so properly dressing is nothing new to me, and I am well trained in how to run an estate. I have been thoroughly educated on what would be expected of me once I wed. But we digress. My qualifications to be Wymar's wife are not what we need to discuss," Ceridwen said starting to feel miffed at Beatrix's bitter words.

"I have no idea what is of such import that we must discuss anything further," Beatrix said with a defiant raised chin.

"You say wedding Wymar would cost you nothing but in truth it would have cost you much."

Beatrix sat back in her chair. "I am listening."

"Then hear my words and hear them well. If you had wed, you would have married a man who would never love you as his heart has already been claimed by another... me. If this alone is not enough, then I am most certain that when the Empress learned of your deception there would have been consequences that would not be to your liking."

"'Twould be too late for her to denounce our marriage if our union had been consummated," she replied with a mulish expression.

Ceridwen did all in her power not to grimace at the thought of another laying with Wymar. "The Empress is a woman who focuses all her efforts on securing her throne and ensuring she has supporters in key locations. Brockenhurst was restored to Wymar because of his accomplishments upon the field of honor in Lincoln, but the Empress's intent was to have a man she could trust in this crucial position. By wedding you, against her decree, he would have forfeited her trust, and I am certain his lands and title would have once more been stripped from him. What would you have done then? Were you willing to become the wife of a mercenary and follow him along living in camp? I assure you, it is not an easy life and there are certainly few comforts to be had," Ceridwen asked already knowing the answer.

"'Twould not have come to that!" Beatrix said but her face betrayed her. This young woman was used to living in luxury. She wanted a husband with land and a title who could keep her in the comfort she was accustomed to.

"Then 'tis a good thing I arrived when I did before a mistake happened that would have been disastrous to all involved. I am here, Beatrix, at the Empress's bidding to marry the man she chose for me. 'Tis what is meant to be. More than that, 'tis what Wymar and I want, because I love him as he loves me."

"You will never love him as I do," Beatrix said. Tears began to glisten in her eyes.

Ceridwen reached over to take her hand and was surprised when Beatrix allowed it. "He does love you in return, Beatrix, but as a beloved sister of his best friend. This alone is reason enough why a marriage between the two of you would have never worked. I can only pray that with time you will accept our marriage and be happy for us. I never had a sister and would like the opportunity to get to know you better."

A gasp escaped her. "You will allow me to return to Brockenhurst?"

Ceridwen smiled and for the first time felt that there might be hope for them after all. "Aye. As I mentioned, you are family to the Norwoods and that will never change. As far as I am concerned, you shall always be welcome within our hall."

Beatrix stood and Ceridwen did the same. "Thank you, my lady," she replied although Ceridwen could see for herself that her words were difficult to utter. "You have given me much to think on."

Ceridwen stepped forward and gave the woman a gentle hug. She did not expect a response. That might have been asking too much given the circumstances but considering Beatrix allowed it gave Ceridwen even more hope that all would be well between them in the future.

"There is nothing to thank me for," Ceridwen said before striding to the door. "I hope we see you at the evening meal. You have been missed."

Heading to her own chamber, she asked a passing servant to summon Agnes, along with a bath to be brought up to her chamber. A good long soak in a tub might be just what she needed to calm her racing heart. Only time would tell if Beatrix would accept the inevitable.

CHAPTER THIRTY-SEVEN

Wymar watched his soon to be bride glide into the chapel as she made her way to stand at his side. She was lovely in a forest green gown that brought out the color of her eyes. A circlet of flowers with colorful ribbons flowing down her back graced her hair which she had left down. 'Twas as if she had done so just to please him and pleased he was. He took her hand and raised it to his lips.

"You are beautiful, Ceridwen," he murmured softly whilst he continued to stare into her mesmerizing aquamarine eyes.

She reached over to finger the sleeve of his green tunic. The golden threads embroidered into the garment matched those at the wrists, neckline, and hem of her own gown. "As are you, Wymar. The ladies did a remarkable job making our garments match."

"As long as you are pleased, then I am happy," he replied, turning toward their priest. "You may begin, Father."

They took their place in the front pew sitting side by side whilst the priest began to perform Mass. The priest began his sermon speaking of uniting the land, talking of the people of Brockenhurst and Wymar's continuing efforts to restore his homeland. Wymar glanced over to Ceridwen to see her staring upon him. He reached over to take her hand and she gave his fingers a squeeze before she returned her attention to the priest.

"Lord Wymar," the priest finally said, "what do you bring to your union with the Lady of Norwich?"

"Scribe!" Wymar called and a man came forward with parchment, quill, and ink to sit at a small table that had been placed near the front pews. "Take this down."

Wymar began to rattle off his holdings, the acreage of land he owned, and the small fortune he had collected over the six years he had been gone from his home. He also had the handsome reward he had received from the Empress in recompense for his service in seeing Ceridwen's return to Norwich. Horses and other stock animals joined the list. Once he had finished, the priest asked Ceridwen to state what she brought to their marriage. As she listed her extensive holdings, 'twas clear they would live comfortably for the rest of their lives together. And while he'd have given up all of his fortune willingly just to have her as his bride, 'twas pleasant to know that he'd have all the resources to be able to give her and their children a comfortable life and leave them well provided for should anything happen to him.

The priest called the couple forward and took a red ribbon to tie the fabric around their wrists. Wymar smiled to see a small black raven stitched toward the bottom, pleased that his family crest was represented this day. But he had no time to further marvel at the needlework of the fabric binding this woman to him for the rest of their lives. Not when he stared upon his lady whilst they gave their vows and pledged their hearts forever.

A cheer rang out in the chapel once the priest proclaimed them husband and wife, and Wymar leaned forward to give Ceridwen a chaste kiss. He smiled as one delicate brow rose up, and he gave her a wink that promised her more to come once they were alone later this eve. The ribbon was untied, and they made their way to the altar where all the necessary documents were signed. Wymar then stamped his seal upon the parchment and Ceridwen was officially his wife. Happiness overwhelmed him. If someone had told him when he had left Norwich months ago that this day would actually happen, he would have told them they were fools. He was filled with joy and gratitude that he had been proven so resoundingly wrong.

Brockenhurst's great hall was full of neighboring gentry, his own knights and their ladies, and of course the Empress's men who had accompanied Ceridwen to witness their marriage. Now if only the celebration could be over so he and Ceridwen would be able to retire to their bedchamber... not that sleep would be on their minds. He delighted in his bride's happiness as she made her way around the room and people offered their congratulations on their marriage. Dancing followed. After he had taken his wife in his arms in the middle of their hall and performed the patterns of a fast-paced dance, others came to follow in his footsteps.

He took a sip of his wine when he noticed Lady Beatrix watching him. He watched her heave a heavy sigh and then began to make her way across the room in his direction. God help him if she once again made some attempt to win his affection. He would not stand for it. Not today of all days. But when she spoke, she surprised him and pleasantly so.

"I must needs ask for your forgiveness for deceiving you with my scheme to have us wed," she began with worried eyes. "I admit 'twas for my own selfish gain and I did not think on what it might cost you had my plan succeeded."

"There is naught to forgive, Beatrix," Wymar admitted, thankful the young woman had finally come to her senses. "As you can see, I am now wed to the woman I love and that is all that matters."

"The Empress will be pleased," Beatrix murmured whilst she, too, watched Ceridwen from across the room. "As long as you are happy, Wymar, then I am happy for you... truly I am."

"I am pleased to hear such a confession, my lady. I was worried you would feel you were no longer welcome here at Brockenhurst."

She gave a small smile. "Your lady made certain when we had speech together to assure me that I would always be welcome in her hall. She was most gracious considering the trouble I caused."

Wymar watched the lady he had known for most of his life. He took her hand and raised it to his lips, watching when her eyes widened. "You are the cherished sister of my best friend, Beatrix. You are the sister I never had. Never feel as if you are not welcome in our home."

Tears welled in her eyes. "Thank you, Wymar. 'Tis more than I deserve."

Before he could respond, she left him. She would need some time, but he hoped that it would not be long before she was able to heal her wounded heart. He could do no more for the lady. The rest was up to her.

He had his cup refilled as he watched the dancing. Ceridwen was currently partnered with Reynard and he only wished that Theobald was also here to join in their celebration. He went to the hearth, his arm leaning upon the mantle when Richard joined him.

"Did my sister dishonor herself again?" he grumbled angrily.

"Get rid of such a hostile look whilst you gaze upon your sister. You shall scare the poor girl," Wymar snapped.

"Did she?"

"Nay, she did not. In fact, she asked most humbly for my forgiveness."

Richard's brow rose. "Humbly? I did not think she had such a trait in her."

"Do not underestimate your sister, Richard. Her motives may have been misguided, but she has a kind heart underneath her determined exterior."

"I am sorry for the difficulties she caused you and Ceridwen."

Wymar placed his arm upon his friend's shoulder. "You have nothing to apologize for and Beatrix has already done so, both to myself and my wife. She will be welcome in my hall as she always has been in the past."

"You are kinder to her than she deserves," Richard said still glaring at his sister.

"And you could use a bit of kindness and forgiveness toward your sister. She is past the age to wed. She saw an opportunity and she took it. 'Twas not the right course of action but you need to find her someone to wed soon or she may just do something rash again."

"I will do my best to find her a man of wealth," Richard replied.

"Wealth?" Wymar asked somewhat annoyed his friend would only think of money. Beatrix deserved more than just that. "Find her a man she can fall in love with, Richard."

"Love? We cannot all be so lucky to find love as you have Wymar," he said, "but I will try."

"You should also find a woman to love, Richard. Trust me when I say you shall not regret it."

Richard mumbled something under his breath. The minstrel's song ended and Reynard began escorting Ceridwen across the hall in his direction. Wymar held out his hand to her, pulling her to his side and placing a kiss upon her cheek.

Reynard chuckled. "I believe your lady would much rather be dancing with you than anyone else in your hall, brother."

Wymar looked down upon his wife; her eyes sparkled like jewels from the torches that lit the room. "Would she now?"

Ceridwen's hand wound around his neck and gently pulled. He leaned down so she could whisper in his ear.

"Mayhap we could retire to our chamber? Surely no one would miss us at this hour of the night," she asked and Wymar's heart swelled with desire to finally have his lady once again.

"I am yours to command, my dear." His husky tone revealed his true feelings, leaving no doubt of where he would rather be. 'Twas certainly not standing in his hall with his guests around him.

"Then let us leave the public celebration of our wedding to others so we may enjoy our wedding in the privacy of our bedchamber. We have waited long enough." Her eyes held a promise of what was to come and he would deny her no longer… nor himself.

He turned to the two men who were closest to him. "If you gentlemen would excuse us, I believe 'tis time Ceridwen and I take our leave."

Reynard laughed. "Time to leave was most likely two hours ago, Wymar. What took you so long?"

Wymar did not bother with an answer. He tucked Ceridwen's arm into the crook of his elbow as they began saying goodnight to those guests who would continue to drink and eat their fill far into the morning hours. He had no objection to them celebrating as long as they pleased, just so long as he was permitted to spend that time having his bride to himself.

Up the winding turret stairs and down the passageway they went until they reached Wymar's bedchamber. He opened the wooden portal and let Ceridwen proceed him into the room. A startled gasp escaped her when she saw that her things had been moved to his bedchamber. He shut the door and put the bolt in place.

"Our servants have been busy whilst we have been downstairs," Ceridwen said smiling.

"I hope the changes make you happy," Wymar replied. He went to a table near the hearth and poured two chalices of wine. Bread and cheese sat on a platter but he was not in the mood for food. He handed a cup to his wife, raised his own in a silent toast and they took a sip.

"All my possessions have been moved here," she stated the obvious as she continued to gaze around the chamber.

"I would not have you sleep anywhere else but next to me. I can have them brought back if you would rather—"

"—you will do no such thing, Wymar. This is where I belong," she stated before setting her cup down. She took his and set the chalice next to her own. "We have waited so long to be together once more…" Her words trailed off in a promise of what was to come.

"Aye, far too long, my love," Wymar whispered.

Her body molded itself to his own and Wymar bent forward to

capture her lips with his in a searing kiss. He could taste the sweetest of the wine she had drunk and he deepened their kiss until he heard a moan escape her. 'Twas all the encouragement he needed.

She undid his belt at his waist and the dress dagger he had attached to the leather hit the floor with a metal clank. He reached up to take the circlet from her hair, tossing it on the table that held their repast. From that point, their hands rushed as they hastened to remove their garments concealing their bodies.

Naked, he picked up his lady carrying her to their bed. "You are beautiful, wife," Wymar whispered as his hands began exploring the woman beneath him.

"My handsome husband… if you do not make love to me this very instant, I shall never forgive you," she teased.

"So demanding…" he replied with a wicked grin before leaving a trail of kisses down her body until he reached the very essence of her.

"Wymar…" his name whispered from her lips was like the sweetest sonnet.

"My dearest wife, I plan on showing you my complete devotion far into the night," he replied before he began to prove to her the depth and intensity of his love.

Her moans only encouraged him to further taste the sweetness that was all Ceridwen. 'Twas almost as though a lifetime had passed since they had made love together and he was determined to prove to her in every way possible that they would never be parted again. But when he felt her take a fistful of his hair giving it a yank, he looked up from between her thighs and saw she was going to make more demands of him.

"Take me now, Wymar, I beg of you," she ordered. With that, he could no longer deny her nor his own desire to finally be inside his wife.

He moved quickly, and knowing she was more than ready for him, he plunged his manhood into her womanhood. Her gasp was one of pure pleasure and together they began the rhythm known to lovers throughout the centuries. Slowly at first to enjoy every sensation that coursed together through their bodies. But soon, there was no longer any sense of needing to wait before they reached the heights of the heavens. And when they finally found their release together, they each cried out one another's name.

They had gone and seen the stars together. The first time making love as husband and wife was a resounding success. Their hearts began to once more settle into a normal rhythm and Wymar rolled over onto his back bringing Ceridwen into his side. Her hand played with the hair on his chest, and he brought her fingertips up to his lips.

She leaned her head back to peer at him with a contented smile. "That was… perfect," she whispered before pushing up to place a kiss upon his lips.

"*You* are perfect, Ceridwen, in every way," he responded before brushing a lock of her hair back from her face. She placed her head once more upon his chest with a satisfied sigh.

"Mayhap once we recover, we can make love again," she suggested with a contented sigh.

He chuckled. "Are you asking or making more demands of me, dearest wife?" he teased holding her close.

He felt her shrug. "Take my words however you wish, my love," she replied. "I am too happy at this very moment to make further demands of you, however."

"You are truly a remarkable woman, Ceridwen."

She rolled on top of him. "Then show me…"

Another grin slowly creased his lips. "As you command, my lady."

Far into the eve did Wymar shower his wife in his devotion and the love he felt for her. They had a lifetime together and even an eternity would never be enough to prove how much this woman meant to him.

CHAPTER THIRTY-EIGHT

THE MORNING AIR was brisk. A blanket of fog hung low over the ground, making the day appear later than it was. 'Twas an eerie sight to behold and did not offer a good omen for those who would travel this day. 'Twould be hard to see anyone who might attempt hiding in the mist so as to lie in wait for an attack. Most of the wedding guests were still abed inside the keep after a night of revelry but Wymar and Ceridwen were up early in order to bid safe travels to his brother along with Richard and Beatrix.

Ceridwen pulled the hood over her head. She was a bit bleary eyed as her husband had kept her up most of the night, not that she would complain. There could be no doubt that their marriage had been properly and most thoroughly consummated.

The Empress's guards stood at the ready and only awaited Reynard. Beatrix was attempting to keep out the cold whilst standing next to a wagon by blowing her warm breath into her hands and shuffling her feet. Her ladies were already seated within the cart and but awaited their mistress to join them. Wymar and Richard stood next to her whilst having speech together. When Ceridwen approached, they cut their conversation off.

Richard bowed before her. Beatrix dropped down into a curtsey. Richard reached out for Ceridwen's hands, and she gladly took them. "Congratulations again on your marriage, Lady Ceridwen. I am sorry we had to roust you from your slumber at such an ungodly hour, but I must needs see my sister home before I again join the Empress's ranks."

"We need not stand on formality, Richard, especially given you are like family. Besides, we fought side by side for the Empress's cause. I do not think 'tis necessary to call each other anything but our given names," she replied squeezing his hands before dropping them when Wymar came and wrapped his hand around her waist.

Richard nodded. "As you wish… Ceridwen."

Ceridwen nodded as well. "Where must you travel to join our Empress?" she asked.

Richard and Wymar exchanged a quick glance before Wymar replied. "Richard is not allowed to say, dearest. You understand."

She felt put in her place with that reminder that she would no longer be privy to information on the movements of the Empress's army. Yet she felt no great loss as a result. Her fighting days were over. She was now the mistress of Brockenhurst, and her duties were here. "Of course. Godspeed, Richard, and to you as well, Beatrix. May your travels home be done in safety."

Ceridwen was surprised when Beatrix came to her and kissed both cheeks. "Thank you again for your graciousness, my lady," she whispered before allowing her brother to assist her into the wagon.

Richard bowed to them again before going to his horse and lifting himself into the saddle. With a brief wave, their party was off, and Ceridwen was unsure when they would see them again at Brockenhurst, especially if Richard was off to further the cause of Empress Matilda.

Wymar kissed the top of her head. "Shall we see my brother off?" he asked, turning her toward where Reynard waited near his horse.

"Somehow I feel this parting for you may be more difficult," she replied, watching him carefully.

"Reynard is more like me than either of us care to admit. Stubborn to a fault and sometimes much too rash, landing him into trouble more often than not. He seems to wreak havoc wherever he may go."

A slight giggle left her. "You? Stubborn?"

His laughter rumbled in his chest. "Mayhap just a little."

They walked across the inner bailey before reaching Reynard and Wymar gave his brother a fierce hug. "Stay safe, you young scamp."

Reynard returned the hug, slapping his brother upon his back before the two broke apart. "You would think he would learn I am no longer wet behind the ears," he muttered before looking at Ceridwen. "Mayhap you could teach him some manners, my lady."

She hid her laughter behind her hand before she wrapped her own arms around her brother-in-law. "Godspeed, Reynard. Please return when you can. You must needs know this is always your home."

"Aye, but thank you for saying so... not that you need me wandering your halls being newly wedded and all," Reynard stated with a grin. He then stepped closer to the couple so his words would not be overheard. "Last I heard, the Empress was in Oxford after failing to be crowned. Rumor has it she is heading to Winchester so we are heading in either direction to meet up with her army wherever they may be upon the road."

Wymar nodded. "Your whereabouts shall be kept between us."

"Aye," Ceridwen agreed. "Spies can be everywhere but you both know such is the case."

Reynard clasped his brother one last time before he, too, alit into his saddle and gave a signal to the Empress's men he was ready. Horses began making their way through Brockenhurst's barbican gate.

Reynard put on leather gloves and took up the reins. "I will give your best to Theobald once I meet up with him. I am certain he was sorry he could not attend your nuptials. If I know him, I am sure he is even now sitting in some pub toasting your marriage and causing chaos with the serving maids," Reynard laughed.

Wymar placed his hand upon his brother's leg. "Just watch each other's back and return home alive."

He gave a jaunty salute. "Until our paths cross again. Take care,

Wymar. My lady."

They watched his retreating form until he was lost from view. Wymar pulled Ceridwen close before bending down and giving her a quick kiss.

"If I have not said the words lately, I love you, Ceridwen," he murmured whilst he watched her features.

"As I love you, my dearest Wymar." She reached up to cup his cheek. "Do not worry, husband. Your brothers and Richard will be fine."

"I would feel better if I was there with them but I know my duties now lie elsewhere."

"You regret not traveling with them to continue your support of our Empress?" She frowned before he took his finger to smooth over the crease that had formed at her brow.

"Nay, I do not. Our fighting days are over as far as I am concerned, Ceridwen. My place is next to you and at Brockenhurst," he said before escorting her back into the keep.

The great hall was starting to fill with the remaining guests who would break their fast and also make their way home. Ceridwen thought they would join them but instead, Wymar continued up the turret and down the passageway leading to their bedchamber.

She smiled, knowing where his thoughts were going. "You do not wish to say farewell to our guests?" she asked whilst a hint of humor lingered in her words.

"Let them wait," he replied, opening the door to their chamber. "We have better things to do this morn that have been neglected."

"Far be it for me to object to the lord of the manor wanting to take care of his lady," she said removing her cloak. She began laughing when he picked her up by flipping her over his shoulder, tossing her upon the bed, and lifting up her gown. "Impatient, are we?"

"Aye!" he said whilst he began unbuckling the belt at his waist. "Any objections?"

"None at all," she said whilst opening her arms to receive her husband.

The was an urgency to their lovemaking and Ceridwen did not mind in the least. She had waited a lifetime to find a love that would last the rest of her days and far into eternity. Ceridwen had found her place in life and 'twas in the arms of Wymar, her Knight of Darkness. He was the love of her life and she looked forward to every aspect of their lives together. Wymar… he was the other half of herself that had been missing. She was now home.

EPILOGUE

Three Months Later
Brockenhurst Castle

WYMAR SAT IN his solar perusing the letter before him even though he had just finished reading it for the third time. He needed answers, or as at least some sign that his brothers were alive and well. Satisfied with the contents of his missive, he put his signature upon it and dusted sand over the parchment. Blowing off the remains, he folded it, took a nub of red wax, holding it over the candle and allowing it to drip over the edges to close the document. He took his seal and applied it before handing it to a waiting servant.

"Send a runner to find my brothers. Mayhap in Winchester or beyond. See that he does not return until they are found and have given him a reply to return with. Ensure he has enough coin to see him through his travels," Wymar ordered before dismissing the man.

"'Twill be done, my lord," the man answered before taking his leave.

Wymar went to a nearby window, opening the shutter to allow the cold winter breeze to clear his head. He was worried. There had not been much news to reach Brockenhurst of late regarding the whereabouts of the Empress or his brothers for that matter. Mayhap Reynard was correct that she was to lay siege to the city of Winchester, but news of her success or failure had yet to reach him. He felt cut off from the Empress's determination to be crowned but at this point he was more concerned that his brothers yet lived. Hence his missive.

'Twould possibly be months before he learned of their whereabouts. Patience had never been one of his strongest traits, but as he noticed how late the morn had become, he knew what awaited him downstairs in his hall to distract his melancholy thoughts.

He made his way down the turret stairs to his hall and held back a grin. Ceridwen stood at the ready, dressed in tunic, hose and boots much the same way she had been attired when he had met her months ago. She gave him a welcoming smile, but he knew underneath such a come-hither look, she was more than ready to prove her worth with her blade. Such had become their routine since winter graced the land. He refused to allow her to train outside any longer in case she slipped upon the icy ground given her condition.

Turbert rushed forward and came to stand before Wymar. The boy held out Wymar's father's sword and he took a moment to relish in the thought that the blade had been found at Norwich and returned to him. Another reason to be thankful to Ceridwen for she was the one who had restored the cherished item back to its rightful owner.

"Milord… yer lady awaits," Turbert said whilst he inched the sword closer.

Wymar gazed down at the boy wondering if he did the lad a disservice by keeping him here instead of sending him on his way with one of his brothers. But mayhap Turbert did not have the same desires for fame and fortune as Wymar once had. "You are happy here, are you not, young Turb?"

The boy's brow furrowed in concern. "Do ye wish to send me away, milord?"

"Nay, of course not, Turb. I only wonder if the domestic life here at Brockenhurst will become you or that you might miss the heat of battle from time to time," Wymar answered.

The boy shuffled his feet. "I have had enough of the bloodshed that is found these days, milord, and am most content to stay here as long as ye will have me."

"Very well, then, Turb. Go take your place amongst those who are here to watch their lord and lady." Wymar took the hilt of the sword and the sweet sense of familiarity fell over him. Briefly, the battles he had won, and lost, flashed inside his mind until he was once more brought back to the present whilst his lady called out his name. Wymar watched Turbert leave his side to take his place along one of the walls. He remained close enough, Wymar supposed, in the event Wymar had need of him.

"Shall we, my lord?" she asked before pulling her blade from the scabbard at her side and examining her sword as if looking for some flaw that would not be found. Her weapon had saved her life on many an occasion. Now 'twas used to only keep her fit in their daily exercises.

"By all means, my lady." He took a moment to stare at the gem in the hilt of his sword. How many times had he been tempted in his past to sell the costly jewel to put food in their mouths? Thankfully, such an act had never come to fruition. Wymar would have regretted such a loss. Returning his attention to his wife, they began to circle one another looking for a point of weakness to begin their attack.

"You kept me waiting," she said whilst she swung her sword back and forth. "You should know better. Have you not learned by now how much I dislike not having your full attention?"

"Business matters," he replied whilst he still accessed her form that was, as always, impeccable. She was just as fierce a warrior as when they first met. "Nothing for you to worry about, my dear."

Her brow rose. "Do you leave me out of such discussions to annoy me? One would have thought by now you have learned better than to do so."

He chuckled. "Nay, my lady. I will fill you in… later. Now… do you wish to have speech all day or shall we begin our training so that I might win and go on with our day?"

She laughed. "Come, my Knight of Darkness, and let us see how you fend against a woman," she taunted bringing her blade before her.

Wymar swung his blade until he too took up his stance. "Do you ever think I will live down such a name?"

Another laugh escaped her lips. "The men will think you soft if they consider you anything other than what you have shown the world. You have a reputation to uphold, my lord. There is no way for you to go back to the day of being some unknown mercenary. Now, let us fight, husband, unless you wish to concede the day."

The sound of sword upon sword began to echo in Brockenhurst's great hall. With the exceptions of the spectators who sat on benches along its walls, one would have thought a small battle was ensuing to cause the keeps' occupants to be fearful. However, the laughter or taunts his wife continued to throw in his direction relieved any who had come to witness the lord and lady of the castle as they performed their daily training. Their friendly bantering at one another only added to the amusement of those watching in the hall. The ladies cheered for their mistress. His knights, of course, praised his efforts to win the match.

"You *are* becoming soft, my lord. We may need to find a new name to call you… Knight of Sunshine, perchance?" Ceridwen teased with a jovial laugh. "Mayhap wedded bliss has made you more vulnerable than you would care to admit."

Wymar chuckled before ducking, narrowly missing her sword before raising his own as the blades were brought together with a loud clang. They stared at one another between the cross of their weapons. "Knight of Sunshine?" he said softly between them whilst he watched her eyes sparkle from the reflection of the torches in their hall. "Surely you can come up with a better name than that."

"I think it suits, considering you are letting a mere woman beat you."

A chuckle escaped him. "Admit it… you are starting to slow down yourself, my lady," he said in a husky tone. "Mayhap the babe you carry is the cause."

"You think because I carry your child that I cannot still defend myself from you?" she asked, her eyes now sparkling mischievously as a slight smile creased her lips. She stepped back with both hands wrapped around the hilt "Prove to me my words are wrong. I believe you and your sword are not adequately performing."

"I am most certain that proof of my adequately performing *sword* is the child that is currently nestled comfortably in your belly, Ceridwen."

Her laughter rang out once more but he could tell she was tiring although she would never admit such to him aloud. "I will bare you a girl child just to spite you, my lord," she taunted before she put her sword away and he held his out for Turbert to take. Once the boy left with Wymar's sword, Ceridwen came over to him, running her hands up his chest and around his neck. The spectators began to take their leave, not that either Wymar or his wife either noticed or cared. He pulled his wife into his chest.

"I have no doubt you will do just that. A girl or a boy makes no difference to me as long as the child pleases you," he murmured for her hearing alone. He took a slight step back and placed his hand upon her stomach. She wasn't showing much but he alone could feel the hardness beneath his hand and knew his seed had planted itself well within his wife.

"We may have to forego these excursions soon," Ceridwen said. "Not that I am yielding the match to you…"

"Would that be so horrible? I believe you have already yielded all to me, my love," he replied, bringing them close again.

She placed her hand upon his chest. "Your heart beats fiercely for me, Wymar."

He returned the gesture. "As does yours for me, Ceridwen. Our hearts will forever beat together as one. You are my match in every way and I will thank God above for the rest of my days that we found each other."

"Our hearts will always find one another across all time, Wymar, for our souls were destined to be together." She gently put pressure on his neck, and he leaned down to kiss her sweet slips.

Aye… Ceridwen of Brockenhurst was his perfect mate. No other woman would ever compare to the love he had found with her. He prayed for the health of the babe she carried and for any more children that God might bless them with. Ceridwen was his to love and they had a lifetime of happiness to look forward to.

He scooped up his wife and carried her to their chamber where he once more began to show her his unending love. He felt a sense of rightness and knew that he was exactly where he was meant to be. He needed to look no further for adventure than his own hall. Ceridwen was all he needed, and she would more than compensate for any excitement beyond his battlement walls. Love… 'twas a miracle that would make Wymar eternally grateful that such an emotion had found him. Aye… he was very grateful and indeed very blessed. His days of darkness were over.

THE END

Sherry Ewing needs your help!

Book reviews help readers to find books, and authors to find readers. Please consider writing a review for **Knight of Darkness**, even a couple of sentences telling people what you liked about the story is helpful.

Reviews can be posted on BookBub, Goodreads, and on most eRetailer websites. For links to this book on those sites, see Sherry's website at

www.sherryewing.com/books

Author Note

Dearest Reader:

Thank you again for purchasing a copy of **Knight of Darkness** (*Book One*) in my brand-new series, **The Knights of the Anarchy**. I hope you enjoyed Wymar and Ceridwen's action-packed journey to finding their happily-ever-after!

How about a little bit of history? My story takes place in 1141, many years from the beginning of this turbulent time period in England's history. The Anarchy began after the death of Henry I and lasted from 1135 to 1153. It would be looked back upon as one of the darkest periods in England's history.

A lot happened before 1135, however, and led up to the succession crisis between Empress Matilda and King Stephen that caused the civil war. It began in 1120 when Henry I's only legitimate son and heir, William Adelin, was killed when his White Ship struck a rock in the English Channel and sank. Henry, fearing for the succession, then married Adeliza of Louvain in 1121, hoping to father another male heir. Although he had other sons, none were legitimate. His second marriage remained childless.

When Henry's only other legitimate child, Empress Matilda (she had married Holy Roman Emperor Henry V), became a widow, she returned to Normandy, which had been an English possession since the time of the Norman Conquest. Henry I then remarried her to Geoffrey of Anjou, heir to the French lands of Anjou, Touraine, and Maine. This formed an alliance securing Normandy's southern borders.

Naming Matilda his heir, Henry then made his court swear an oath to follow her. His decision wasn't popular, so the agreement from the nobles was reluctant. Up to this point in her life, Matilda hadn't spent much time in England and her husband wasn't popular with the English nobility. Added to this was the fact that England had not had a reigning queen since it was united under the Saxon King Egbert in 827. The people were suspicious of a woman on the throne.

Henry's relationship with his daughter and son-in-law was strained during his final years. As part of her dowry, Matilda had been promised several castles in Normandy, but her father never gave any indication of when she would take possession of them. Matilda and Geoffrey finally demanded these castles in 1135 and insisted that the Norman nobility swear allegiance to the couple. Henry refused, causing a rebellion to break out in Normandy. Matilda and Geoffrey sided with the rebels against Henry.

Henry I died on December 1, 1135. Some nobles declared this released them from their oath to Matilda. The Norman barons believed that Theobald of Blois, Henry's nephew via his sister, would be the better choice for England's next monarch. Theobald's younger brother Stephen, however, disagreed. Stephen was a well-liked member of Henry's court and had the support of the Church via their younger brother – another Henry, the Bishop of Winchester. Wasting no time, Stephen crossed the Channel to England from Boulogne, seizing the crown on December 22nd.

Matilda refused to renounce the crown. Her claim was upheld by her half-brother, Robert of Gloucester (one of Henry I's illegitimate sons), as well as her uncle King David I of Scotland. Robert's declaration of support for Matilda caused a rebellion to rise up across the southwest of England as well as Kent, while Geoffrey of Anjou invaded Normandy and David I attacked northern England.

In 1139, Matilda arrived in England to claim her throne. She stayed at Arundel Castle with her stepmother. Meanwhile, Robert tried to rally support for her across the country. Stephen besieged the castle, effectively trapping Matilda inside. Since she hadn't announced herself as a threat to him, he allowed her safe passage to connect with Robert in Bristol. She then established a base in the southwest. Over the next several years, there were minor skirmishes and an attempt at peace while Stephen attempted to reclaim the region.

This brings us to 1141 and the time of our story when Stephen besieged Lincoln Castle. His army was attacked by enemy forces led by Robert of Gloucester and Ranulf of Chester. Defeated in what is known as the Battle of Lincoln, Stephen was indeed taken prisoner and held for close to nine months at Bristol Castle.

In my upcoming series, you'll see Theobald Norwood continuing his brother's vow of fealty as he, too, takes up the cause for the Empress Matilda in **Knight of Chaos, The Knights of the Anarchy (Book Two)**. This book will continue the historical story as Theobald makes his way to Winchester after the Empress fails to be crowned Queen in London.

I would like to thank Kathryn LeVeque and Dragonblade Publishing for accepting this series into their collection of books. I hope your readers love it as much as I loved writing it.

Thank you to authors Jude Knight and Caroline Warfield for giving me insight into what needed to be fixed. I appreciate you both taking time out of your own busy schedules to beta read **Knight of Darkness**.

I would also like to offer my thanks to my editor Elizabeth Mazer. Your developmental edits and suggestions made this story stronger. You made me dig deep into these characters and what motivated them. I cannot thank you enough for all your hard work to improve **Knight of Darkness**!

Thank you to my family for always supporting me in every possible way. With a day job, you know how little time I have to write these days and I appreciate your understanding when I don't have a lot of sparkling conversation left in me at night. And special thanks to my daughter Jessica. She continues to be my sounding board when I have plot twists running amuck through my head.

Thank you to all my readers for your continued support. I hope you never forget that I appreciate each and every one of you. You are the reason I continue to write, and your reviews, emails, and kind words on social media give me strength to write another page. Thank you from the bottom of my heart!

Until the next time, I hope you enjoyed this bit of historical information on The Anarchy. Take care and watch out soon for **Knight of Chaos**. I just know you'll love Theobald's story as much as you did Wymar's!

All the best,
Sherry

OTHER BOOKS BY SHERRY EWING

Medieval & Time Travel Series

To Love A Scottish Laird: De Wolfe Pack Connected World
Sometimes you really can fall in love at first sight...

To Love An English Knight: De Wolfe Pack Connected World
Can a chance encounter lead to love?

If My Heart Could See You: The MacLarens, A Medieval Romance (Book One)
When you're enemies, does love have a fighting chance?

For All of Ever: The Knights of Berwyck, A Quest Through Time (Book One)
Sometimes to find your future, you must look to the past...

Only For You: The Knights of Berwyck, A Quest Through Time (Book Two)
Sometimes it's hard to remember that true love conquers all, only after the battle is over...

Hearts Across Time: The Knights of Berwyck (Books One & Two)
Sometimes all you need is to just believe... Hearts Across Time is a special edition box set that combines Katherine and Riorden's stories together from *For All of Ever* and *Only For You*.

A Knight To Call My Own: The MacLarens, A Medieval Romance (Book Two)
When your heart is broken, is love still worth the risk?

To Follow My Heart: The Knights of Berwyck, A Quest Through Time (Book Three)
Love is a leap. Sometimes you need to jump…

The Piper's Lady: The MacLarens, A Medieval Romance (Book Three)
True love binds them. Deceit divides them. Will they choose love?

Love Will Find You: The Knights of Berwyck, A Quest Through Time (Book Four)
Sometimes a moment is all we have…

One Last Kiss: The Knights of Berwyck, A Quest Through Time (Book Five)
Sometimes it takes a miracle to find your heart's desire…

Promises Made At Midnight: The Knights of Berwyck, A Quest Through Time (Book Six)
Make a wish…

It Began With A Kiss: The MacLarens, A Medieval Romance (Book Four)
Sometimes you need to listen when your heart begins to sing…

Knight of Darkness: The Knights of the Anarchy (Book One)
Sometimes finding love can become our biggest weakness…

Regency

A Kiss For Charity: A de Courtenay Novella (Book One)
Love heals all wounds but will their pride keep them apart?

The Earl Takes A Wife: A de Courtenay Novella (Book Two)
It began with a memory, etched in the heart.

Before I Found You: A de Courtenay Novella (Book Three)
A quest for a title. An encounter with a stranger. Will she choose love?

Nothing But Time: A Family of Worth (Book One)
They will risk everything for their forbidden love…

One Moment In Time: A Family of Worth (Book Two)
One moment in time may be enough, if it lasts forever…

Under the Mistletoe
A new suitor seeks her hand. An old flame holds her heart. Which one will she meet under the kissing bough?

A Mistletoe Kiss in the Bluestocking Belles boxset *Belles & Beaux* (2022)
All she wants for Christmas is a mistletoe kiss…

A Second Chance At Love
Can the bittersweet frost of lost love be rekindled into a burning flame?

A Countess to Remember
Sometimes love finds you when you least expect it…

To Claim A Lyon's Heart: Lyon's Den Connected World
A gambler's bet. A widow's burden. Will one game of chance change their lives?

You can find out more about Sherry's work on her website at www.SherryEwing.com and at online retailers.

Social Media for Sherry Ewing

You can learn more about Sherry Ewing at these social media links:
Amazon Author Page: amzn.to/1TrWtoy
Bookbub: bookbub.com/authors/sherry-ewing
Dragonblade Publishing: dragonbladepublishing.com/team/sherry-ewing
Facebook: facebook.com/SherryEwingAuthor
Goodreads: goodreads.com/author/show/8382315.Sherry_Ewing
Instagram: instagram.com/sherry.ewing
Pinterest: pinterest.com/SherryLEwing
TikTok: tiktok.com/@sherryewingauthor
Twitter: twitter.com/Sherry_Ewing
YouTube: youtube.com/SherryEwingauthor
Newsletter Sign Up: bit.ly/2vGrqQM
Facebook Street Team: facebook.com/groups/799623313455472
Facebook Official Fan page: facebook.com/groups/356905935241836

About Sherry Ewing

Sherry Ewing picked up her first historical romance when she was a teenager and has been hooked ever since. An award-winning and bestselling author, she writes historical and time travel romances to awaken the soul one heart at a time. When not writing, she can be found in the San Francisco Bay Area at her day job as an Information Technology Specialist.

Learn more about Sherry where a new adventure awaits you on every page:
Website: www.SherryEwing.com
Email: Sherry@SherryEwing.com

Printed in Great Britain
by Amazon